PROLOGUE

I am slumped on the bus, head resting against the window, my hands clasped around the holdall on my lap. Outside, people go about their business, oblivious to my impending ordeal. An old woman shuffles along the pavement behind a scuffed brown shopping trolley. A teenage boy on a BMX bike swerves to avoid her, raising his middle finger in anger as he passes. Beady-eyed pigeons watch the bus trundle past from their rooftop eyries. Office workers head for the park to spend their lunch hours working on their melanomas.

A trickle of sweat crawls between my shoulder blades and I shift on the sticky seat. It is hot. Too hot. The sky is as blue as a forget-me-not and there's not a cloud in sight. By rights rain should be lashing against the grubby bus window, the sky leaden like my heart. You might say I'm being fanciful, but I couldn't give a toss what you think. This relentlessly sunny summer's day is obscene.

My eye is caught by a harassed-looking woman standing on a street corner with a pushchair in front of her and a toddler by her side. The toddler, chubby almost to the point of being obese, is dressed in a flesh-pink princess costume, fairy wings and spotty wellies. She looks like a grotesque salmon-coloured slug. To add insult to injury her mother has scraped her fine blonde hair into a single pigtail that protrudes from the top of her head like pampas grass. It looks ridiculous.

My heart rate quickening, I crane my neck to see inside the pram, but the baby is hidden from view by a navy parasol. Does it look like its sister, I wonder, then give my head a little shake. Who actually cares? All babies look like Winston Churchill anyway.

The bus grinds to a halt at a set of traffic lights, the air brakes hissing like an angry cat. I check my watch. I'm cutting it fine. I'm supposed to be there at eleven and it's already twenty to. I reach into my bag for the letter, the action a reflex. It's right at the bottom, hidden under my pyjamas and wash bag. I unfold it and re-read it, even though I know it off by heart. Seeing it in black and white makes it feel real, and my throat tightens.

My eyes skim the time of my in-patient appointment, the name of the ward, the date. The letter flutters as my hands tremble. I tighten my hold and keep reading. Dos and don'ts. Don't eat or drink anything from midnight the night before the procedure. Do make sure there's someone to look after you afterwards. A bitter little laugh escapes my throat before I have a chance to swallow it down and a pensioner two rows in front throws me a puzzled look. I ball the letter in my fist and slide further down the slippery orange plastic seat, hugging the holdall to my chest.

Procedure. Such an inoffensive word for such an invasive act. My stomach is churning at the very thought of it.

It's the right thing to do, I tell myself for the gazillionth time. The procedure will give me a fresh start, a new begin-

For Adrian, Oliver and Thomas.

ning. It'll wipe the slate clean. I'll be sparkly and new. Without it, my future's uncertain, hopeless. I know I'm being fanciful again, like some angst-filled heroine in a bleak Victorian saga.

So fucking what?

The pensioner turns around a second time, his salt and pepper eyebrows raised. Did I say that out loud? Maybe. Probably. I glare at him until he looks away, muttering under his breath.

The bus turns right into the road that leads to the hospital. Reaching up, I press the bell and the air brakes hiss again. I sway along the aisle until I'm standing next to the driver. He smells of coffee and cheap aftershave.

'Thanks,' I mutter as the doors open and I jump onto the pavement, careful as always to avoid the cracks. Like I need any more bad luck.

I hitch my bag onto my shoulder and gaze at the slab building, an ugly jumble of glass and concrete. My heart is pounding and my stomach is turning somersaults. For a moment I contemplate turning away and catching the next bus home. Should I? Could I?

Deep down I know it's not an option. My choices ran out a long time ago. I lick my lips and head for the hospital doors.

CHAPTER ONE

NOW

Canterbury is busy. Shoppers wander aimlessly in front of me and on every street corner groups of French and Belgian schoolchildren jostle each other as their teachers count heads and consult clipboards.

I shoulder my way past them all as I head towards Fenwick, as focused on the department store as a cruise missile is on its target. I promise myself I won't get waylaid in White Stuff. No point at the moment, anyway. I give my belly a rub; I'm rewarded with an answering kick.

Out of habit I ferret around in my bag, pull out my phone and check to see if there's a text from Matt. There isn't, so I slip the phone back into my bag with a sigh. We argued again last night. Without warning, one throwaway remark escalated into a full-blown row and although we eventually made up, the sporadic texts we've pinged back and forth since have none of their usual warmth or humour. They're devoid of both emoji and emotion.

That's why I'm determined to find the perfect birthday present for him - to apologise and show him how much I love him. Need him.

The men's department is on the ground floor, sandwiched between handbags and the café. I wander past the rails of designer clothes, fingering cashmere sweaters and holding shirts aloft, narrowing my eyes as I picture Matt wearing them.

'Need any help today, madam?' says a shop assistant, sidling over. He has a neat beard and a sharp suit. Probably had avocados on toast for breakfast.

'I'm looking for a present for my husband. He's thirty-five tomorrow,' I add, as if Mr Avocado could give a toss.

'What about a leather jacket?' He's already heading over to a row of stylish biker jackets.

I swallow. Money is tight, especially with my maternity leave looming. 'I was thinking more of a shirt.' I say with an apologetic smile.

To his credit he doesn't miss a beat. 'Then you're in luck. The Paul Smith shirts go on sale in the morning. I'm marking them up now. See if there's anything you think he'd like.'

My eye is drawn to a cornflower-blue shirt already sporting a thirty per cent off sticker. 'This is nice,' I say, knowing it'll bring out the blue of Matt's eyes.

'What size?'

Although Matt has the broad, muscular shoulders of a swimmer he likes his shirts fitted to show off his pecs, his one vanity.

'Medium, probably.'

The shop assistant hums to himself as his fingers march along the rail of shirts. Just when I think I'm out of luck he pulls one out with a 'Ta da!'

I pay and thank him for his help, and he heads towards the Hugo Boss suits, still quietly humming to himself.

Relieved to have bagged a bargain and hopeful Matt

will love the shirt I take the escalator down to the basement and choose a funny card and some Star Wars wrapping paper I know will make him laugh.

I'm about to head back up to the ground floor when the lift doors open behind me and a willowy woman pushing a buggy steps out. I pause. I'd forgotten the children's department was down here. I always avoid baby shops. I'm superstitious like that. And who can blame me? But something is drawing me towards the rails of tiny sleepsuits, dresses and dungarees. Surely it wouldn't hurt to have a quick look? I glance down at my bump, as if seeking approval. I'm not sure what I'm expecting. A somersault for yes and a kick for no? *Stupid Sophie.* And to prove me right the baby is still. I wrestle with myself for a second or two. Heart wins over head and I follow the willowy woman to the children's department.

'When are you due?' the woman at the till says as she rings through what now seems a hideously extravagant pile of sleepsuits and bodysuits in shades of sugared almonds.

'Two months,' I tell her, wondering whether I should put some back. 'It's the first time I've bought anything. Haven't wanted to tempt fate, you know?'

She folds a pair of powder-blue dungarees and slips them into a carrier bag. 'I'm sure everything will be just fine.'

I blanche as she tells me how much I've spent and press my credit card into her hand before I change my mind. She hands me four bulging bags.

'Just make sure you keep the receipt.' She nods at my bump. 'In case it's not.'

Guilt at the amount of money I've spent morphs into an uneasy fear that by splurging on baby clothes I've somehow provoked the Fates, and my stomach is churning as I step onto the escalator. I've allowed myself to be seduced by the dream of a picture-perfect future and I berate myself for my weakness. I should know better. My hopes have been dashed too many times by fertility specialists wearing white coats and concerned expressions.

That's when I see him. A wave of shock hits me so forcefully I sway and have to grab the handrail to stop myself toppling backwards. In the blink of an eye I'm seventeen again. I drink in his features. Messy brown hair. Broad, untroubled forehead. A trace of a smile on his face. My heart flutters in my chest and I squeeze the handrail until my knuckles whiten.

'Ed?' I whisper.

He laughs and I flinch, old insecurities resurfacing. White leads trail from his ears to an iPhone in his hand. He wasn't laughing at me. He must be listening to a podcast. I remind myself that podcasts didn't exist when I was seventeen and no-one our age had mobile phones. I remember I'm the wrong side of forty, with grey roots and crow's feet, and I'm staring at a boy young enough to be my son with my tongue virtually hanging out. I flush and look away.

As our escalators rattle past each other I sneak another look. I can't help myself. Our eyes meet for the briefest of moments. But something's out of kilter. His eyes are brown, not hazel, flecked with green. There's a dimple in his chin that Ed never had. Ed was tall and rangy. This boy is too stocky. And yet...

The escalator reaches the ground floor and I step off. A

floor below the brown-haired boy disappears from view. I could catch the escalator back down, find him, ask who he is, why he's here. But deep down I already know. I've always known. Past hurts and grievances rise to the surface like scum on an incoming tide and I fight a wave of nausea. Seeing him here, in my city, was inevitable, I realise that now. It was only ever a matter of time.

CHAPTER TWO

NOW

The carrier bags hidden underneath a tartan picnic blanket in the boot of my car, I drive past the police station towards the south of the city. By the time I've turned onto Stone Street, the old Roman Road linking Canterbury to Lympne, I've convinced myself it's a complete coincidence the boy on the escalator happened to look like a boy I once knew. Seven-and-a-half billion people live on this planet. It's hardly surprising some of them look like each other.

After a couple of hundred metres I indicate left and bump up a gravelled driveway following signs to Camomile Community Garden. The closer I get, the calmer I feel. The garden has that effect on people. I noticed it when I first came here to volunteer almost eight years ago. I've worked here ever since.

Based in what was once the kitchen garden of a 12th century manor house, Cam is a therapeutic garden for people with learning disabilities and mental health problems. We have just over thirty on our books. Social Services call them our 'service users'. To us they are simply gardeners.

The manor house was ravaged by fire over a century ago and the four flint and brick walls of the garden and the old wine cellar where we store our tools are all that remain. We're an island in a sea of apple orchards and acres of wheat in the heart of the Garden of England.

I park, push open the studded oak door and head for the office which, blissfully, is empty bar Mr Pickles, the tabby cat we adopted a couple of years ago. He's sprawled, sloth-like, across Angela's neat-as-a-pin desk.

'She'll have your guts for garters,' I tell him.

He regards me through narrowed green eyes and yawns.

'Don't say I didn't warn you.' I take out my sandwich and fire up my computer. I've a heap of emails to answer and a grant application that needs finishing. Instead I stare out of the window, my chin in my hands, lost in a maelstrom of memories.

The crunch of gravel followed by the piercing voice of my boss interrupts my reverie and I sit up with a start.

'Sophie, are you back?' Angela calls in that quavering voice that sets my teeth on edge.

'In here,' I answer, shooing Mr Pickles from her desk. He jumps to the floor in high dudgeon, his tail quivering, and stalks off to his bed next to the filing cabinet. Angela sweeps into the office, bringing with her a waft of garlic and red wine.

'I had lunch with Bob. He says he still hasn't received the plan for the recruitment evening.'

'Tell him it'll be with him by close of play,' I say. 'But only if you happen to be talking to him again,' I add. A dull flush creeps up her neck and I smirk into my sandwich. Her affair with the married chairman of Cam's board of trustees is well-known, despite her best efforts to keep it hidden.

I'm deep into my recruitment evening plans when there's a gentle tap at the door.

'Come in,' I call, and Rosie's familiar face appears around the door. She's beaming from ear to ear and I beckon her inside.

'Is it that time already?' Angela tuts. The gardeners are a constant source of irritation to her. Why she decided to work here is beyond me.

I pat the seat next to mine and Rosie crashes past Angela's desk, knocking over her in tray, and sits down with a thump.

'Sorry Angela,' she says automatically. Rosie is always apologising for something, whether it's accidentally standing on a row of newly-planted seedlings, colliding with one of the visitors or having Downs Syndrome. It breaks my heart.

'No harm done, I suppose,' Angela says. I stifle the urge to let rip. Honestly, my hormones are all over the place today.

'What are we doing this afternoon, Sophie?' Rosie asks.

'I thought we'd plant out the runner beans. We shouldn't have another frost now.'

'Cool,' she says, holding out her hand to pull me up.

'Don't forget that plan,' says Angela as we head out of the door, Rosie's hand still tucked in mine.

Once we're outside I turn around and make a show of sticking my tongue out at my boss. Rosie collapses in giggles and then looks horrified, pressing her fingers to her lips and whispering, 'Sorry.'

I smile. 'Nothing to be sorry for.'

By half past two Cam is a hive of activity. All our usual

Tuesday afternoon crowd are here. I send Rosie off in search of gardening gloves, kneeling mats and trowels and head over to where Geoff, the only other member of staff, is helping Martin Miller deadhead the roses.

'How's it going?' I ask.

Geoff knows I'm not talking about the deadheading. Martin's behaviour is becoming increasingly erratic and it's a cause for concern. We know from his support worker that the last time he had a psychotic episode he ended up being sectioned for six months.

'We're fine, aren't we, Marty?' Geoff says.

The younger man doesn't appear to hear. He has zeroed in on a blown pink Chatsworth rose. He raises his secateurs and deftly snips the head off. It drops into his hand and his fingers curl into a ball, crushing the dark pink petals inside.

'Got it!' he says, raising his fist in the air.

'Good job, son.' Geoff holds out a trug. Martin drops the rose into it and they move onto the next one. He is so focused on the task I'm not even sure he knows I'm here.

I spy Rosie by the runner bean wigwams and join her. The next hour passes quickly as we ease the young plants out of their pots and into their prepared beds. The early summer sun beats down on the back of our necks and for the first time I feel my bump getting in the way.

Rosie notices, too. 'Baby's getting big now,' she says, pointing at my belly.

'He is, isn't he?' I wait for her inevitable response.

She doesn't disappoint. Her eyes widen. 'It's a girl, and you're going to call her Rosie, remember!'

'If she's a she. I don't want you getting your hopes up.'

Rosie gives a little shake of her head. '*When* she's a she.'

The truth is, Matt and I don't know what we're having. We decided not to find out at the twenty-week scan.

'It'll give us something to focus on during labour,' I told him, as the sonographer squirted gel over my bump and began running the ultrasound probe over it. I wasn't fooling anyone. Matt knew as well as I did that knowing whether the baby was a boy or girl would just make it harder if the worst happened.

Twelve weeks after the scan our baby is still very much here. I know the statistics off by heart. Ninety per cent of babies born at twenty-seven weeks survive. But they are still considered premature if they are born before thirty-seven weeks. I do everything in my power to keep our baby where it should be.

When the last runner bean is planted I sit back on my haunches and stretch my back. Rosie is bent over the smallest plant trying to coax it around the bamboo pole, but every time she winds it around it uncoils in her hand. She growls in frustration and I lay a hand on her arm.

'Don't worry, they'll surprise you. They always find their own way up the poles in the end.' I pull off my gardening gloves finger by finger. 'Cuppa tea?'

'Cuppa tea,' Rosie agrees, the runner beans forgotten.

It's been a busy afternoon and it's not until I'm standing in the tiny kitchen at the back of the office waiting for the kettle to boil that I remember the boy on the escalator. I picture the familiar contours of his face. The features that don't belong to Ed are Lou's, I realise.

The knowledge is like a punch in the gut.

I saw her today. In Canterbury. Flaunting her pregnancy. Rubbing her belly and smiling this secret smile, as if she and the baby were in on some private joke, just the two of them. It made me want to puke.

I had nothing planned so I followed her, keeping my distance so she wouldn't see me. Not that I needed to worry. She was too caught up in her perfect little world to notice me. I may as well have been invisible.

She bought a shirt. Blue to match his eyes, of course. Such a cliché. Then she headed down the escalator to the children's department. I was surprised, knowing how superstitious she is. I loitered behind a display of Orla Kiely storage jars while she trailed through the aisles, fingering soft-as-down sleepsuits, running her hands over embroidered blankets and pulling tiny outfits from the rails and holding them up to the light to examine the intricate stitching.

I made a mental inventory of her haul, for later.

She dithered before she walked over to the till, wrestling with her conscience. Sophie's so open, I can read her like a book.

She's worried she's tempting fate.

Thing is, she just might be.

CHAPTER THREE

NOW

N o-one likes to admit to a bit of Facebook stalking, so I force myself to wait until I've finished my dinner and cleared up before I sit down at the kitchen table and open the laptop. I'll just take a quick look. Clicking on the familiar blue logo, I ignore the half a dozen notifications awaiting my attention. Instead I type Edward Sullivan into the search box and, holding my breath, hit enter.

Of course there are hundreds of them. It's not exactly an unusual name. I scroll down, dismissing various Edward Sullivans from Nottingham, Dublin, Vancouver and Oregon. I know the further down the list I go the less likely I'm going to find my Ed. Facebook's famous algorithms will have seen to that.

My Ed. I swallow. He hasn't been that for more than twenty years. What does he look like now? Have the years been kind to him? Have his features softened with age? Does he have a bald patch, a paunch? What would he think if he saw me? When people voice surprise that I'm six years older than my husband I laugh and tell them you're as young as the man you feel. The fact is I work hard at staying young.

I chew a nail. Perhaps he's not on social media.

'Bet Lou is,' I mutter. I'm about to type her name into the search box when I realise there's a quicker way. I scroll down my friends list until I find Jasmine Carter, former head girl at our school and prize busybody. If anyone's kept in touch with all the girls in our year, she will have.

I click on Jasmine's profile and find her friends list. It's no surprise that she has nearly two thousand. Impatient, I whizz through them until I find who I'm looking for. The familiar face of my former best friend, Lou Stapleton. My hand hovers over the keyboard, my index finger itching to press enter. But I hesitate. What long-buried feelings am I about to disturb? Why on earth would I want to dredge up all that unhappiness now? I have a good life, a happy life. I know it's not too late to stop. I can shut down my laptop, pretend I never saw the boy. *Their* boy. I'm teetering at the edge of a cliff. I could step back. Retreat with my dignity and sanity intact. But I'm weak. Curiosity gets the better of me and I click Lou's name.

Luckily she hasn't bothered to set a single privacy setting. She was always lax about things like that. I used to tell her off for keeping her pin number on a piece of paper in her purse, right next to her bank card. She'd just laugh and tell me to take a chill pill.

I study her profile photo. She's on a beach, somewhere exotic like the Maldives or the Bahamas. Behind her the sea sparkles azure-blue. She's sitting on the end of one of those wooden-slatted sun loungers you get in country house spas and is holding a cocktail that is a radioactive shade of orange. Lou always liked a drink. Before we went out she'd raid her parents' drinks cabinet, taking a small swig from each bottle so they didn't notice. Cherry brandy, whisky, pale sherry and aniseed-flavoured Ouzo. She didn't care what she drank, said it helped her get into a party mood. By the time we left the house her eyes would be glittering and her voice a few decibels louder than normal.

She's wearing a strappy dress in the photo. Huge sunglasses. Her hair, cut in a choppy bob, is blonder than it was at school, but I expect she has highlights to hide the grey. She's laughing, the dimple on her chin clearly visible. Is Ed behind the camera, pulling silly faces or prompting her to say "sausages"? Is she happy with the way her life turned out? I hope so, after everything she took from me.

Feeling as though I'm standing behind a locked door, peeking through a keyhole into Lou's life, I scroll down her feed. Frustratingly, she's one of those people who only post photos of inanimate objects so there are dozens of pictures of beautiful sunsets, restaurant meals and views of the countryside but none of any actual people. I keep scrolling, hoping someone who does take photos of people may have tagged "Lou Sullivan nee Stapleton" in a post.

I'm about to give up when a photo of an American football team catches my eye. It's a standard team photo. Eleven players wearing helmets, royal blue jerseys and cream pants. I heard on the grapevine Ed and Lou moved to New England after Ed got a job at a prestigious Boston law firm. My heart beats faster as I zoom in, scanning the players for Ed, but it soon becomes apparent they are boys, probably aged around fourteen or fifteen. I check the date. The photo was taken four years ago. That would fit.

By the look of it the woman who posted the photo has

tagged every parent and most of the players. There are lots of all-American names like Brad and Chuck. And then, last but one, is the name I'm looking for. Josh Sullivan.

My iPhone starts buzzing, brashly loud in the silence of the kitchen, and I start. It's Matt, wanting to FaceTime. I hold my hands to my burning cheeks, arrange my features into a smile and press accept.

'Hello, Sophie.'

My heart constricts. No 'Hey baby' or 'Hi gorgeous' tonight. Just a bald, wary hello. He's still mad at me. Not that I blame him.

'I'm sorry,' I say.

He loosens his tie. He's sitting at the desk in his digs. On the wall behind him is an enthusiastic oil painting of the Scottish Highlands by his landlady, Moira.

'I know. You already said. It was just a drink with a couple of mates from work, Soph. I don't see what the problem was.'

Neither do I, now. But when Matt told me he was off to the pub last night I hit the roof. Virtually accused him of having an affair. Spent the rest of the evening smouldering with jealousy and resentment and checking Find My iPhone to make sure he was where he said he was.

'I don't know what got into me. My hormones...' I trail off.

His face softens and I know I'm forgiven, this time at least. 'Speaking of which, how's that baby of mine? Still cooking nicely?'

I push the chair back and stand so he can blow the bump a kiss. He leans towards his phone so closely I can see his five o'clock shadow.

'I swear you're bigger than you were yesterday.'

I wiggle my eyebrows. 'And that's supposed to make me feel better how exactly?'

He finally laughs. 'The bigger you both are, the more there is to love. What have you been up to today?'

I fish around for an interesting story that doesn't involve seeing the son of my ex-boyfriend and former best friend and then stalking them on Facebook. He wouldn't be jealous - he's not the type - it's just that it's all too complicated to explain.

I remember the Paul Smith shirt. 'I bought your birthday present.'

'Is it an Aston Martin in Volcano Red for my mid-life crisis?'

I snort. 'No, it's not. Anyway, you're too young to have a mid-life crisis.'

'A new road bike then?'

'Nope. And it's not a Bang and Olufsen sound system or a smart TV either, I'm afraid.'

He pulls a sad face and starts telling me about his day but I'm only half-listening. He's halfway through a long and convoluted story about his deputy manager taking the afternoon off when he stops, waiting for my response. I smile. 'That's nice.'

'I said Cheryl's dad was rushed to hospital with a suspected heart attack. He's in intensive care. Were you listening to a word I said?'

I hit my forehead with the palm of my hand. 'Sorry. You know my brain is mush. Blame the baby.'

He lets out a long sigh. 'I hate being away from home, especially at the moment. I should be there for you both.'

'We're OK. Only two more sleeps.' I smile again, as if it doesn't matter, even though I would give anything to have him here, to feel his arms around me. When the bank offered him the role of manager at its busy Brighton branch just over a year ago I was the one who convinced him to take it. We'd spent all our savings on fruitless rounds of IVF and I knew the pay rise would fund another attempt. At that point I would have gladly sacrificed a kidney to have one last shot at having a baby, so sending my husband to work ninety miles away was a small price to pay.

But I worry the weeks spent apart are taking a toll on our marriage. We're becoming too used to our own company. We spend Saturdays remembering how we fit together. And just when we do it's time to say goodbye again.

'Two more sleeps,' Matt agrees.

We blow kisses and end the call and I set my phone face down on the kitchen table. The room feels empty now he's gone. My laptop sits in front of me. Lou's Facebook page has been replaced by the screensaver and I'm glad. What on earth was I thinking, trying to track down Ed? I need to forget all about him and Lou. Matt's the only one who matters. He's my world. The father of my unborn child. Why would I do anything to jeopardise that?

CHAPTER FOUR

THEN

W e're sitting cross-legged on the carpet, surrounded by our Superdrug spoils. Wella Shaders and Toners - light ash blonde for Lou, rich mahogany for me - cucumber face masks, pearlescent-pink nail varnish and lip gloss. We have splurged at least a month's wages on our haul. And that's not including my sapphire-blue satin slip dress and Lou's crushed red velvet number, which are hanging side by side on the doors of Lou's pine wardrobe.

Her walls are plastered with posters of Marti Pellow and *Love is all Around* is playing on a loop on her Sony stereo system. It's been number one for two months now and it's seriously beginning to get on my nerves, but Lou is a massive Wet Wet Wet fan and it's her bedroom, so I can't really complain.

'You have the first bath,' she says generously.

'You sure?'

'Yeah. You need to look your best if you're going to pull Sexy Ed. I'll take one for the team. Just remember not to pull out the plug. I'd rather have your dirty water than a stone-cold bath, even if you are shaving your legs.'

'Thanks Lou.' I blow her a kiss. My stomach is a swarm of butterflies as I tie back my hair and apply the face mask. I'm light-headed with anticipation. The speech day disco is one of the highlights of the school year, a chance for everyone to let their hair down after months of study. As we primp and preen in Lou's bedroom the school hall is being transformed with hired disco balls, balloons and lights into a den of infinite possibilities.

'Do you think he'll even notice me?' I mumble through closed lips, for fear of cracking the face pack.

''Course he will. He's been giving you the glad eye all term,' says Lou, who is wrestling with her mum's eyelash curlers.

'Glad eye?' I scoff. 'Who are you, your nan?'

She tuts. 'You know what I mean. It's obvious he fancies you.'

'So why hasn't he asked me out?'

'I dunno. Perhaps he's shy.'

'But I'm shy, too! What if we're both too shy to make the first move? I'll die a lonely spinster and he'll turn into a sad old man shuffling around the supermarket with plastic meals for one.'

Lou abandons her eyelash curlers and reaches under her bed. 'That's where I might be able to help.'

I blink. 'Not pills, Lou.'

She shakes her head. 'It's just vodka. It'll relax you, give you a bit of Dutch courage. And it won't smell on your breath.'

'I don't know -'

'I'm having some even if you're too chicken.' She unscrews the top of the half-bottle and takes a slug.

'I'm not chicken. It's just that pissed people are so

annoying, all shouty and aggressive one minute and puking up in the bushes the next.'

She fixes her brown eyes on mine. 'I'm not though, am I?'

''Course not,' I tell her. But I'm lying. Booze changes Lou's character, and not for the better. Sober Lou is funny, warm and loyal. Pissed Lou is argumentative, stroppy and has a nasty habit of disappearing with boys at parties leaving me on my own. Give me Sober Lou any day of the week.

'Go on, just a wee dram,' she says in a terrible Scottish accent.

I giggle. Maybe it wouldn't hurt just this once. I'm worried if Ed and I don't get it together tonight we never will. He's been shooting me smiles from the other side of the common room for ages, and he always makes a beeline for me in the lunch queue, but we just chat about inconsequential things, like how soggy the chips are, and what an old witch Mrs Evans, the head of sixth form, is. I get the feeling he likes me, but he's never asked me out. Perhaps he never will. So, unless I make the first move...

'Oh alright,' I say, taking the bottle and grimacing as the alcohol scorches the back of my throat.

'Good girl.'

Basking in her approval, I take another slurp. Once we've blow-dried our newly-coloured hair and painted our nails, the nerves have disappeared and I'm ready to take on the world. I slip into my dress and help Lou with her zip. We stand in front of her mirror and pout.

'We look a million dollars.' Lou drops the half-empty bottle of Smirnoff into her bag and links arms with me. 'Ready?' she asks, raising one of her perfectly-plucked eyebrows.

I grin. 'As I'll ever be.'

CHAPTER FIVE

NOW

My resolve not to track Ed down lasts all of two days. Work is busy as I prepare for our recruitment evening and when I'm there it's easy to push him to the back of my mind. But on Thursday night when I'm updating our Facebook page with photos I've taken of the vegetable garden, my curiosity gets the better of me. I type in Josh Sullivan before I can talk myself out of it.

The moment I see his profile picture I wish I hadn't. But I should know better than anyone that you can't turn back time. I force myself to take another look. Josh's arm is draped around his father. Ed's eyes burn with the same intensity they did when he was seventeen. But that's where the similarity ends. His cheeks are sunken and his complexion is as grey as ash. His hair, that beautiful chestnut-brown hair I would run my fingers through, has disappeared, replaced by a chemo-induced wispy white fuzz.

My dad died of a brain tumour. I know what stage four cancer looks like. And there's no dressing it up. Ed looks like a dead man walking. Terrified what the photo might mean, I slam the laptop shut.

That night I sleep fitfully. Whenever I do nod off my dreams are filled with Ed. Not the boy I remember but the gaunt shadow of a man he is now. Or was. Once upon a time we promised each other we'd always be together. Now I don't even know if he's alive or dead. I realise I gave up my rights to know a long time ago, but it doesn't make it any easier. Is that why Ed and Lou's son is in Canterbury? Perhaps they wanted to come home for Ed's final weeks. Lou's family moved up north soon after I left school, but I assume Ed's parents and older sister are still in Whitstable. I'm surprised I haven't bumped into them over the years to be honest, but even in a small city like Canterbury it's easy to hide.

As the dawn chorus begins I give up any hope of sleep, even though it's my rostered day off and I could have enjoyed a guilt-free lie in. I pad downstairs, flick the kettle on and reach for the teabags. Unlocking the back door, I take my tea into the garden, hardly noticing that the dew is soaking my bare feet. I sit on the love seat under the Japanese flowering cherry at the end of the garden and rest the mug on my bump. There's a swirling sensation as the baby shifts inside me.

Hidden in the branches above my head a blackbird is singing its heart out. The tree was heavy with shell-pink blossom when we first viewed the house six years ago. Matt loved the red-bricked Victorian semi's spacious rooms and proximity to the station, but I fell in love with the cherry blossom. It reminded me of Nakameguro in Tokyo where cherry trees, lit by lanterns after dark, line the canal.

We were planning to go there together, Ed and I, after we'd finished our A-levels. Not for us the usual gap year destinations of Thailand and Australia. We wanted to explore Japan, visit Buddist temples, buy sashimi from street-sellers and ride the bullet train from south to north. We never stopped to consider how much it would cost to travel across one of the most expensive countries in the world. We thought we were so grown up, but we were naive, artless. I went on my own in the end, although I had to spend a couple of years working as a waitress to save up first.

Japan was everything I hoped it would be and more. And although he was two years into his law degree at UCL by then, I felt Ed's presence as I took baths in Japanese onsen and climbed to the summit of Mount Fuji.

I hope with all my heart that I've read too much into the photo and that Ed's in remission. If he is, would he see me? There's so much I wish I'd said to him when we were kids, so much I bottled up inside because I thought it was for the best. Like an aggressive cancer, regret has eaten me up from the inside for decades. Only now, happy with Matt and seven-and-a-half months pregnant, I'm finally hovering on the verge of contentment. Perhaps making my peace with Ed would bury my remaining demons.

The pips for the ten o'clock news have barely finished beeping when there's a knock at the door. I know without looking through the spy hole that it'll be Roz, here for my cut and colour. Roz is one of those precise people who always arrive exactly on time, not a minute early, not a minute late. Like a Japanese bullet train. Not like me. My reputation for tardiness is a standing joke among all who know me. That's not to say I like being late because I don't. But I can't seem to crack punctuality.

Roz's preciseness is one of the things I admire about her. She's fastidious to the point of being anal, but that's a pretty good trait to have in a hairdresser. I went to Toni and Guy for years, it was my one extravagance, but you don't get much change from a hundred quid for highlights and a cut and blow dry, and when we signed up for the latest round of IVF I was happy to sacrifice my trips to the salon.

Finding Roz was serendipitous. A couple of months after I decided I couldn't afford Toni and Guy, a flyer was pushed through the letterbox advertising her mobile hair-dressing business. Thirty quid for a cut and colour, and all in the comfort of my own home. I rang the number there and then.

Roz has been cutting my hair for almost eight months now and we've become friends. We meet in Canterbury for a coffee every couple of weeks. I was taken aback when Roz first suggested it, the second time she cut my hair.

'Too soon?' she said, her head cocked to one side.

'Of course not,' I replied. Tell the truth, I was flattered. I was also lonely. Matt hadn't long started working in Brighton and my days felt empty without him.

We have lots in common, me and Roz. She, too, is small and dark-haired, although she's more fine-boned than me. Matt always jokes I have the hands of a farmer. She went through several rounds of IVF with her husband Phil, just like me and Matt, and they now have a beautiful toddler, Caitlyn, who goes to a childminder when Roz is working.

Having been through IVF she knows what it's like to yearn for a baby above all else. She has experienced the unadulterated joy of a positive pregnancy test and tasted the salty tears of disappointment. She is happy to pore over grainy scan photos, pointing out fingers and toes with wonder when others would have glazed over in boredom. She reminds me to eat properly and rest up when I'm tired. She reassures me when I'm anxious.

Roz is only thirty-two but she's a wise head on young shoulders, as my mum used to say. I often find myself offloading to her. She is always so sympathetic, listening intently as she considers my latest beef with Angela or quarrel with Matt and offering down to earth advice.

I smile as I undo the door chain and let her in. As usual her arms are full of bags and cases. It's amazing how much equipment she carries around with her.

'Let me take that,' I say, reaching for a black holdall.

'Not in your condition.'

I give the bag a half-hearted tug but she's surprisingly strong. Admitting defeat, I close the door and follow her into the kitchen.

'Was the patch test OK? No irritation?' she says, whipping a sheet of PVC from the holdall and laying it on the kitchen floor.

I hold my ear back so she can inspect my skin. She nods. 'Looks good to me.'

'Do we really need to do a patch test each time? I've been using the same brand for years with no problem. It would save you a journey.'

'Can't be too careful. I don't want to risk you having a serious allergic reaction, do I? And you know I don't mind.'

I flick the kettle on while she's unloading mixing bowls and brushes, dye and scissors. Strong black coffee for Roz, another cup of tea for me. She takes the mugs, motions me to sit down and wraps a towel around my shoulders. It's nice to be mothered, even if it's only for an hour or so every couple of months.

Roz starts telling me about Caitlyn's first proper pair of sandals and how she surprised the young assistant at Clarks by opting for blue not pink. But I can't concentrate on her story. Ed's atrophied face is dominating my thoughts.

'I don't think she's going to be a girly girl, if you know what I mean?' Roz says. And then, 'Sophie, are you alright?'

I only realise she has asked me because she has stopped applying colour to my roots and her hand, encased in a copper-stained latex glove, is resting on my shoulder.

'Of course I am.'

'You're very quiet. There's nothing wrong with the baby is there?'

I rub my belly. 'No, the baby's fine. I didn't sleep well last night, that's all. Too hot, I expect.'

'Good. Not that you didn't sleep.' She laughs. 'You know what I mean.' She rinses her gloves under the tap and checks her watch. 'Half an hour should do it. Fancy another cup?'

I shake my head. 'Roz, can I ask you something?'

'Sure, fire away.'

'Do you keep in touch with your exes?'

She spins around and shoots me a curious look. 'Why do you ask?'

'Do you?' I press.

'Depends what you mean by keeping in touch.'

I shrug. 'I don't know. Not meeting up to reminisce about old times. Following them on Facebook, I suppose. Perhaps the odd text.'

She takes a sip of her coffee and watches me, her lips pressed together. 'Is there something you want to get off your chest? A problem shared and all that.'

I blush and I know she's noticed because she stares into her mug to give me time to compose myself.

'When I was seventeen I fell in love with a boy at school. We split up for reasons I won't bore you with and he ended up marrying my best friend.'

'Ouch,' says Roz with feeling. 'That must have been hard to swallow.'

'It was,' I agree. 'Ed and Lou, a double betrayal. But I got over it eventually and met Matt. And you know the rest.'

'I do indeed. So why are we talking about your childhood sweetheart?'

'I lost touch with them both. Haven't seen them for twenty-odd years. They moved to the US. And then I saw their son in Fenwick the other day. I tracked Lou down on Facebook and it looks like Ed has cancer.'

'And?' says Roz.

'They've moved back to Canterbury... '

'And you're wondering whether you should get back in touch?' Roz finishes.

My shoulders slump. 'That's about the sum of it, yes.'

'What are you worried about?'

'That it'll upset Matt, upset the equilibrium.'

Roz raises her eyebrows.

'I wouldn't like it if he got back in touch with an old girl-friend,' I say.

'I don't suppose you would.' She aligns her scissors and comb on the kitchen table. 'So, don't contact them.'

'But what if Ed's still alive?'

'You think he might be dead?'

'He looked so ill in the photo I saw, and I've no idea how long ago it was taken.'

Roz picks up a shank of my hair and inspects it. 'Another ten minutes,' she says. 'So, *do* contact them then.'

'But what if -'

'Sophie,' she says in exasperation. 'Where's your laptop?'

'On the dining room table. Why?'

She disappears, reappearing seconds later with my laptop under her arm. She plonks herself on the chair opposite me, her hands poised over the keyboard.

'Password?' she demands.

'Camomile nineteen seventy-eight. Why, what are you doing?'

'You obviously want to see Ed again, so I'm helping things along.'

'What?' I cry in alarm.

Ignoring me, she peers at the screen. I curse silently, remembering I left Josh's Facebook page open.

'I see what you mean. He does look on death's door. I'm guessing Lou Sullivan is your Lou?'

'She's not my Lou. What are you doing?'

'I'm sending a message to Not-Your-Lou saying you've heard she's back in town and asking if she fancies meeting up for a coffee sometime.' Roz smiles. 'There, all sorted.'

Part of me is speechless. I can't believe what she's done. I don't want to become entangled in the Sophie-Ed-Lou triangle again. It ended so catastrophically last time. But part of me is relieved. From the moment I saw Josh I've been vacillating between contacting my old friends and staying well away. At least this way, if it all goes wrong it's not my fault. I didn't start it.

I am not culpable.

When I was a small cog in a large corporate wheel I was

well-versed in the four stages of successful project management.

Initiation, when you identify a need, problem or opportunity and brainstorm ways that you could meet that need, solve the problem or seize the opportunity. A bit of blue-sky thinking involved here, if you'll pardon the jargon.

Planning, the vital second stage, when you break your project into smaller tasks, identify the timeline and anticipate risks and potential problems that could throw your carefully-planned project off-track. Working through a myriad of potential outcomes and scenarios, covering all the bases. Asking yourself what if - and having a quick fix in place if needed. Anyone will tell you planning is the most crucial part of any project.

Execution, the third stage, when you action your plan and it finally becomes a reality. If you've done your homework this stage should be a breeze, a veritable walk in the park.

And, last of all, closure, when you sit back and assess the success of the project. Did you meet the need? Did you solve the problem?

Did you seize the opportunity?

CHAPTER SIX

NOW

M att seems tired and distracted. The journey from Brighton took an hour longer than usual due to a shunt on the M25. To make matters worse the air conditioning in his old Volvo packed up halfway along the A249. I was debating whether to begin dinner without him when he let himself in the front door just before eight. He handed me his bag of dirty laundry and I joked, 'I remember when you used to give me flowers.'

It was the wrong thing to say.

'I tell you what, I'll do it,' he said, snatching the bag back.

'Don't over-react. It was a *joke*. Give it to me.'

I tried to wrestle it from him and we had a ridiculous tug of war until I gave up and said, 'Suit yourself. But make sure you don't put the colours and whites in together again.'

He muttered something under his breath and I left him to it.

As I serve up our overdone lasagne and pour him an extra-large glass of wine I wonder how we've managed to get the weekend off to a bad start already, without even trying. It's happening more and more. The smallest slight can escalate into an argument and before I know it we're bickering like siblings. But I refuse to go down that well-trodden path tonight. Instead I paste a smile on my face and carry his tray into the sitting room where he is slumped on the sofa watching a re-run of *Top Gear*.

'Your favourite. Sorry it's a bit on the dry side.'

'I suppose that's my fault, too,' he says, taking the tray from me, his eyes still on the television.

'That's not what I meant.' I perch on the coffee table in front of him so he can't avoid me. 'Come on, Matt. I've been looking forward to seeing you all week. Let's not fight tonight. Please?'

He finally looks at me. His skin is pale, save for the dark circles under his eyes. He looks knackered.

'Alright.'

'Sorry for before. I really was only joking.'

'Sorry I snapped,' he says. 'Bitch of a day.'

'Trouble at t'mill?'

'I've been tipped off by Susie at head office that the regional manager is making a "surprise" visit on Monday.' Matt draws speech marks in the air with his knife and fork. 'I'm expecting a bollocking. There's no getting away from the fact that our figures are down.'

'Surely that's down to the economy, not you?'

'Maybe. But Mike's the type of grade A dickhead who likes to blame everyone but himself. I'm pretty confident it'll be yours truly in the firing line. Aren't you eating anything?'

I smack my palm against my forehead. 'I told you my brain is mush at the moment. I'll go and get mine.'

The kitchen is in darkness, but I don't bother to switch on the light. As I reach into the cupboard for my tray Matt's phone lights up. I'm surprised he's left it in the kitchen. He's usually glued to the damn thing. I glance at the screen and put the phone on the tray along with my plate and a glass of water and carry them into the sitting room.

'Your phone just rang but it was on silent so I didn't hear it, I'm afraid. Unknown caller.'

'Probably work,' he says through a mouthful of lasagne. He swipes the phone and places it face down on the coffee table in front of him.

'At this time of night?'

He shrugs. 'Probably. Or it's some loser telling me I've been involved in an accident -'

'That wasn't your fault -' I play along.

'And I may be entitled to some compensation,' Matt finishes. It's only when he smiles - his first this evening - that I realise just how strained he looked before.

'Is everything OK?'

'Of course. Why wouldn't it be?'

The last thing I want to do is start another argument so I choose my words carefully. 'You look a bit tired. Is it too much - the job, living in digs, that long drive? Because we can talk about moving again. I don't mind.'

'We've been over it a million times. We love this house. Prices are so high in Brighton we'd barely afford a two-bedroom flat. You love your job.' He ticks the list off on his fingers. 'I only ever saw the job as the next step up the ladder. As soon as a position comes up closer to home I'll ask for a transfer. I just have to bide my time.'

'But it could take years. And this is killing you. Let's at least get an estate agent around to value this place.'

Matt shakes his head. I push the lasagne around my plate. Matt's right. I do love our house and I'd hate to leave Cam. But I'd do it for him, for our little family.

'We've got enough on our plate what with the baby coming. I'm not throwing a house move into the mix. The subject's closed, OK?' Matt places his knife and fork together and slides the tray onto the coffee table next to his phone. 'What else is new?'

This is the perfect opportunity to tell him about seeing Josh and tracking down Ed on Facebook. I almost do. Almost, but not quite. We never had the 'how many lovers have you had' conversation when we first got together. It seemed a bit tacky to broach it and Matt never asked. He's a very private person. In fact, he hardly talks about his past at all and I've always respected that. And for the moment I'm more than happy to keep the topic safely buried.

'Angela's been on the warpath again, wanting to vet my talk for the recruitment evening, can you believe it!'

Matt tuts. He has no time for Angela. 'Don't let that silly bint get under your skin. Everyone knows you basically run the place. You organise the volunteers, you oversee the grant applications, you're responsible for the planting plans and rotas. Angela knows that too, so she's trying to exert what little control she has by micro-managing you.'

'I wish she wouldn't. I'm nervous enough as it is. What if she completely re-writes my presentation?'

'She won't. She's far too idle. When's the big day?'

'Wednesday.'

I know it's irrational but the very thought of giving a talk to a roomful of people fills me with dread. This is Cam's first ever recruitment evening and as deputy manager I'm in charge of volunteers, so it's fallen on me to give the presentation. I've spent hours preparing it, trying to paint a picture of the vital work we do for people like Rosie and Martin. I'm pleased with the result, but whether I'll be able to deliver it is another matter.

'You'll be fine.' Matt reaches for my hand and gives it a squeeze. His touch still sends a shiver down my spine, after all these years. 'Sorry I won't be there for you.'

'That's OK. Not your fault. Anyway, you haven't asked me what I've planned for tomorrow.'

'Tomorrow?'

'Your birthday!'

He rubs a hand over his face. 'Of course. Silly me. So, what are we doing?'

'I said we'd pop into Cam for a quick coffee. Rosie's baked you a cake. And I've booked a table for lunch at The Sportsman.'

Matt gives a low whistle. 'Very nice. Can we afford it?'

'You took me to Venice for my thirty-fifth,' I remind him.

'I know, but we were young and carefree in those days. We've got Junior to think about now.' He lays a hand on my belly and grins as the baby kicks against his touch. 'Lionel Messi, eat your heart out. This little one's going to play for England, you mark my words.'

I roll my eyes and reach over to take Matt's tray but he shakes his head. 'You put your feet up. I'll clear up tonight. I expect you've been on the go all day.'

I sink into the sofa with a contented sigh. 'You sure?'

'Absolutely. Nice hair, by the way. Toni and Guy?'

'You're hopeless. I told you ages ago I don't go there anymore.'

'So you did. Sorry. Head like a sieve. Must be the pregnancy hormones.'

I bat him on the arm. 'Idiot!' I say fondly. But at least he's noticed.

I pick up the remote and flick through the channels looking for some trashy TV to lose myself in. Matt drains his wine glass, picks up his tray, slips his phone into his back pocket and leaves the room.

CHAPTER SEVEN

THEN

L ou's dad drops us off at the school gates.
'I'll pick you up at half eleven, OK? Have fun.
And don't do anything I wouldn't.'

'As if we would,' Lou says wide-eyed.

We wave as he drives away.

'You're lucky. Your parents are so laid back,' I tell her.
Mine would insist on picking me up at ten at the latest and
if they saw my skimpy dress they'd completely freak. They
think I'm wearing the floral monstrosity I was made to wear
to my cousin Rachel's wedding last summer. But I'm an
only child whereas Lou's the youngest of four, and her sister
and two brothers are all working or at uni. It's easy for her to
duck under the parental radar. That's why it's always
simpler to stay at Lou's when we're going out.

The thumping beat of the disco grows louder as we join
a swarm of kids heading for the main entrance. Lou totters
up to the door on her enormous wedges, peers through and
darts back.

'Shit, I knew it. They're checking everyone's bags.' She
scrabbles around in her clutch for the vodka and offers it to

me. I shake my head. I've had plenty. She drains the rest and lobs the bottle over her shoulder. It lands with a clatter on the tarmac. A couple of boys from the Upper Sixth cheer and she curtseys unsteadily. I'm glad it's soft drinks only inside, otherwise I know I'd be spending another evening holding her hair back while she decorates a toilet bowl.

'Excited?' she asks, linking arms with me.

'Terrified.'

She tilts her head. 'Why? He won't bite.' She pauses. 'Or maybe he will, you lucky bugger.' She explodes into gales of laughter and half a dozen pairs of eyes swivel in our direction. Horrified, I elbow her in the ribs.

'Stop it,' I hiss. 'It's not funny.'

She holds a finger to her lips with exaggerated care and nods. 'You're right. Not funny.' She stumbles and suddenly her face is millimetres from mine. I can feel the warm puff of her breath on my cheek as she bends to whisper in my ear.

'Remember what I said. All you have to do is open your lips and let your tongue do the rest.' She laughs again as I shove her away and fold my arms across my chest.

It's alright for Lou. She lost her virginity at a party last summer. I've never even kissed anyone. Not properly. Tom Bennett tried to snog me in the back row of the cinema while we were supposed to be watching *Braveheart*, but I managed to wriggle out of his reach. He probably told all his mates I was frigid, but I don't care. It's not my fault I don't fancy him.

Lou, on the other hand, already has a bit of a reputation at school for being a good-time girl. I try to keep her in check, but when she's pissed she's out of control.

The queue edges forwards and I smooth my hair down. By my side, Lou is singing softly to herself. The tune is familiar, but it's not until the disco beat fades for a moment that I recognise the song.

'Sophie and Ed, sitting in a tree,' she sings. 'K-I-S-S-I-N-G.'

Once we're inside the main doors we head for the girls' loos to check we haven't got lip gloss on our teeth and then weave our way into the hall. The DJ is playing *Don't Turn Around* by Ace of Base and I let the music pulse through me as we find an empty table and stow our bags.

'Can you see him?' I shout.

'Don't worry about him yet. Let's dance!' Lou cries, pulling me onto the dance floor. We find a small gap in the throng of people and I give myself up to the music. My body feels supple and relaxed and I dance with the kind of abandonment I never would when sober. But all the time I'm scanning the crowds, searching for a glimpse of Ed's messy brown hair.

And then I see him. He's leaning against the closed canteen hatch at the back of the hall watching us. My insides turn to liquid. I glance at Lou. She's swaying to the music with her eyes half closed, lost in her own little world. I tap her on the shoulder.

'Gotta pee. Won't be long,' I shout in her ear. She nods and I shoulder my way across the dance floor. A thickset fifth-former with a ginger buzz cut stands on my foot and a girl in my maths set swears loudly when I accidentally knock some of her Coke over her, but I don't care. I only have eyes for Ed Sullivan.

Emboldened by the alcohol coursing through my veins, I sashay up to him.

'Come here often?' I say in a pseudo-husky voice, like some old tart out on the pull.

He laughs. 'Every weekday in term-time, regular as clockwork.'

He totally gets that I'm being ironic, and I love him for it.

'Me too! Wonder what else we've got in common.'

He's looking at me steadily, those hazel eyes of his staring deep into my soul. Goosebumps prickle my skin.

'You cold?' he asks, draping his denim jacket over my shoulders before I have a chance to answer.

'Thank you.' My knight in shining armour.

'My pleasure... Soph?'

Anything. You don't need to ask.

He bends his head and I tilt my face towards him, hoping Lou is right about the vodka. But instead of kissing me he whispers in my ear, 'Where's Lou?'

'Lou?'

'Lou,' he repeats, looking over my shoulder onto the dance floor. 'Is she with you?'

My eyes narrow. 'Not right now, no. Why?'

He rubs the back of his neck and gives a self-conscious titter. 'No reason.'

His eyes are still ranging over the mass of bodies now throbbing to *Things Can Only Get Better* by D:Ream. The irony isn't lost on me.

'There's always a reason,' I shout over the music. He turns back but can't look me in the eye and a tiny piece of me dies. How can I have been so wrong? He doesn't like me at all. He fancies her, just like everyone else. Blonde, bright, bubbly Lou, not shy, sensible Sophie, always lurking in her shadow. I draw back.

He must have noticed because he frowns.

'Hey, what's up?'

I shake my head and turn away. 'Nothing. Nothing's up.' I shrug off his jacket, letting it fall to the floor behind me, and march towards the toilets. *Don't cry don't cry don't cry.*

He's calling my name over and over but I ignore him. He reaches me by the doors to the hall.

'Sophie! Wait, what did I say wrong?'

'Nothing!'

'I don't believe you.' He takes my elbow and guides me out into the fresh air.

'Sit,' he orders, pointing to the much-graffitied bench under the huge oak tree that dominates the front of the school.

I do as I'm told and he sits next to me and offers me his jacket. I shake my head but he wraps it around me anyway.

'Why are you here? Shouldn't you be looking for Lou?' My voice is bitter.

He blinks. 'Why would I be looking for Lou?'

'You asked where she was.'

'You think I fancy her?'

I stare at the ground. 'What am I supposed to think?'

'Oh Sophie, you couldn't be more wrong. Lou's not my type at all.'

'So why were you asking about her?'

'Because I wanted to make sure you were on your own! You two are practically joined at the hip. It's impossible to have a conversation without her butting in. I wanted to talk to you. Just you.'

'You did?'

'I did.' He smiles. 'There's something I want to ask you.'

I hold my breath. Time stands still. I don't know how, but suddenly his lips are kissing distance from mine. His

47

breath smells of spearmint. He clears his throat. 'Sophie Williams, will you go out with me?'

Six little words that mean so much. If I could bottle this moment I would. I feel euphoric, as light as air. I realise we're holding hands. Lou and the rest of the world are forgotten as I meet his gaze and smile.

'I will.'

CHAPTER EIGHT

NOW

Monday morning arrives far too quickly. The weekend was perfect, despite its rocky start. Matt loved his shirt and declared his sea bass at The Sportsman faultless. After lunch we strolled along the sea wall at Seasalter watching families enjoying a day at the beach.

'That'll be us soon,' I said, as we passed a young couple helping their toddler build castles in a small strip of sand between the pebbles.

Matt squeezed my hand. 'Can't wait.'

On Sunday morning we had brunch in Canterbury and spent the rest of the day pottering in the garden. But on Sunday night an anxious little knot settled in my chest and I still feel twitchy when I wake up. Knowing Matt's so far away as my due date approaches makes it harder to say goodbye every time.

'I don't want you to go,' I tell him as we stand in the hallway saying our goodbyes.

'Only four sleeps,' he says, holding me close. But I can sense he's impatient to be off. I pull away.

'Text me when you arrive.'

He nods and pats his jacket to make sure he's remembered his phone. As he does it rings, but instead of answering it he gives a little shake of his head and opens the front door.

'Shouldn't you have taken that?'

'They'll phone back if it's important. But it's probably just another claims chaser. I seem to be very accident-prone at the moment.'

Sun is streaming through the open door and his face is in shadow. I feel a prickle of fear like an icy draught on the back of my neck and I clutch the bannister for support.

'Don't say that. You might tempt fate.'

'I won't.' He cups my chin. 'I love you. See you Friday.'

He picks up his holdall and disappears through the door. My eyes smart with tears and I brush them away with an impatient hand.

'I love you, too,' I whisper. But my words are lost in the swirl of dust motes in the now silent hallway. Matt has long gone.

Angela is already at her desk when I hurry into the office at ten past nine. She looks at her watch.

'Bloody traffic,' I say unnecessarily, as the city's ring road is a giant car park during rush hour most weekdays.

She gives a little harrumph. 'I found your presentation on the shared drive and read it yesterday. It's not the approach I would have taken -'

I slam my bag on the table and await the next brickbat.

' - but at this late hour it'll have to do. I know public speaking's not your thing. Would you like to have a run-through this afternoon?'

I'd rather stick red hot pokers in my eyes.

'That's very kind of you, but I'm sure I'll be fine,' I say.

'You know the Lord Mayor's coming, don't you?'

'How could I forget? And a reporter and photographer from the Gazette.'

'I am nervous about one thing,' Angela says. I glance over but she refuses to meet my eye.

'Yes?'

'Are you sure it's a good idea to have Rosie and Martin doing their little bits?'

'And why wouldn't it be?' I say with an edge to my voice.

'You know what Rosie's like, she's so hard to understand when she gets over-excited. And what if Martin has one of his episodes? It'll be a PR disaster!'

'I think you're forgetting one vital fact, *Angela*.' I spin out her name to hammer the point home. 'Camomile Community Garden was set up precisely for people like Rosie and Martin. Yes, they're unpredictable. They don't always read from the script. That doesn't mean we should keep them on the sidelines or treat them like second-class citizens. They love the garden and their enthusiasm is infectious. Any new volunteer worth their salt will see how rewarding working with them is. And if they don't, I'd rather not have them on the books.'

'I didn't mean -' Angela blusters, but I cut her short.

'Don't worry. I know exactly what you meant.'

She watches in silence as I retrieve the day's job list from my desk and stalk out of the room.

My blood's still boiling as I stomp across the garden to the cellar to find the tools we need. Geoff's outside, rinsing a trowel off under the tap.

'That bloody woman!'

He doesn't need to ask who. He and I loved working for Richard, Angela's predecessor, and we were devastated when he suffered a stroke and took early retirement. Geoff urged me to apply for Richard's job, but after much soul-searching I decided not to, preferring to be hands-on in the garden rather than spending my days worrying about funding streams and schmoozing local councillors. Bob Wittershaw, the chairman of our board of trustees, gave the job to his bit on the side. Angela's background is allegedly in business management, which is ironic, as she's the most ineffective manager I've ever had the misfortune to work for, and I worked for a few during the years I spent travelling. She's completely out of her depth and relies on me and Geoff to run the place. So I've ended up worrying about funding and doing my fair bit of schmoozing anyway.

Geoff chuckles. 'What's she done now?'

'Honestly, she's totally out of order. She's worried Rosie and Martin will make a show of themselves at the recruitment evening. Why come and work for a charity if you don't like the people we're here to help?'

'Rise above it,' Geoff advises. 'It's a lovely idea to include them.'

I shoot him a grateful smile. Geoff has more common sense in one little finger than Angela has, full stop. He's been a bit of a father figure to me since Dad died.

'I'll try. Although I've had it up to here. I'm going to completely lose it with her before long.'

'She's not worth getting in a tizzy over.' Geoff washes his hands and dries them on his shorts. 'Those runners are looking good.'

'I know. Rosie will be pleased. She's here this afternoon but I'll text her a photo of them in a sec.'

I fill a wheelbarrow with forks, hoes, shears and secateurs and push it over to the runner beans. Taking my phone from my back pocket, I'm about to slide the screen straight to camera mode when I see a notification from Messenger on the home screen. My heart lurches. It's from Lou. My eyes flicker down. The few lines I can see are littered with exclamation marks and capital letters, just like the notes she used to pass me in class when we were thirteen. Typical Lou. I sit down on one of the many benches dotted around the garden and read.

Hello stranger!!! Long time no speak! I was only thinking about you the other day. I happened to drive past school. It brought back SO many memories. Mostly happy ones!! I'm SO GLAD to hear from you! I was hoping you might turn up at the funeral but it's probably just as well. I was a MESS!! I assumed you'd moved away so I couldn't believe it when I got your message. Good old Facebook!! You don't know how much I'd LOVE to see you. How about coffee and cake in the café at Waterstones? God, it will be so good to see you. It's been TOO LONG!! Lou x

A single tear is running down my cheek and I bat it away. But it's soon followed by another, and another, until they're streaming down my face. I take a shuddering gulp of air but still the tears come. It's no wonder. Inside my ribcage my seventeen-year-old heart is breaking. Because despite all Lou's shouty capital letters and cheery exclamation marks I can only focus on one word.

Funeral.

When the first gardeners arrive I've managed to collect myself and, although a quick glance in the tiny mirror in the ladies' loo reveals I look on the pale shade of alabaster, at least the tears have stopped. But I still feel shaky, as though I've had a near miss with an articulated lorry, and when Rosie asks if I'd like 'a cuppa tea' I astonish her by asking for two sugars.

Martin is sitting on the edge of Cam's small lawn hugging his knees to his chest. I say his name and touch his shoulder. 'Hey, want to come and help prick out the lettuce?'

A smile spreads across his face. Pricking out seedlings is one of his favourite jobs. I'm with him on that. Sure, it's repetitive, but it requires dexterity and patience and it's so rewarding to give all those new plants space to grow.

'What do we need to remember?' I ask him as we carry trays of oak leaf lettuce seedlings into the greenhouse.

He's silent for a moment. 'Hold them by the leaf, not the stem.'

'That's right. Because if we damage a leaf they can grow another.'

He nods. 'But they can't grow another stem.'

He bounces on his toes and stretches his arms as if he's limbering up for a race. His grey teeshirt and baggy jeans hang off his slight frame and his muddy-brown hair is sticking up on one side. I stifle the urge to smooth it straight. Angela's always telling me off for mothering the gardeners.

We fill up a couple of dozen plant pots with potting compost and I hand Martin a plastic green dibber before reaching into my back pocket for the Swiss Army knife I always have with me. Monty Don uses one for pricking out, and if it's good enough for Monty Don, it's good enough for me.

Martin eyes the knife with longing.

'Can I use it? Please, Sophie.'

I check over my shoulder. There's no sign of Angela.

She'd have a pink fit if she knew I was even considering giving a knife to one of the gardeners, but Martin's used mine before. A little trust goes a long way at Cam. He leans forward, his eyes wide. He seems calm enough today.

'Alright then. But don't tell Angela.'

He grins and holds out his hand. I pass him the knife, blade towards me, and we ease the delicate seedlings out of the tray. I push all thoughts of Ed and Lou out of my mind and concentrate on guiding the tiny plants into their new pots.

'It's too crowded in there,' says Martin, waving the knife at the seed tray in front of him. 'They need head space. I need head space, too.'

'We all need head space.' I brush the compost from my hands. 'We'd better get these watered and then I've promised to help Rosie pick some flowers for the recruitment evening. Are you looking forward to it?'

He pats his jeans pocket. 'I've been practising and practising and practising. My mum says she knows it off by heart. But I'm still nervous.'

I make a play of looking over my shoulder to check no-one's in earshot. 'I'll let you in on a secret. I'm nervous, too.' I hold out my hand for the knife, and Martin hands it over reluctantly. 'It's OK, you can borrow it another day. Just remember -'

He laughs manically. 'Don't tell Angela!'

It was Rosie's idea to decorate the hall we're using for the recruitment evening with some of the flowers and vegetables we grow at Cam.

'The boys can do the tomatoes and stuff, and you and me can do the flowers,' she said.

I'd looked at her in admiration. 'It's a wonderful idea, Rosie. You clever thing.'

She'd beamed with pleasure and is still smiling now as we walk along Cam's gravel paths choosing the most beautiful flowers to use in our displays.

'You seem happy now, but you looked sad before,' she says out of nowhere. 'And you asked for two sugars!' she marvels. Her bottom lip wobbles. 'It's not little Rosie is it?'

I am quick to reassure her. 'Little Rosie is fine. I'd just heard from a very old friend who I haven't seen for a long, long time and I felt a bit sad.'

'As old as my granny?' she says, her eyes wide.

I laugh. 'When I say old, I mean old as in from a long time ago, not how old she is. Lou's the same age as me. Which is quite old enough.'

'She's called *Loo*? Like *toilet*?'

I laugh again. 'No, Lou, short for Louise. She was my best friend when we were at school. But we lost touch and she moved to America. I haven't seen her for more than twenty years.'

'That's a shame.' Rosie snips off a pale pink carnation and lays it in the trug I'm carrying. 'Why did Lou make you sad?'

'She told me her husband had died. He used to be my friend, too.'

'That *is* sad.'

'And now Lou's moved back to Canterbury and wants to meet for coffee.' I shift the trug onto my other arm. 'But I'm not sure it's a good idea.'

I'm thinking aloud, but Rosie spins around, her mouth hanging open.

'Why? She was your *best friend*. You *must* want to see her again!'

I shake my head. Rosie doesn't understand. Seeing Lou will unleash emotions I've kept suppressed for years. I'm not sure I can deal with her, let alone her grief, right now. I'm like an unseasoned traveller turning up for a low-cost flight. I have too much baggage.

And yet I've missed Lou. She left a hole as big as Ed did when I walked out of their lives. Ed's gone, but I have a chance to make things right with her.

'So, you think I should see her?'

Rosie nods. 'Have a nice cuppa with Lou. But remember, no sugars!'

CHAPTER NINE

NOW

I'm sitting in the back row of the church hall half an hour before the recruitment evening is due to start when my phone buzzes with a text from Matt.

Good luck sweetheart. Hope you're managing to keep a lid on your nerves. Just be yourself. They'll love you as much as I do xx

I tap a quick reply back.

I just want to get it over and done with TBH. But the hall looks great at least. Love you xx

It's true. The hall looks amazing. We've set out enough chairs for sixty people, which is probably a bit optimistic, and Geoff and Bob Wittershaw's wife Mary have done a brilliant job with the display boards, which are plastered with photos of the gardeners at work from spring right through to winter. The top table, where Rosie, Martin and I will sit, has been decorated with an emerald-green table-cloth and two beautiful floral arrangements using the flowers Rosie and I picked. Another table along the back of the hall bears crates of lettuce and French beans, mange tout and early tomatoes from the greenhouse, which we're offering our guests in return for a small donation.

Even Angela couldn't help but be impressed.

'You've done a good job. Let's hope the talk goes just as well.'

The remark was so typical of Angela that I couldn't help but smile. She's queen of the back-handed compliments.

I check the time. It's twenty to seven. Mary and Rowena, another of our volunteers, are pouring orange squash into plastic cups and filling bowls with crisps. Angela wanted to serve wine and platters of finger food but for once I put my foot down. I'm not frittering our meagre budget on nibbles and booze.

My nerves are jangling. What if no-one turns up? The local paper published a page feature on Cam and its work last week and I've sent details of the recruitment evening to all the parish magazines within a ten-mile radius. We even had a mention on Radio Kent's Sunday gardening show, but I still have no idea how many to expect.

The baby is pressing down on my bladder. Do I have time for another quick trip to the loo? I smile as I remember Rosie's confusion yesterday. After a bit of dithering I took her advice and arranged to meet Lou in Waterstones after my midwife appointment in the morning. I don't know what I'm more nervous about - talking to a roomful of people or chatting one-to-one with my former best friend.

The double doors at the back of the hall swing open and a grey-haired woman with a kind face steps inside. I walk over to welcome her. As she does the doors open again and over the next ten minutes a steady stream of people arrive.

At five to seven I nip to the ladies'. As I'm washing my hands I stare at my reflection in the mottled mirror above the sink. I look pasty apart from areas of brown pigmentation on my cheeks and forehead. Pregnancy mask, they call it. It appeared despite my religious application of factor 50 sunscreen every morning and no amount of foundation covers it. I hate it, but Matt says I should embrace it, like the morning sickness and thick ankles. Easy for him to say.

Outside the toilet I can hear the hubbub of people in the hall. I catch my breath as fear sweeps through me. *I can't do it.* I hold out my hands. My fingers are trembling like a drunk on a detox. Why did I ever think this was a good idea? I press my head against the cool mirror and wait for my nerves to subside.

This is how Mary Wittershaw finds me a few minutes later.

'Sophie, are you alright?'

The concern in her voice fills me with shame. I'm only giving a talk to a couple of dozen people, for Christ's sake. It's not as though I even have to give it off the cuff. It's all there, on my PowerPoint presentation.

'I'm fine. Just taking a moment.' I rub my trembling hands together as if relishing the task ahead. 'Let's get this show on the road!'

Mary's husband Bob is already at the top table.

'I've told him to keep it short,' Mary whispers out of the corner of her mouth. 'But I'm afraid he does enjoy the sound of his own voice. He lives up to his name. He'd witter on for England given half the chance. Feel free to cut him off when you've had enough.'

This makes me grin, and I'm still smiling as I take my place next to him. Rosie is also beaming, but Martin is sitting hunched over with his head down, picking at the translucent skin on the inside of his wrist. It's a nervous habit that's always exacerbated when he's anxious. I feel a stab of guilt that I'm putting him through this. I touch his shoulder and mouth, 'You OK?' but he just stares at me with vacant eyes.

The hall falls silent as Bob pushes his chair back and stands.

'Welcome to Camomile Community Garden's first ever recruitment evening. Tonight you'll learn about the charity and the work we do for people like Rosie and Martin and how you can help. But first I'd like to tell you about the history of the project, which celebrated its tenth anniversary last year.'

I zone out as Bob burbles on about how Cam was set up and how it relies on charitable donations and grants to survive. Instead I scan the hall, curious to see the kinds of people who might be joining our ranks.

It's no surprise they fit the profile of a typical volunteer at Cam - middle class and newly retired. I'd love to see a few younger faces on the books. After all, a lot of the gardeners are in their early twenties. But most twenty-some-things are working and playing too hard. At least their grandparents' generation is reliable and keen to help.

I spot a familiar face. It's Roz, sitting on her own in the back row, her handbag on her lap. She must have sensed me watching her because she smiles and gives me a little wave. I smile back. I'm surprised she's here. She doesn't strike me as the gardening type. Perhaps she came along as moral support as Matt couldn't make it. I can't remember mentioning the evening to her, but I can't remember anything much at the moment.

A couple of people in the front row are growing fidgety. I know I need to take control and cut Bob off. Trying to ignore my racing heart, I take three deep breaths and shuffle to my feet, hoping no-one notices my trembling knees.

I clear my throat. 'Thank you, Bob, for your very comprehensive insight into the history of Camomile Community Garden, or Cam, as it's known to its friends.'

There's a small ripple of applause and Bob sits down reluctantly. I open my laptop, tap in my password and navigate to the shared drive on which I've saved my presentation.

The file is sandwiched between a funding application and last year's accounts. I click on it and wait for it to open. The first slide is a group shot of all our gardeners and volunteers at last year's open day. But there's no sign of it now. Instead a small window opens. My eyes slide over the words with a feeling of dread.

The file is corrupt and cannot be opened.

CHAPTER TEN

NOW

I close the window and try opening the file again. The same message pops up on the screen. I try a third time. Out of the corner of my eye I see a man wearing a frayed Panama hat sneak a look at his watch.

This can't be happening. What am I going to do? All those carefully-crafted words, the dozens of photos I've taken, all stuck in cyber hell. There's no way I can give this talk without them. The urge to flee is so intense I have to grip the edge of the table to stop myself pushing the chair back and sprinting from the room.

My eyes slide over to Angela, who is sitting in the front row flanked by the Lord Mayor and the reporter from the Kentish Gazette. Her arms are crossed and she's staring at me flinty-eyed. I know I have to say something, but my tongue is sticking to the roof of my mouth and I seem to have lost the power of speech.

Seconds tick by. Beside me, Rosie is humming to herself, oblivious to my predicament. Martin is still plucking at his wrist. Every sound is amplified in my heightened state of anxiety. The scrape of a chair at the back of the hall; the scratch of the reporter's pen as he doodles in his notebook; the distant rumble of a lorry on the ring road. *Think, think, think.* How did the talk begin? I search my memory but draw blanks. My palms are clammy and I wipe them on my dress. As I run them over my belly the baby kicks. It's the catalyst I need to pull me from my inertia.

My baby, whose precious life began in a petri dish, has survived this far against the odds, clinging on with the gritty determination of a battle-scarred warrior, while I'm paralysed with terror at the thought of talking to a roomful of people eager to hear about my beloved Cam. *Pathetic.*

I reach for the glass of water on the table in front of me and take a small sip. The baby kicks again. I think of the petri dish and the moment of conception. Just start at the beginning, says a tiny voice inside my head and I take a deep breath.

'I remember the first time I walked through the gates into Cam.' My voice sounds shaky, but I plough on. 'It was love at first sight. A little slice of horticultural heaven on the edge of our beautiful city. I began as a volunteer just like you all.' I raise my chin and smile. 'Just like you all will be by the end of the evening, anyway...I hope.' There's a small murmur of assent. It's enough to give me confidence. 'I fell in love not just with the plants but with the people, people like Rosie here, and Martin. And when the opportunity to work at Cam came along I grabbed it with both hands.'

I pause, relieved to see I have their attention. 'Gardening has such a positive impact on both physical and mental health. Being in the garden keeps us connected to other living things. Studies have shown that self-absorption can contribute to depression. Gardening allows us to be nurturers, it gives us a sense of responsibility and helps us be less insular.'

My gaze wanders to Roz, sitting on her own at the back of the hall. She's listening intently.

'If the plants are Cam's oxygen, the volunteers are its lifeblood. Without them we couldn't function. We need people like you to support our gardeners and to help us fundraise to keep this vital amenity flourishing. Working with our gardeners is immensely satisfying and rewarding and it's also great fun. I give you my personal guarantee that you'll love it. In fact, I promise that after your first week you'll be wondering why you didn't volunteer years ago.'

A couple of people chuckle. They're finally on my side.

'I'd like to hand over to two of our gardeners, Rosie and Martin, who would like to say a few words.'

Rosie leaps to her feet and grins at the audience.

'I'm Rosie and I'm twenty-two. I'm *always* getting into trouble. Angela says I'm like a bull with two left feet in a china shop. But I think that's a bit mean to bulls. Cam is my favourite place in the whole wide world, and I love working with Sophie and Geoff and the others, even Angela. *When* she's in a good mood.'

There's an awkward pause and I hardly dare look at my boss. She's bound to think I've put Rosie up to this, but I really haven't.

Rosie screws up her face as she tries to remember what comes next. 'My favourite thing about working at Cam is eating the things I've grown with my own hands.' She holds out her hands and wiggles her fingers. 'It always tastes scrumdiddlyumptious! And now I'm going to tell you a secret. Sophie's having a baby and when she's born she's going to call her Rosie, just like me!'

Everyone claps as she sits back down. I give her the thumbs up before turning to Martin.

'Ready, Marty?'

Avoiding eye contact, he reaches for the tatty piece of paper on the table in front of him. As he does his sleeve slips back and I notice beads of blood on his wrist. My heart lurches. Why did I ever think this was a good idea? He's been showing the occasional sign of manic behaviour over the last couple of weeks. What if this sends him in a downward spiral? Subconsciously I rub a thumb over the jagged scar on the underside of my forearm.

Martin pulls himself to his feet and crumples the paper in his hand. He wraps his thin arms around himself and stares at an electric bar heater suspended from the ceiling above us.

'I'm Martin and I'm twenty-six and I have schizophrenic disorder and I'm bipolar which means sometimes I'm very happy and sometimes I'm very sad and sometimes I'm very hyper and sometimes I'm very angry but I'm always happy when I'm at Cam almost always anyway because being with the plants helps me keep calm and gives me head space because we all need head space don't we Sophie?'

His entire discourse has been delivered in an emotionless, almost robotic monotone. He sits down abruptly and glances at me.

I touch his hand. 'We certainly do. Thank you, Martin and Rosie, for telling us why Cam is so important to you. And thank you to everyone for coming along tonight to learn about the work we do. If you'd like to join us, please see Mary to fill in a form and if you have any questions don't hesitate to ask.'

There's another round of applause and I exhale slowly. My legs still feel like jelly, as if I've just swum the Channel or climbed Scafell Pike.

'Did I do OK?' Rosie says, her forehead crinkling.

'You did brilliantly. You both did.'

Martin is still hunched in his chair. 'I did it for you, Sophie,' he mumbles. 'I wouldn't have done it for anyone else.'

'I know, and I'm so grateful. You both made a great impression. Look at all those people filling in forms!'

Rosie claps her hands in delight. 'Fan-bloody-tastic!'

I spy Martin's mum Maureen sitting on the end of a row and head over to her. She must have come straight from work as she's still wearing her navy polyester cleaning overalls. Years of worry are etched on her face. It can't be easy caring for someone with such complex mental health problems as Martin, yet I've never once heard her complain.

She pats the chair beside her and I sit down.

'I hope Martin wasn't too anxious about speaking today.'

'He did get himself a bit worked up about it,' she admits. 'But he'll be pleased he did it.'

'How is he in himself?'

Maureen shakes her head. 'Not great. He promises me he's taking his medication, but he's having problems sleeping again.'

I know from experience this is not good.

'Any hallucinations or delusions?'

'He says not. I've managed to get an appointment with his care co-ordinator next week. Just to have a chat with him and check his med levels.'

'Let me know if there's anything I can do.'

She brushes my offer aside. 'Nonsense! You've enough on your plate getting ready for the baby. Don't you worry about Martin. He'll be right as rain. Look, there's someone to see you. You take care, and I'll see you soon.' And she scurries off to see her son.

Roz takes her place.

'This is a nice surprise,' I say. 'You didn't tell me you were coming.'

She shrugs. 'It was a spur of the moment thing. I remembered you telling me about it ages ago and I thought I'd come along and sign up. Do my bit, you know? And besides,' she pats her concave stomach and pulls a face, 'I could do with the exercise.'

'Hardly. You've got an amazing figure! You make me feel like a big fat frump.'

'Ah, but you're pregnant. You have the perfect excuse. Was it the baby brain that made you lose it up there?'

I grimace. 'Was it that obvious?'

She gives me an amused look. 'I was waiting for the tumbleweed to blow past. What happened?'

'I get really nervous about public speaking, but I thought I'd be OK because I had my PowerPoint presentation to use as a crutch. When I tried to open it, the bloody thing had corrupted.'

'Files don't corrupt for no reason. You can't have closed it down properly the last time you used it. Unless there's a virus in the application.'

'I didn't know you knew so much about computers.'

'What, for a mobile hairdresser? There's a lot you don't know about me.' She fixes her green eyes on mine. 'And I you. You didn't tell me you're having a girl.'

'We're not. Well, we might be - there's a fifty-fifty chance obviously - but we don't know. We don't want to find out until the birth. I told you that.'

She nods to herself. 'That's what I thought. So why did that girl say you were?'

'Rosie? It's wishful thinking. She wants us to name the baby after her.'

'She knows you're not going to, right?'

I'm not sure why it matters so much to Roz. 'Probably not, no. You know me, I don't like to think too far ahead.' I have a sudden compulsion to change the subject. 'So, I haven't put you off?'

For a second she looks confused and then her face clears. 'No. It sounds like fun. And we'll get to spend more time together, won't we?'

She smiles and rests her hand on my bump. Her touch is reassuring and my shoulders relax for the first time all evening. She's such a good friend to me. I have more in common with Roz than I ever did with Lou.

Her hand slips away as I pull myself to my feet. 'We will indeed. I'd better go and find you a form before you change your mind.'

CHAPTER ELEVEN

THEN

Sunlight from a crack in the curtains dances on my eyelids, dragging me from a deep sleep. I stretch and yawn. Beneath me the blow-up bed sighs like a disappointed parent.

I glance up at Lou. She's lying on her back with her mouth open, snoring gently. She's out for the count. Rubbing my face, I reach for the glass of water on the floor beside me. My mouth is paper dry and my lips feel bruised...but in a good way. Hardly surprising. After Ed asked me out and I said yes he cupped my face in his hands and kissed me like it was our last day on earth.

We stayed on the bench, our bodies entwined, lips nibbling, tongues probing, for what seemed like hours. Ed traced my face with his fingers while I drowned in his eyes. We kissed and kissed and kissed. The effects of the vodka had long worn off, but it didn't matter. I was drunk on happiness.

Lou broke the spell when she burst out of the school hall, spied us and stumbled over. Her pupils were tiny pinpricks and her voice was slurred.

'There you are! I've been looking for you all over!'

The accusation in her voice was unmistakable and my heart sank. Ed tipped me off his lap and ran his fingers through his hair.

'Everything alright?' I asked her.

'Couldn't be better. I've been abandoned by my best friend, I've drunk all my booze, and they're playing slow songs and nobody's asked me to dance. Not a single anybody.'

'Don't be melodramatic. I haven't abandoned you. I just needed a bit of fresh air.'

She squinted at me and jabbed a finger in Ed's direction. 'Fresh air my arse. You got off with him, didn't you? Sexy Ed. Said you would, didn't I? I'm very pleased for you both. But now it's time to come and dance with me. I'm loneleeee.' She attempted a twirl, only to lose her balance halfway round. If Ed hadn't grabbed her elbow to steady her she'd have ended up kissing the concrete.

'My knight in shining armour,' she slurred, as he guided her onto the bench next to me.

Pop! My bubble of happiness was pierced by a dart of jealousy, just like that.

'My knight,' I said, eyes narrowed. She was too pissed to notice the barb in my voice, but Ed did, and a pained expression flickered across his face. Muttering something about needing a drink, he mooched off towards the school hall, his hands in his pockets.

Once he was out of earshot Lou turned to me, her eyes wide. 'So, what's he like, then? Is he a good kisser?'

'How would I know? I don't have anything to compare him to, do I?'

'The back of your hand?' Lou roared with laughter. I bit

my bottom lip. She has a cruel streak when she's had a drink. Verging on vindictive.

'You know, he's actually quite hot. You've snared yourself a babe. You should be chuffed to bits. So, why are you looking so bloody miserable?'

'I'm not.'

'When are you seeing him next?'

I held up my hands. 'Stop with the cross-examination. I don't know, alright? We didn't get a chance to arrange anything before we were interrupted.'

Lou pulled a face. 'Oops. My fault. Anyway, forget about him. Can we go and dance now? Pretty please?'

I stood up and tugged at the hem of my dress as I tried to gather my thoughts. They were dominated by Ed. Where did we stand? Were we a couple? Could I call him my boyfriend if we hadn't arranged a date? I had no idea.

Lou grabbed my hand and pulled me back into the disco. My eyes raked the hall, but I couldn't see Ed anywhere. I followed Lou back onto the dance floor. This time my limbs felt wooden and my feet as heavy as bricks. I danced half-heartedly until the beat slowed for the last song, Seal's *Kiss from a Rose,* and we drifted to the edge of the hall. One of the boys from the Upper Sixth who'd cheered Lou earlier appeared by her side and within seconds they were necking, her arms around his neck, his meaty hands clasping her backside.

My mood was growing darker as I watched them sway to the music. It was fine for her to leave me on the sidelines. God forbid I should do the same to her. I scanned the hall for the hundredth time. Ed wasn't on the dance floor, smooching with another girl. That was something, at least. Had he gone home? If so, why didn't he say goodbye? Where did that leave us?

Hands snaking around my waist from behind made me yelp in surprise. I turned to see a pair of already familiar hazel eyes smiling down at me.

'Where were you?' I demanded, but he put a finger to my lips and led me onto the dance floor. My bad mood melted away as he bent his head to kiss me...

———

'You awake?' whispers a croaky voice and I'm back in Lou's bedroom, curled up on a sagging blow-up bed.

'Uh huh. How's your head?'

She winces. 'Not great. Gimme your water.'

I sit up and hand her the glass. Her long blonde hair is tangled and there's the unmistakeable crimson bloom of a lovebite on her neck.

She empties the glass and wipes her mouth with the back of her hand. 'What a night!'

'You and that guy from the Upper Sixth seemed to hit it off.'

She fans herself and laughs. 'Dan? He's lush. I'm meeting him at the park later for more of the same. Wanna come?'

'Thanks for the generous offer, but I can think of things I'd rather do than sit there while you two fumble in the grass. Like eat my own intestines.'

'You're so funny.' She pauses, eyes narrowed. 'Hey wait, you and Ed finally got it together, didn't you? I nearly forgot you're an item! 'Spect you're seeing him this afternoon.'

I'm about to tell her that yes, we've arranged to meet outside McDonald's at two, but something stops me. I don't want her to know. I don't want her quizzing me on everything Ed's said or done. I don't want her unpicking our fledgling romance, over-analysing our every action with rapt fascination. At the moment Ed and I are held together by a gossamer-like thread. We need to learn to be a couple without the scrutiny of Lou Stapleton, even if she is my best friend.

I let my fringe fall over my eyes. 'No,' I lie. 'He never asked me out. We're not anything.'

CHAPTER TWELVE

NOW

The health centre's waiting room is about as far removed from healthy as it's possible to be. Two seats down from me a snotty toddler in a grubby white teeshirt and faded red shorts is systematically ripping up an ancient copy of *Take a Break* while his mum scrolls through her phone, oblivious to the pile of torn paper growing at her feet. Opposite me an elderly man with bloodshot grey eyes and bushy eyebrows is scratching a large area of psoriasis on his forearm. Behind me two women are comparing notes on their bed sores.

I shudder. I bet if I licked my finger and held it in the air a gazillion microscopic pathogens would be glued to it within seconds. I check my watch. The midwife is running twenty minutes late. I hunker down in my seat and breathe as shallowly as I can, as if that's going to make a difference.

Finally, when I've just about given up hope of ever seeing her, a door opens. A heavily pregnant woman waddles out and Jackie, my midwife, calls me in.

'How's it going?' she asks as I hand her my plastic pot of urine.

'OK, I think. I'm finding work a bit tiring now.'

She unscrews the top of the pot and dips a plastic stick into it. 'Remind me when you're planning to go on maternity leave?'

'Thirty-six weeks.'

'You can't go any earlier?'

'My boss wanted me to stay until thirty-eight.'

'And let me guess, she doesn't have children?'

I give a wry smile. 'Spot on.'

Jackie reaches for her blood pressure monitor and I roll up my left sleeve. She fixes the cuff around my arm and pumps it up, her eyes on the monitor as she releases the air and scribbles something in my notes.

'One hundred and fifty over one hundred. That's high for you.'

'It's been a stressful week. We had a recruitment evening last night and after this I'm meeting a friend I haven't seen for over twenty years. I'm a bit nervous, to tell you the truth.'

'As long as that's all it is. But come back and see me in two weeks rather than three.'

I grip the side of the chair. 'Do you think I might have pre-eclampsia?'

'No. Your blood pressure's what we'd describe as moderate, not severe. And there's no protein in your urine. We'll put it down to your stressful week. But if you start getting severe headaches or blurred vision, or if your hands, feet or face start to swell, call me, OK? Better safe than sorry.'

She must have noticed I've gone quiet because she pats my hand and says, 'Worrying will only make it worse, and there's nothing to worry about, I promise. Shall we listen to the baby's heartbeat?'

'Yes please.'

Jackie rolls a length of blue paper onto the couch and I slip off my shoes and lay down. At first she can't find the baby's heartbeat, which probably sends my blood pressure into the severe bracket, but eventually the static-filled sound of a rapid-fire beating heart fills the small room.

'See, nothing to worry about.' She wipes off the gel with another length of blue paper and has a prod and a poke. 'And the baby's the right size for your dates. You're both doing a great job.'

'Thanks. It's hard not to be paranoid when you've been through as much as we have to get here.'

Jackie smiles. 'I know. But try not to worry. When that baby comes kicking and screaming into the world you'll look back at your pregnancy with longing. In fact, you'll be harking back to the days when your bladder was the only thing keeping you up in the middle of the night.'

The baby kicks me in the ribs as if agreeing and I say goodbye, promising to ring her if I notice any signs of pre-eclampsia.

I walk along Old Dover Road, following a gaggle of university students across the pedestrian crossing and into the underpass. It's a couple of degrees colder down here and I wrap my cardigan around me.

I wasn't lying when I told Jackie I was nervous. The thought of seeing Lou again has stirred a welter of injurious emotions that I'm finding hard to pick apart. Resentment, jealousy, grief, shame, guilt, anger - they're all there, coalescing in my psyche like a particularly unpalatable one dish supper.

I turn into Whitefriars and stop at HSBC to take out some cash. As I'm waiting for the ATM to spit out my money I look up at Waterstones. The café is on the first floor of the bookshop and I can see a blonde woman sitting in an armchair by the wall-to-ceiling windows. Even though her head is dipped as she studies her phone I know it's her. Lou. I can tell by the narrow taper of her shoulders and the way she's sitting, knees together and feet crossed at the ankles, like she always did.

I thrust the money into my purse. I don't think she's seen me. It's not too late to leave. I could dart into the bank and send her a message, tell her sorry, so sorry, but the car's broken down/I've been called into work/we have a gas leak/the cat has been rushed to the vet's. Of course there's no leak and we don't even own a cat, but she doesn't know that. I'm good at excuses.

Running away is so bloody tempting. I did it before, didn't I? But I know deep down I can't run away forever. I hitch my bag onto my shoulder and start walking.

'Sophie darling!'

Eyes swivel in our direction as Lou leaps from her chair and embraces me extravagantly. She holds me at arms' length, looks me up and down and declares, 'Look at you! Absolutely blooming! It's wonderful to see you, darling. *Wonderful!*'

Christ alive. It's like I've stumbled onto the set of *Absolutely Fabulous*. When did she get so flamboyant, so OTT? I can feel the eyes of half a dozen people in the café boring into my neck.

'Another coffee?' I ask quickly.

'Flat white for me. Two shots. Heavy night.'

I retreat to the queue at the counter, glad to have a moment to collect myself. From this distance Lou looks impossibly elegant. Skinny jeans, strappy sandals, a white fitted shirt and a navy jacket. Chunky bracelets on her wrists and sunglasses perched on her head. Her lips and nails are painted scarlet and her teeth are as pearly-white as her shirt. I took time over my make-up and dressed with care this morning, choosing my favourite soft grey Vertbaudet cross-over teeshirt and matching cardigan, white maternity leggings and grey ballet pumps, but I still feel dowdy in comparison.

'What would you like?' says the girl at the counter, interrupting my thoughts.

I give her my order and carry Lou's coffee and my pot of Earl Grey over to the table.

Lou is staring out of the window at the shoppers on the street below and when she turns to me her eyes are bright with unshed tears. 'It's so good to see you.'

'You too,' I say.

'You know why I'm back?'

I don't want her to know I've been digging around on Facebook, so I pick my way around the truth. 'Someone told me a while ago that Ed had cancer, and then you mentioned the funeral in your message. I'm so sorry.'

She reaches for her coffee with trembling fingers. 'It's been an absolutely shit year. He started complaining about feeling tired and rundown last autumn but refused to go to the doctors. You know how stubborn men can be. When he began losing weight I made him an appointment and drove him there myself. But by the time he'd been diagnosed with bowel cancer it had already spread to his liver and lungs. He had surgery and a couple of rounds of chemo at the beginning of the year, but it was too little, too late. We lost him in April.'

Lou places her cup in its saucer without having taken a sip.

I reach for her hand. 'It must have been awful.'

'You have no idea.'

I do, actually. I went through it with Dad, stage by painful stage. But now isn't the time to point it out.

'And your son? How's he coping?'

Her voice thickens. 'Josh? Outwardly he seems fine, but I don't know. He won't talk to me about it. And he was so close to his dad. He's at Kent Uni reading law. Wants to be a solicitor, same as Ed. That's why I moved back to Canterbury. He's in halls but I wanted to be close by in case he needed me.'

She picks up her coffee and stirs it. 'I wasn't sure you even knew we were married, if I'm honest. We sent you an invite to the wedding care of your parents' address but you never replied.'

'Never saw it.' I'm on safer ground now. 'I went travelling while you were at uni. I was away for years. Japan, Australia, South America. Mum and Dad only knew where I was when I managed to phone home. And of course there was no internet or mobile phones in those days. They looked after my mail, but they never mentioned a wedding invitation.'

'Probably trying to protect you. I don't blame them. I'm so sorry.'

'Water under the bridge.' I smile. 'I always thought you fancied him.'

'When we were kids?' she says, appalled. Her dismay seems genuine. 'I didn't, I promise. I hadn't seen him for years and then we bumped into each other on New Year's Eve 1999 in Alberrys wine bar of all places. I was wait-ressing there while I was looking for my dream job in publishing and Ed had just started at law school in Guildford. We got talking. The first thing he asked me was whether I was still in touch with you.'

My throat constricts and I take a sip of tea, not trusting myself to speak. But Lou doesn't notice. She's lost in her trip down memory lane.

'I told him you and I had lost touch after I started at Warwick. He hadn't spoken to you since the day you dumped him. He still seemed cut up about it. We exchanged phone numbers and that was it. I doubt I'd have ever seen him again, but I got a job as a publishing assistant at a small imprint in Guildford. Everyone there was in their forties and married with kids. I was Billy No Mates. So I gave him a ring to see if he wanted to meet up. He did. I'd just come out of a long-term relationship and he was between girlfriends. We went out on a few dates. We had a laugh, but I don't think either of us ever thought it was serious.'

She looks sidelong at me. 'And then I found out I was pregnant.'

Her words are like a right hook in my diaphragm and for a moment I am breathless.

'Pregnant?' The word is barely a whisper.

'With Joshie,' Lou confirms. 'It knocked Ed for six when I told him. Becoming a dad at twenty-two wasn't part of his life plan at all. But you know what a gentleman he is. Was. He asked me to marry him. And I said yes.'

'Why didn't you -'

' - get rid of it? I just couldn't.'

I stare at her, speechless. I literally have nothing to say. This close up she looks every one of her forty-one years. Lines fan out from her eyes and there are webs of tiny broken capillaries on her cheeks.

'OK, so it wasn't the love affair of the century. Not like

you had with him. And we may have married for the wrong reasons. But we had a happy marriage and a good life, and there wasn't a single day I regretted becoming Mrs Sullivan. And now he's gone and I don't think I can cope without him.' Her voice, steady up to this point, disintegrates into a series of gulps and splutters and I fish around in my bag for a clean tissue.

She blows her nose, flips open a compact and grimaces at her tear-streaked face. 'God, I look shit.'

'You've been through a tough time.'

She reapplies her lipstick and snaps the compact shut.

'Let's not talk about it anymore. Too bloody depressing. Tell me your news instead, darling. Is this your first baby?'

Taken aback by the clinical speed in which she's switched from maudlin widow back into *Ab Fab* mode, I can only mumble, 'Yes. Well, sort of.'

'And when's it due?'

'First week in September.'

'I see you're married,' she says gesturing to my ring finger. 'Who's the lucky man?'

'Matt.'

'And how did you meet?'

I can't help smiling. 'He spilt a glass of red wine down my white dress in the bar at The Marlowe Theatre. We'd both gone to see Dara O'Briain.'

'No way!' squeals Lou, and it's only then I glimpse the girl I knew behind the red lipstick and affectations.

'He bought me dinner afterwards to apologise. We were married six months later.'

'And how long ago was that?' says Lou, clearly enjoying the story.

'We had our seventh wedding anniversary in May.'

'Got a photo of him?'

'Sure.' I scroll through the pictures on my phone looking for one I took on the beach in Corfu last summer. Matt looks tanned and relaxed and ridiculously handsome. I know it's shallow, but I want her to know I hooked myself a babe. I hand her my phone and she gives a low whistle.

'He's hot! And what does this hot husband of yours do?'

'He's a bank manager.'

'Bloody hell, Soph. Brains and brawn. You really hit pay dirt, you lucky bugger. No wonder you waited so long to have children. I'd have wanted him to myself if I were you, too.'

Once again it's like I've been punched in the stomach. Her thoughtlessness astounds me. She of all people should realise why we might have waited so long to have a baby. I twist my hands in my lap, so agitated I can't speak. But Lou's too busy studying the photo of my husband to notice.

I identified the opportunity late last year. If I said it was kismet, that this last chance of happiness was preordained, I'd be lying. Fate, destiny - call it what you will - had fuck all to do with it. I made this happen. Correction. Am making it happen. And I take full credit for that.

I spent years dreaming, months searching, weeks carrying out the legwork, until I eventually found what I was looking for.

I wanted what was rightfully mine.

And I'd have been happy with that.

Then fate did play its part. I was given a golden ticket. An all-star bonus. An added extra. Two for the price of one. I was presented with not just my past and my present, but my future, too.

The gods were smiling on me. They offered me everything I always wanted, everything I deserved. Everything that bitch took away from me.

And Sophie, sweet Sophie, has absolutely no idea what's coming her way.

CHAPTER THIRTEEN

If I was worried Lou would find out about me and Ed, I needn't have been. It's been easy to keep our relationship secret. She's so wrapped up in Dan, the boy from the Upper Sixth, that she barely remembers I exist.

Normally, I'd be wounded. Aggrieved. But now it suits me just fine. It means Ed and I can get to know each other without Lou sticking her oar in.

Ed can't understand why I haven't told her. He says the longer I leave it, the harder it'll be. Today, after school, as we sit on our favourite bench in the Westgate Gardens, I try to explain.

'I love Lou, I really do. She's been my best mate since I can remember. But she's so outgoing, so larger-than-life, that I've always lived in her shadow, you know?'

Ed is pensive as he watches the River Stour glide by. 'I can see why half the school fancies the pants off her. She's a babe.'

His words are slivers of ice in my heart.

'But you shouldn't feel inferior to her. You're bright and

funny and beautiful. Yours are the only pants I want to get into.'

'You really don't fancy her?'

His hand reaches for mine. 'I really don't. Never have, never will.'

I nod to myself. I believe him. 'But it's not just that.' I poke at the grass with my toe. 'If she knew about us you'd become hers, too. She'd want to hang out together all the time. I wouldn't be able to keep you all to myself.'

He grins. 'That I do understand.' He drops my hand and wraps his arms around me. I smile as I sink into his chest. Ed doesn't fancy Lou. Never has, never will.

But Ed and me? We're perfect together. Soulmates. Nothing can come between us.

Weeks turn into months, and before I know it, we are a day away from our six-month anniversary. Lou is yet to discover we're an item. She's still obsessed by Dan. When we're together she spends the whole time droning on about him. Dan's favourite films, the music Dan listens to. What Dan likes to eat. Dan, Dan, Dan, until I want to scream.

Dan's planning on taking a gap year after his A-levels. I'm not sure Lou figures in those plans. She's obviously beginning to feel a teensy bit insecure, too, because she's started wanting to spend time with me again. I'm her human safety net.

She seeks me out at lunchtime. 'Shall we go and see *Batman Forever* tomorrow night? Val Kilmer's so cool. Do you know who he reminds me of?'

'Dan?' I hazard. 'I can't. I... I promised Mum I'd go to legs, bums and tums with her.'

Lou pouts, as I knew she would.

'Sorry.' I shrug. It's a lie. My parents are out for the evening and Ed's coming around. I'm cooking him a special anniversary dinner with flowers on the table, candles, the lot. 'Maybe Saturday?'

'Not Saturday. Dan's mate Chris is having a party. You should come, too. There'll be loads of boys there.'

'Yeah, maybe. I'll let you know, OK?'

But Lou has spied her boyfriend heading towards the sports field with a couple of his mates. She blows me a kiss and heads towards them. One of Dan's friends sees her approach and whispers something in Dan's ear. They crease up with laughter. My throat tightens and I shoot daggers at Dan and his Neanderthal friends. Poor Lou. I have a sneaky suspicion her heart's about to be broken.

I stand back and survey the room. Soft mood lighting. Tick. Flowers on the table. Tick. Candles lit. Tick. The bolognese is bubbling away on the hob, and the two bottles of cider Dad grudgingly agreed we could have are chilling in the fridge.

Ed's not due for another fifteen minutes so I race upstairs, shower in record time, and pull on the blue satin slip dress I wore to the speech day disco. It seemed fitting to wear it again today, our six-month anniversary. I brush my hair and apply smoky grey eyeshadow and black-as-midnight mascara. I'm running a slick of gloss over my lips when the doorbell rings. My pulse quickening, I run back down the stairs and throw open the front door.

Lou is standing there, dressed in a white sports vest and

purple leggings. The smile on her face freezes when she notices I'm not exactly dressed for an exercise class.

'Dan's out with his mates again, so I thought I'd come to legs, bums and tums with you and your mum.' She gazes over my shoulder into the empty hallway behind me. 'But something tells me your plans have changed.'

I sneak a glance at the clock on the sideboard. It's almost seven. Ed will be here any minute. How the hell am I supposed to explain that?

Lou pushes past me. 'Where is your mum, anyway?'

'Out.'

I scurry behind her as she stomps along the hallway, peering into every room. She stops in the doorway of the dining room and turns on her heels to face me, one eyebrow raised.

'A romantic dinner for two. I'm assuming it's not your parents' date night, because that would be gross. Is there something you've forgotten to tell me?'

I bite my lip. 'Actually, yes. I'm going out with someone.'

She narrows her eyes. 'Who?'

As if on cue, the doorbell rings again.

'Ed S-Sullivan,' I stutter, inching past her to the door.

Ed is standing on the doorstep with a huge bunch of velvety-red roses. As he gives me a peck on the cheek I whisper in his ear, 'Lou's here.'

His eyes widen as he sees her scowling in the hallway, her hands on her hips. I take a deep breath and brazen it out.

'Mum had to go to a work do with Dad at the last minute, so I invited Ed round. We've been seeing a bit of each other recently.'

'So I see. Nice of you to tell me.'

'I would have, but you've been so wrapped up in Dan... '

She's silent for a moment, then lets out a long sigh. 'You're right, I have. But I think I'm going to knock it on the head. He can be a bit of a dick when he's with his friends.' She shakes her head, then holds her arms wide and grins. 'But I'm so pleased for you guys. It's fantastic news! C'mon, group hug!'

My eyes meet Ed's for a split second as we shuffle forwards into Lou's arms and a look of understanding passes between us.

'You don't mind if I hang out with you guys until I meet someone else, do you?' she asks.

'Of course not,' I mutter.

'Wicked.' She pulls away and licks her lips. 'So, what's for dinner? I'm bloody ravenous!'

CHAPTER FOURTEEN

NOW

R osie is still buzzing from her performance at the recruitment evening.

'I was good, wasn't I?' she says again as we set to work weeding the rose garden.

'You were a natural. They loved you,' I agree.

She nods. 'They did. How many are coming to help us?'

'Nineteen signed up there and then and another half a dozen are going to come and have a look around to see if it's for them. I think we can call it a success.'

'Bet Angela's pleased.'

'Hard to tell. You know Angela. Doesn't like to crack a smile unless she can help it.'

Rosie points her trowel at me. 'Cheeky!'

'I just wish I knew what happened to my presentation.'

I know I should forget it, but it's still bothering me. I'm meticulous about saving my work and in all the years I've used PowerPoint I've never had a problem with a corrupted file. For it to fail just when I needed it most seems suspicious to say the least.

'What did happen to it?'

I'm not sure how much Rosie understands about the intricacies of PowerPoint so I say, 'Someone hid it so I couldn't find it.'

'On purpose, so you'd forget your lines?'

'They must have.'

'Who would do that?'

There's only one other person who has access to the shared drive.

'Angela.' The name escapes my lips before I can stop it.

Rosie frowns. 'Angela's a bit grumpy sometimes, but she's not nasty. She wants helpers, too, remember.'

I'm not convinced. I love Rosie. She's the kindest, most straightforward person I know. But she has one major flaw - she only sees good in people. And then she surprises me.

'It might be Martin.'

'*Martin?*'

Her brow wrinkles. 'He's very angry. His hands are always like this.' She drops the trowel and curls her hands into fists. 'And I heard him having an argument with someone the other day. A really cross one. And when I looked to see who he was having an argument with *there was no-one there!*'

'He sometimes hears voices in his head, especially when he forgets to take his pills.'

'Well, this voice was a really angry one and it sounded real to me. All deep like this.' She lowers her voice and says in a raspy tone, 'You can't trust anyone here. They're all out to get you. You need to fight back.' Rosie's eyes are wide. 'That's why I think it might be him. He must be doing what the voice told him to.'

Rosie's words follow me around all day and I'm still mulling over them when I let myself in the front door after work. Bending down to pick up the post isn't easy these days, and I find myself grunting like an old sheep as I straighten my back.

I step back in surprise when Matt appears in front of me.

'I didn't see your car,' I squeak.

'I had to park halfway up the street.' He takes the post from me and gives me a quick peck on the cheek. 'I took a couple of hours' flexi so I could beat the rush hour,' he says, flicking through the envelopes. His eyes narrow when he comes to a plain white envelope with his name and address handwritten on the front.

'Anything interesting?'

'Credit card bill, the bank statement and a belated birthday card from Auntie Jan by the look of it.'

'I'm surprised she remembered. She hasn't sent you one since she's been in the home. Aren't you going to open it?'

'It'll keep.' He slips the card into his briefcase and takes my hand. 'Follow me. I've got a surprise for you.'

A bouquet of raspberry-pink peonies is waiting for me on the kitchen table.

'My favourite!' I bury my head in them and inhale their delicate rose-like scent. 'What have I done to deserve these?'

'I suppose you could call them an apology.'

I raise an eyebrow. 'Why? What have you done?'

'I should have been there for you for the recruitment evening. I knew how nervous you were. And I missed your midwife appointment yesterday. I feel like I'm letting you down all the time at the moment.'

'Don't be silly. You can't help it. I'm fine.' I rub my bump and smile. 'We're both fine.'

'I almost forgot. I've a confession to make.'

He reaches into his briefcase and produces a fleece blanket in the palest of yellows.

'I know we promised we wouldn't, but I bought this, too. I saw it in a baby boutique when I popped out for lunch yesterday. You don't mind, do you?'

I take the blanket from him. It's as soft as silk with scampering rabbits embroidered in the corners. 'It's beautiful. And I've a confession to make, too.' I picture the bags of baby clothes I bought in Fenwick, hidden at the back of my wardrobe. 'But first, let's take a drink into the garden. It's such a beautiful afternoon.'

We sit under the cherry tree and Matt drapes an arm over my shoulder. As I relax into his chest I know it's time to tell him about Lou. I describe how we were best friends at school but lost touch when she went to uni. How she's moved back home after her husband died. I conveniently omit the fact that her late husband and I had history.

'It was weird. The last time I saw her we were eighteen. Now she's all grown up. Terribly middle-class and gushing and a bit showy.' I feel a stab of disloyalty. 'But I think the real Lou's in there somewhere, underneath all the bullshit.'

'Will you see her again?'

'I've invited her round for dinner on Sunday night. You don't mind, do you?'

'Not at all. I'm curious to meet her. You hardly ever talk about your past.'

'That's because my life only began when I met you,' I say playfully, and then, 'To be fair, you don't either.'

He takes a long draught from his bottle of Peroni. 'That's because there's nothing worth saying.'

We have our traditional Friday night curry, even though I know it'll give me heartburn later, and watch a heist movie Matt finds on Sky Cinema. I'm sprawled on the sofa with my feet in his lap feeling like a giant beached whale. His phone, face down on the arm of the sofa, pings a couple of times. Each time he ignores it.

'Who's texting you this time of night?' I ask the third time it beeps.

'It's just Daily Mail news alerts. Sorry, I know it's annoying. I need to change the notification settings.'

'Anything I should know about?'

He looks confused for a second.

'The news alert. What was it?'

He picks up the phone and squints at the screen. 'Hold the front page - Donald Trump is being an arsehole about South America again.'

'They're playing catch-up. That was on the radio this morning.'

Matt pats my leg. 'They don't call it the Daily Fail for nothing.' He yawns. 'I'm shattered. I'm going to head up. Leave the clearing up. I'll do it in the morning.'

'If you're sure. I won't be long. I just want to watch the weather.'

'You know there are apps for that,' he teases.

'I know. But I'm a gardener and gardeners are old school. We like to watch the weather on the TV.'

Once the impossibly petite weather presenter has assured me we have a settled few days ahead, I switch off the television and head upstairs. As I cross the hallway I stub my toe on Matt's briefcase. Swearing under my breath, I pick it up, intending to leave it on his desk in the tiny box room at the back of the house we grandly call the study, when I remember the card he said was from his Auntie Jan.

I fish it out and stare at the handwriting. Something about it looks familiar, but it's not Jan's. She has the spidery cursive script of someone with chronic arthritis. Matt's name and our address, however, are written with a spiky, decisive hand. I check the postmark. The card was sent from Portsmouth, Matt's home city. His parents retired to Spain a couple of years ago, but Jan still lives in an old people's home on the seafront in Southsea. Perhaps her hands are so bad now she asked one of the carers at the home to write Matt's card for her. It would make sense.

I prop the card against his Mac, leave his briefcase by the side of the desk and close the door. When I reach our bedroom the light is already off. I ease myself into bed and drop a kiss on Matt's bare shoulder. I want him to turn over and give me a hug, but all I get is a muttered, 'Not tonight, Soph,' as he pulls the duvet under his chin.

I stare into the darkness, wondering about the late-night texts, the mystery birthday card and the flowers and what they could mean. I taste sourness at the back of my throat. It's either reflux or misgivings, I can't quite be sure. I reach for the glass of water on my bedside table and swallow the acid back down.

Planning. The most crucial part of any project. After all, failing to plan is planning to fail. And please believe me when I say I don't intend to fail.

I have an Excel spreadsheet dedicated to my little project. There's a list of everything I need to acquire and a countdown to the optimum time for the execution phase. But the part I'm most proud of is my 'what if?' column.

Remember those gamebooks that were massive in the

eighties and nineties? Choose Your Own Adventure Books, *they were called. The reader became the hero and, through the choices they made, determined the plot's outcome.*

That's what I've done. I, of course, am the reader. The hero. So, I've envisioned countless different scenarios. If 'so and so' does this... I need to do that. If they then change their mind, I need to...

You get the picture.

Or maybe not. Because, if you hadn't guessed already, I'm deliberately trying to obfuscate you.

Anyway, back to the spreadsheet. I've broken down my project into smaller tasks and I'm working through them one by one. I spend hours on the internet every day, tracking down the things I need, poring over relevant papers and studying instructional videos. Covering all the bases until I'm ready to execute my master plan.

CHAPTER FIFTEEN

NOW

I spend the weekend giving the house a spring clean. I'd like to say I was nesting, but I'm not. I just want to impress Lou. I despise myself for it, but at the same time know it's inevitable. I always sought her approval when we were teenagers and even though more than twenty years have passed I'm self-aware enough to realise I'm reverting to type.

By Sunday evening Matt's peonies have pride of place on the gleaming sideboard in the dining room and the table is laid with our best cutlery and the heavy crystal glasses we were given for our wedding, which normally only come out on Christmas Day and New Year's Eve. I've cleaned the downstairs windows and both bathrooms. I've hoovered under the sofas in the sitting room and changed the sheets in our room and the spare bedroom. I've even cleaned the fridge.

When Matt sees the recipe for beef Wellington on the kitchen table he raises his eyebrows. 'You're going to a lot of trouble. What time's the Merry Widow gracing us with her presence?'

'Matt, you can't call her that!' I pretend I'm scandalised but really I love it.

'You should be taking it easy, not slaving over a hot stove. I told you I was happy to pick up a Chinese.'

'She and Ed have spent the last two decades living the high life in Boston. I don't want her turning her nose up at a takeaway. Mustn't let the side down.'

'She's a mate. I'm sure she wouldn't mind.'

I'm sure he's right, but I'm too proud not to make an effort, so I spend the next hour wrestling with Gordon Ramsay's beef Wellington recipe, topping and tailing green beans and preparing a buttery dish of Dauphinoise potatoes. The ramekins of rich chocolate mousse I made earlier are in the fridge along with a couple of bottles of Sauvignon Blanc.

By half past six, satisfied I've done everything I need to, I head upstairs to run a bath. While I wait, I study my face in the bathroom mirror. On a good day I used to be able to pass for mid-thirties. Not anymore. When Matt and I met I was thirty-two and he was twenty-seven. Age really was just a number. But the older I get the more I worry our age gap has amplified. Matt looks as youthful as he did the day he spilt his wine over my dress. My face is now a well-worn map of crow's feet and brown spots. Quite frankly it's a relief when the mirror steams up and my haggard reflection disappears in the fog.

Lou, inevitably, is late. When the doorbell finally rings at a quarter to eight Matt puts down his bottle of beer and goes to the door. I wait in the sitting room. Lou is in relentless *Ab Fab* mode again.

'You must be Matt. You're even more gorgeous in the flesh! I'm Lou, Sophie's oldest and most glamorous friend. I'm *so* pleased to meet you!'

I can almost hear the mwah mwahs as she air kisses him on both cheeks. I haul myself to my feet and join them.

'Darling, there you are. This is for you.'

She waves a bottle of Piper-Heidsieck at me. I try not to mind that she should know I'm not drinking.

'Gin and tonic or a glass of fizz?' says Matt, guiding her along the hallway to the kitchen. I follow, clutching the champagne dutifully, like a maid in waiting. The bottle is so cold my hands stick to the glass.

'Oh, fizz please, Matthew. Just what the doctor ordered.'

I set out bowls of olives and vegetable crisps on the kitchen table while Matt busies himself opening the champagne. Even though I know it's coming the pop of the cork still makes me jump.

'What a luxury to have a handsome man to open the champers,' Lou says, smiling at Matt as he passes her a glass. 'It was always Ed's job. I suppose I'll have to learn how to do it now. Perhaps you could teach me?'

'Of course,' Matt says gallantly. He picks up the cork. 'The trick is to hold the cork in one hand and the bottom of the bottle in the other. Don't twist the cork. Instead you need to hold the cork firmly and turn the bottle towards you.'

I watch Lou watching Matt demonstrate. Her eyes are glittering and her speech is very precise. I realise she's halfway to being pissed already and is trying very hard not to show it.

'Olive?' I say, offering her the bowl.

'No thanks.' She waves it away and instead takes a large slug from her glass.

'Did you drive?'

She shakes her head. 'Joshie was home. He dropped me off.'

'Joshie?' Matt says.

'My son. He's just started at Kent, reading law. Didn't Sophie mention him?'

'Oh, erm, probably. I'm always being told off for not listening.' Matt gives a sheepish grin.

Lou laughs. 'I don't suppose she did. Sophie always was a dark horse and you know what they say, a leopard never changes its spots.'

Wondering if they have even remembered I'm in the room, I thrust a crisp bowl under Lou's nose. Anything to soak up the booze. 'I'm confused. Which am I, a horse or a leopard?'

'Neither,' Lou says, dipping her head towards Matt. 'You're a fucking cougar, darling.'

The champagne bottle is in the recycling bin and they've started on the Sauvignon Blanc when I serve the beef Wellington. Lou is regaling Matt with stories of our school years, most of them at my expense. I try really hard not to mind, but she's flirting with him outrageously and Matt, always the gentleman, is doing nothing to discourage her. He has such an easy charm that women are always falling at his feet. He won over Mum in a matter of minutes and Rosie worships the ground he walks on. Even Angela isn't immune to his charms.

Being the only sober person in the room makes me feel disconnected from the others. Almost invisible. But it gives me a chance to observe my husband and my former best friend as they parry back and forth. Lou is pushing her food about her plate, making me wonder why I bothered with Gordon bloody Ramsay's bloody beef Wellington. But she's still knocking back the booze. Her eyes are glazed and she's playing with a strand of her blonde hair. Every now and then she runs a finger around the rim of her glass. Matt is laughing at her witticisms and topping up her glass, but I don't think he's flirting back. He's just pissed, and he's a loud, amenable drunk who would laugh at anyone's jokes.

Lou gets unsteadily to her feet. 'I need to powder my nose. Where's the little girls' room, darling?'

'First door on the left at the top of the stairs,' I say. And then, when I see her sway, 'Need me to show you?'

'Would you mind? I seem to be a little tipsy.' She hiccups and giggles. 'Oops-a-daisy.'

I roll my eyes at Matt and mouth, 'No more booze!' and take Lou's arm. Under the silk shirt and capri pants she's as thin as a stick. How many other meals has she pushed around her plate without eating recently? Compassion for her hits me like a wave.

'Come on, you old lush,' I say, leading her up the stairs. 'Need me to come in with you?'

'Just like old times. Do you remember that time in your mum and dad's bathroom when you -'

'Not now, Lou.' My voice is firm. 'Are you going to be OK?'

She hiccups again and waves her hand at me. 'You go back to that scrumptious husband of yours. I'll be fine on my own. I've got to be, haven't I? I don't have a choice.'

'Do me a favour and don't lock the door, just in case,' I tell her, before heading back downstairs.

Matt is attempting to load the dishwasher. 'Bloody hell, I had no idea Lou was such a game old bird,' he says.

'She's the same age as me!'

'You don't look it.' He dumps a couple of plates on the side with a clatter, crosses the kitchen and takes me in his arms. 'You are beautiful, Sophie Saunders, and I love you so very much. I really do. You do know that, don't you?'

I give him a gentle shove. 'Enough. You're pissed as a

fart.'

Unperturbed, he murmurs in my ear, 'Let's have an early night, shall we?'

The scent of the lemony aftershave I bought him for Christmas mingles with the sour smell of wine. I'm at once attracted and repelled. He gives my backside a squeeze and whispers, 'Get rid of Lou and come to bed.'

'Christ, Lou!' My blood runs cold. 'She's been up there ages. I'd better go and check she's OK.' I push him out of the way and take the stairs two at a time. I'm out of breath when I reach the landing. I knock on the bathroom door. 'Everything OK in there?'

There's no answer. I press my ear to the door but all I can hear is a running tap. I give her a couple of minutes and knock again but there's still no reply. Anxiety gnaws at my insides. No-one takes that long to wash their hands, drunk or not.

'Lou, I'm coming in.' I turn the handle, but the door won't budge. She's locked it from the inside, even though I told her not to.

'Lou! Are you alright?' I call. I'm really worried now. What if she's lost her balance, hit her head on the side of the rolltop bath and is lying unconscious on the floor? I yank the brass door handle again, then give it a shove with my shoulder, but the door remains stubbornly closed. As of course it would. None of the original Victorian pine doors had their keys when we bought the house, so Matt fitted a heavy-duty bolt to the bathroom door soon after we moved in. It'd take a battering ram to open it.

'Lou!' I yell again. I kneel on the floor and squint through the keyhole. All I can see is the sink, which is directly opposite the door. The tap is still running but there's no sign of Lou. I shift my weight, my cheek squashed against the smooth pine door so I can see the rest of the bathroom. It's carnage. I open my mouth and scream.

CHAPTER SIXTEEN

NOW

Matt is by my side in an instant. 'What on earth -?'

I point at the door. 'Lou,' I croak. 'She's -' But I can't finish. I don't know what she is. All I know is that our white bathroom looks like a crime scene. A bloodbath.

He rattles the door handle.

'She's locked it!' I cry. 'Look through the keyhole.'

He kneels beside me and, as he stares through the keyhole, I replay the scene in my head. Splatters of blood as bright as holly berries on the cream rug and smears of it on the side of the bath. My nail scissors, their blades open, discarded on the floor. Lou curled up in a foetal position between the toilet and the shower. Her white capri pants sodden with blood.

'Jesus Christ,' Matt says. 'What the hell has she done?'

'Shush, what's that?'

A quiet keening is infiltrating the landing. The sound's so pitiful it makes the hairs on the back of my neck stand up. I give the bathroom door another rap.

'Lou, it's me, Sophie. Everything's going to be alright.

But you need to let us in so we can help you. Do you understand? You need to unlock the door.'

The keening quietens. Matt is about to say something, but I hold my finger to my lips.

'I don't want your help,' says a feeble voice. 'I want to die.'

In the steady, neutral tone I use at work when one of the gardeners is agitated, I say, 'I know things seem bad at the moment, but they will get better, I promise. You're not alone. I'm here for you. And so is Josh. He needs you. We all do. Let me in, please.'

The metallic sound of the bolt being drawn across is followed by the click of the door handle. I let out a huge breath. Whatever she's done to herself, we can fix it.

I push the door open, gather her in my arms and hold her tight.

———

Much later, Lou is sitting at the kitchen table in a pair of my pyjamas while I warm milk for a hot chocolate for us both. I've cleaned and bandaged her wrists as best I can. Matt wanted to call an ambulance, but Lou became so distressed at the thought of going to hospital that I promised we wouldn't. Luckily the cuts weren't as deep as I first feared, and soon stopped bleeding when I applied pressure to them. It was only when I was washing them and noticed older scars crisscrossing her wrists that I realised this wasn't the first time she's self-harmed.

I place the mugs on the table and sit opposite her. 'Do you want to talk about it?'

Lou glances at the door.

'It's OK. Matt's gone to bed.'

She gives the barest of nods and reaches for her mug with trembling fingers.

'What is there to say? I'm a fucked-up piss-head and the world would be better off without me.'

'Don't be silly. Of course it wouldn't.'

Mascara is caught in the creases at the corners of her eyes and her cheeks are leached of colour. She looks like a particularly sorrowful Pierrot doll.

'No-one would notice if I went,' she sniffs.

'What about Josh?'

'I'm a burden to him. A millstone around his neck.'

I raise an eyebrow. 'He's told you that, has he?'

'Of course not. He's far too nice. Too much like his dad. But it's true.'

'You're being ridiculous. You're his mum. He needs you.'

It's as though she hasn't heard me. 'It's alright for you, with your lovely house and your lovely husband and your lovely baby on the way. Everything's so fucking *lovely*. You're a walking advert for the perfect little family. *Bless.*'

She spits out the word with so much venom I flinch.

'Perfect Sophie. Everyone loves you, don't they?' she adds, glaring at me with open animosity. The speed at which she's morphed from melancholy drunk to embittered Fury terrifies me. I had no idea she felt like this.

'Lou -'

'Ed loved you, that's for sure. He never got over you. I was always second best.'

'I'm sure that's not true.'

'Are you kidding me? You were 'The One', the love of his life. He worshipped the ground you walked on. I was there, remember. You were the original star-crossed lovers. Romeo and Juliet eat your fucking heart out.'

'We were seventeen. Everyone falls head over heels when they're that age. It would have fizzled out eventually.'

'Ah, but you didn't give it a chance to, did you?'

I ball my fists and press them into my eyes. I don't want to go there, not tonight.

'You know why,' I say. 'I had no choice.'

The fight leaves her and she buries her head in her hands. She mumbles something indecipherable.

I touch her arm. 'What did you say?'

'I want to go home.'

'I don't think that's a good idea.'

'I don't care what you think. I want to go home.' She reaches in her bag and pulls out her mobile.

'What are you doing?'

She looks at me blankly. 'Calling a cab.'

'Don't be silly. I haven't had anything to drink. I'll take you.'

We sit in silence as I drive through the quiet streets. I was surprised when Lou gave me her address. I'd pictured her in one of the grand Georgian townhouses in St Dunstan's, but she actually lives in a small cul-de-sac off Forty Acres Road where most of the houses are student lets.

I park outside and follow her to the front door. She fumbles around in her bag for her keys. I pretend not to notice the pile of empty wine bottles by the wheelie bin.

'You can go now,' she says, standing with her back to the door and the keys in her hand.

'I'll just see you in, shall I?' I give her a bright smile. 'Might as well, now I'm here.'

'Just go home, Sophie. I'm a big girl. I can look after myself.'

I think longingly of my bed. I'm dead on my feet. 'Are you sure?'

She nods.

A light goes on upstairs, making me jump.

'Josh,' Lou says.

I picture the boy on the escalator. Messy hair and laughing eyes. Half of me wants to see him again, to see if he really is the mirror image of his father. The other half wants to put as much distance as possible between me and all these reminders of the past. While I'm faltering, Lou makes up my mind for me.

'For Christ's sake, just piss off home!'

I hold up my hands in surrender.

'Alright, I'm going. I'll text in the morning, check you're OK.'

I retrace my steps down the path to the car. As I fix my seatbelt I glance back at the house. Lou's still fumbling with her keys. Before she's had a chance to place the key in the lock the door opens and a man is framed in the rectangle of light. My heart starts thumping. Logic tells me it's Josh. But it's as if I've stepped back in time...

CHAPTER SEVENTEEN

THEN

Isn't it funny how much brighter the world seems when you're in love? Colours are more vivid, food tastier, jokes funnier. I've never been a cup-half-full kind of person - I'm too cautious, too much of a pessimist - but at the moment my cup isn't full, it's overflowing. There's a spring to my step and a twinkle in my eye, and all those other clichés you think of when you pass a smiley person in the street.

Because I'm the happiest I've been in my life, and I glide around with a grin on my face and little bubbles of pure euphoria in my heart. Nothing can touch my elation. Not the dire news about the economy, or the bombing of the Israeli Embassy in London. It's the middle of the summer holidays and I'm fizzing with excitement as the bus transports me to Whitstable and the love of my life.

'For Christ's sake, can you please wipe that soppy smile off your face. It's getting on my tits,' huffs Lou, sitting next to me.

'Sorry,' I say, even though the corners of my mouth refuse to turn down. 'I can't help it.'

'Who else is going to be there? I'm fed up playing gooseberry to you two lovebirds.'

'Erm, I think Kate and Toby are coming, and Toby's mate Chris. He's pretty cool.'

'The rugger bugger?'

I nod and she appears mollified. Chris is just her type. Tall, blond and brawny. Not dark and gorgeously geeky like Ed.

'Is tonight the night?' she says, nudging me.

I flush. We haven't done it yet, though we've come pretty close.

'Well?'

'I dunno. Maybe,' I hedge, thinking of the cerise-pink lacy bra and matching pants from Knickerbox I'm wearing under my denim shorts and teeshirt. Ed has invited us over for a barbecue as his parents and sister are away for the weekend. Mum and Dad think I'm staying the night at Lou's. I don't want to count my chickens, but tonight in all probability *will* be the night.

'You might need these then,' Lou says, scrabbling around in her bag and handing me a packet of Fetherlite.

'Lou!' I hiss, glancing over my shoulder, worried someone will have clocked the instantly-recognisable logo and assume I'm a good-for-nothing tart.

She laughs. 'Don't be coy. It's about time you lost your cherry.' She slips the condoms into my shoulder bag. 'You do need to be careful, though. You don't want one night of passion to wreck your whole life.'

I give her a withering look and stare out of the window, my stomach churning with nerves and excitement, as the bus chugs down Borstal Hill and into Whitstable. We jump off in Oxford Street and make our way to Ed's house, a neat

Victorian semi just off Island Wall and a stone's throw from the pebbly beach.

Ed sweeps me into a bearhug and showers my face with kisses. 'God, I've missed you,' he mutters into my newly-washed hair.

'You only saw me yesterday, you twit,' I say, melting into his embrace.

'Seriously, you two. You need to get a room.' Lou shakes her head and makes a beeline for the garden where Toby, Kate and Chris have already started on the cider.

It's an idyllic afternoon. After we've stuffed our faces on burnt sausages and burgers we take what's left of the cider down to the beach and watch the sunset.

When the others decide to play truth or dare Ed whispers in my ear, 'Shall we head back?'

I nod, liquid with anticipation, and scramble up the beach after him. At the top, where the shingle meets the sea wall, he pulls me towards him and kisses me until my legs go weak and I feel lightheaded with lust.

Finally he breaks away and cups my face in his hands. 'I love you, Sophie Williams.'

My heart contracts. It's the first time he's said the L word. Darts of happiness prickle my skin like goosebumps. 'I love you, too.'

So much it hurts.

He takes hold of my hand and we slip along the alley to the house. Later, as we lie beside each other in his single bed below posters of Suede and Pulp, he strokes my cheek and murmurs, 'Are you sure about this?'

'Oh yes,' I breathe.

Because I've never been surer of anything my whole life.

CHAPTER EIGHTEEN

NOW

I'm sitting in stationary traffic on the ring road, watching as the clock edges ever closer to nine. I try not to think about the grief I'll get from Angela if I'm late for the first of the induction days we're holding for our new volunteers. They aren't due to arrive until half past, but I need at least half an hour to run through the work sheets with Geoff and Mary.

The car in front of me edges forwards. On the radio John Humphrys is grilling the Health Secretary on the funding shortfall in social care. I'm half listening, because the current crisis in mental health services has a huge impact on our gardeners, but I'm also wondering how Lou is feeling this morning. I check in my mirror for police cars and, when I'm happy the coast is clear, pick up my mobile and send her a quick text.

How's the head this morning?

The phone pings within seconds.

Sore. Can't remember much TBH. But I expect I owe you an apology. Ed always said I was a Jekyll and Hyde drunk. Sorry if Mr Hyde made an appearance x

No worries, I type back. *Just glad you're OK. Talk later.*

Whether Lou really can't remember the things she said last night or chooses not to is irrelevant. She flipped so quickly from happy to hostile. It was the same when we were kids. Usually she was just loud and uninhibited when she was bombed. Drink fuelled her wild side. When we went clubbing she was happy to pop an E and spend the night dancing with strangers while I watched from the side-lines, worrying about how we'd get home. Every now and then she would turn spiteful, dripping venom like a poisonous snake, and then acting like nothing had happened the next day. At least this time she knows she was bang out of order. I will forgive her, but I can't forget. There was real hatred in her eyes.

The driver behind me blasts his horn, making me jump. On the radio, John Humphrys announces the nine o'clock news and the traffic starts moving. I push all thoughts of Lou aside and make my way to work.

The new volunteers are sitting around the wooden-slatted table we use for our tea breaks. They're a mixed, but promising bunch. A retired couple in their late sixties called Bev and Trev who 'want to give something back' now they've sold their cleaning business; Mary's friend Margaret from the WI; a widower called Derek who worked on the land all his life but now lives in a sheltered flat with only a window box for a garden; a muscular-looking man in his seventies called Mike who is sporting an orange tan and impossibly dark hair for someone his age, and Roz, who is at least thirty years younger than the rest of them and looks completely out of place.

Ignoring the flutter of nerves in my stomach, I open my arms wide. 'Welcome to Cam. We're delighted you'll be joining our team. For your first few sessions you'll be working alongside me, Geoff or Mary, just so you get a feel for how we do things. Once you know the ropes you can choose which section of the garden you'd like to work in. There's no point sticking you in the rose garden if veggies are your thing.'

I consult my clipboard. 'Today Bev and Trev are with Geoff and Nancy lifting the spring bulbs. Mike and Margaret are with Mary and Rosie weeding the raised borders, and Roz and Derek are with me.' I smile at them both. 'We'll be in the greenhouse with Martin potting up plants to sell at our open day in a couple of weeks' time. If you'd like to follow me, I'll show you where we keep the tools.'

We cross the garden to the cellar. I turn the key in the mortice lock and pull the heavy door open.

'I don't know how much you know about local history, but Cam is based in what was once the kitchen garden of Holborough House, a very grand 12th century manor house that was the ancestral home of the Holborough family. There's a print of it in our office if you're interested.'

'What happened to the house?' Trev asks.

'It burnt to the ground in the late 19th century. The four walls of the kitchen garden and the wine cellar are all that's left. By then the Holborough family had squandered all their money on gambling and dodgy business ventures so the house was never re-built. A local farmer bought the land and rents the garden to us for a peppercorn fee.'

I reach inside the cellar for the light switch and the cavernous space is bathed in a feeble yellow light.

'There's a handrail to the left. The steps are pretty steep so please be careful.'

'This is some tool shed,' says Derek, as he takes in the rows of neatly-ordered forks, rakes, brooms, spades and hand tools.

'It's Geoff's domain.' I laugh. 'He's a great believer in the old adage that there's a place for everything and everything in its place. Woe betide you if you muck up his system.'

I hand everyone the tools they need and we tramp back up the steps. In the car park a diesel engine emits a phlegm-like splutter. The minibus has arrived. I smile at my new recruits. 'Time to meet the gardeners!'

The moment I see Martin I know something's not right. His shoulders are hunched and his chin is tucked into his chest as if he's battling against a force ten gale. When I introduce him to Roz and Derek he mutters something under his breath, and when Derek offers his hand to shake he shrinks back as if he's on the receiving end of a lethal uppercut.

If ever there was a stereotype of someone with severe mental health issues, today Martin is that person. He's rocking back and forth from heels to toes, toes to heels, and every couple of minutes his head jerks to the side. He's had facial tics before, but never this bad.

Derek seems unfazed, but Roz is silent. Watchful. Perhaps she'll decide working at Cam isn't for her. I over-compensate for Martin's behaviour by being over-the-top chirpy, giving a running commentary as we repot the plants we've spent the last few months growing from cuttings and seeds.

WHEN SHE FINDS YOU

'Can I have your knife, Sophie?' Martin says.

Roz's head shoots up. Her eyes are wide.

'Not today, Marty. We don't need knives for potting on, do we?'

'I want your knife.'

'I said no, Martin. No knives today.'

His head jerks again and he takes a step towards me.

'IwantyourknifeIwantyourknifeIwantyourknife!'

I'm aware of someone slipping out of the greenhouse behind me. I can't tell if it's Roz or Derek. But I don't turn around. I can keep Martin calm if I can get through to him. He always listens to me.

'KNIFEKNIFEKNIFEKNIFE!' he chants, stamping his foot in frustration. He's so close I can smell his stale sweat. My hands slide around my stomach, holding my baby close.

'Martin, look at me,' I say, with as much authority as I can muster. But his eyes are glazed. Whoever's voice he's hearing, it isn't mine. I step backwards, bumping against the bench we were potting plants on moments earlier. Martin swings his arm above his head and I cower, waiting for the punches to rain down.

A movement to the left catches my eye. It's Roz. She lunges forwards and in one fluid movement grabs Martin's right wrist with her right hand, pushes his right shoulder with her left, and places her right leg in front of his, pushing him down. Taken unawares, he crumples to the floor.

'Call the police!' she says breathlessly. She's holding Martin in an armlock, his cheek pressed to the ground. His body has gone limp. He meets my eye.

'Not the police,' he whimpers.

'Not the police,' I agree. 'I'll call his mum. You can let him go. He'll be OK.'

'Are you serious?' shrieks Roz. 'He tried to attack you!' Her eyes are blazing.

'I didn't. I just wanted the knife to prick out the lettuce,' Martin pants.

'Roz, please let him go. He'll be fine, I promise.'

She loosens her grip on his arm reluctantly, stands up and dusts her hands off on her jeans. Martin pulls himself to a sitting position and clasps his arms around his legs. He's trying to make himself as small as possible. He used to do it a lot when he first came to Cam. The fact that he's back in that dark place fills me with trepidation.

I'm reaching in my back pocket for my phone when Geoff appears with Derek at his side. Geoff assesses the situation with one glance and, to my relief, takes over.

'Derek, perhaps you could join Mary and the gang for the next hour or so? Roz and Sophie, go and have a cup of tea in the office. Martin, you come with me and I'll call your mum, shall I?'

Martin gives a tiny nod and Geoff shoos us out of the greenhouse. Roz follows me in silence to the office. For once I'm glad Angela has a mid-morning 'meeting' with Bob Wittershaw. If she finds out I've been letting Martin use my knife she'll hit the roof.

Roz holds the office door open. 'Sit down,' she orders. 'I'll make the tea.' She fills the kettle and switches it on, lines up two mugs, drops a teabag in each and takes the milk out of the fridge. Her actions are economical and precise.

'Where did you learn to do that?'

'What, make a cup of tea?'

'You know that's not what I meant. When did you learn to restrain someone?'

'Oh, I worked in a nursing home for a while. A lot of residents had dementia. We were taught the different types of restraint during our induction. I've never had to use it before.' She hands me a mug. 'Should you be working here?'

I frown. 'What do you mean?'

'When you said you worked with people with learning difficulties and mental health problems, I assumed they'd be autistic, ADHD or Downs. A bit doolally but basically harmless. I didn't think they'd be as bad as him.' She jerks her head towards the door. 'What's wrong with him, anyway?'

I hesitate. We take client confidentiality very seriously at Cam. But then I remember Martin telling everyone himself at the recruitment evening. Roz must have forgotten.

'He has schizoaffective disorder. He's also bipolar. He's fine when he takes his medication.'

'And I've seen what happens when he doesn't. He's dangerous. Who knows what he would have done if I hadn't been there. These people kill, Sophie. In the blink of an eye. Like that.' She clicks her fingers. 'You hear about it on the news all the time.'

'Martin would never hurt me. He's harmless.'

'Why are you defending him? What did he want the knife for? Imagine if he'd stabbed you in the stomach, stabbed the baby? Would you still be defending him then?'

Blood drains from my face. 'Don't say that. He's more likely to hurt himself.' An image of Lou using my nail scissors to score gashes in her wrists forces its way into my head. Christ, what a mess.

'I'm only thinking of you and the baby. What's Matt going to say when he hears what's happened?'

'I wasn't going to tell him.'

'Because he'd go ballistic and tell you to start your maternity leave right now?'

I can't disagree because we both know she's right. Instead I say, 'I can't go before the open day. There's too much to do.'

'You're not the only one who works here. Let one of the others take the slack for a change. You have to put the baby first.'

I lean towards her and touch her shoulder. 'We'll be fine, I promise. There's nothing to worry about. But I love you for caring, I really do.'

Isn't it just amazing what you can find on the internet? For instance, while I was browsing online last night I happened to discover that self-inflicted Caesarean sections are actually a thing.

Not a very common thing, admittedly. But cases of DIY C-sections have been reported since the 18th century. Who knew?

Most times the mother, baby or both have died, but according to Wikipedia there are five successful documented cases.

My personal favourite is a woman called Juliana Sanchez, who lived in rural Columbia and in 2005 performed a Caesarean section on herself when she went into premature labour.

Juliana sent her nine-year-old son to the nearest shop half a mile away to buy a kitchen knife, downed a couple of cups of almost neat alcohol, sliced through her abdomen from the bottom of her ribs to her pubic bone, rummaged around a bit and pulled her baby out by his feet.

She then cut the baby's umbilical cord with a pair of scissors and put her organs back in place as best she could before a man from the village attempted to stitch the wound with a sewing needle and thread.

'Blood came out of me like a fountain,' she told reporters.

She and the baby both lived, despite the risk of bleeding out, the potential for infection, the very real danger of dying from shock.

She knew the risks, yet she went ahead anyway. A mother's ultimate sacrifice to save her baby.

Her story moves me beyond words.

CHAPTER NINETEEN

NOW

I check my wing mirror to see if Roz is still following me. As we were leaving Cam she offered to wash and blow dry my hair, and although all I want to do is snuggle up on the sofa and watch trash on the TV, I felt it would be churlish to say no.

'You've had a crap day,' she'd said. 'Let me come over and spoil you for an hour. On the house.'

'Won't you miss Caitlyn's bedtime?'

'They are staying at Phil's mum's for a couple of days. I couldn't go with them because of today.'

'You should have said. We could have fixed your induction for another time. Where have they gone?'

'I just told you. To see Phil's mum.'

'Sorry, I mean where does she live?'

'Oh, I see. Brighton.'

'Same as Matt!'

'Same as Matt,' she'd agreed.

'Hey, seeing as we've both been deserted, why don't you stay for dinner? Nothing fancy, just a bowl of pasta.'

She'd smiled. 'That'd be great. Thank you.'

I pull up outside our house and Roz reverses into a space a couple of cars down.

'I still can't believe you'd want to spend a precious evening off washing my hair,' I say, opening the front door and ushering her inside.

She shrugs. 'I'd rather be here. The house feels so empty without them.'

I deposit my keys and phone in the ceramic bowl on the sideboard in the hall while Roz sets out her hairdryer, mirror and brushes on the kitchen table.

'Cuppa?' I ask.

'Wouldn't say no.'

As I lean against the kitchen counter waiting for the kettle to boil the baby kicks me so sharply under my ribcage that I gasp.

'Hey, you OK?'

I rub my belly and smile. 'Junior's trying out some karate moves.'

Her eyes light up. 'Mind if I feel?'

''Course not.'

I take her hand and place it on the side of my bump where the baby was kicking. Her hand feels warm and firm. Her head dips as she gazes at my belly. The baby kicks again and her face breaks into a smile.

'If you press here you can feel its foot.'

'Got it!' She's silent for a while as the baby wiggles and fidgets. When she does speak her voice is thick with emotion.

'It's amazing to think there's a whole new little person in there, isn't it? A person who is as pure and perfect as freshly-laid snow. A completely blank slate, untainted by life.'

'It is,' I say. It's a strangely intimate moment and I feel

my own voice wobble. Roz is so clearly moved by the baby it's hard not to be affected. It must remind her of being pregnant with her own hard-fought for baby.

'I think it might be a boy,' I tell her. 'People say they are more active in the womb. I know it's only an old wives' tale but there's got to be some truth in it, don't you think?'

Roz's hand is still on my belly and the baby is treating her to some fearsome kicks.

'What was Caitlyn like?'

'Caitlyn?' She pauses. 'It was so long ago I barely remember. Does that make me a bad mum? Let's think... She was quite placid. Yes, very quiet. Not like she is now, running rings around me, the little madam.'

The kettle boils and I pull away to make our tea. 'I bet. I'm not sure I'm looking forward to the terrible twos. Mum says I was a monster.'

Roz takes her mug and sits opposite me. 'Do you believe in nature or nurture?'

Her question takes me by surprise. 'I don't know,' I admit. 'I've never thought about it.'

'You should. It's important. Are we defined by our genes or by our history? Is our behaviour a product of inherited or acquired characteristics? You, for example. I can tell from their wedding photo that you inherited your brown eyes from your mother and your curly hair from your father.'

The only photo I have of Mum and Dad's wedding is on the mantelpiece in our bedroom. I hadn't realised Roz had seen it. But she's right, I always blame Dad for my unruly curls and Mum for my muddy-brown eyes. I nod.

'So where did your cautious personality come from?'

'Cautious? Am I?'

133

Roz snorts. 'You're the most cautious person I know. Do you take after your mum or your dad?'

'Dad, I suppose. He was a very prudent man. The type to hope for the best and plan for the worst, you know?'

Roz nods in satisfaction. 'So, you agree with me. Genes determine our character traits. Your dad was cautious, hence you are, too. There's nothing we can do about our personalities. We are all pre-wired.'

'I suppose I could have learnt through his cautious behaviour -'

But Roz has started fixing her shower attachment to the kitchen tap and doesn't hear. She beckons me over. My bump's never felt bigger as I lean forwards and dangle my head over the sink.

She holds the shower head over the exposed nape of my neck. 'How's that?'

'Bit hot,' I say in a muffled voice.

She fiddles with the mixer tap.

'Much better.'

She washes and conditions my hair and wraps a towel around my head, turban-style. My back has set and an old lady 'ouff!' escapes my lips as I straighten and hobble over to the table.

Roz uses clips to separate my hair into sections. 'Straight or curly?' she asks, watching me in the mirror.

I grin. 'Let's stick two fingers up to my genes and go straight for a change.'

'And there I was saying you were cautious.'

She plugs her hairdryer into the socket behind me and sets to work drying sections of my hair. It's too noisy to talk and I let my mind drift.

I hope Martin's OK. Geoff took me to one side just before I left for the day. 'I've spoken to Maureen. She's really worried about him. Says he's retreating into himself more and more. His support worker is popping round in the morning to see if he needs to be admitted.'

'I hope not. He hates it in there,' I said.

'It's the best place for him if he's deteriorating. They can adjust his meds, re-start his talking therapies. Get him back on an even keel.'

'I know but -'

'And you must tell Angela what happened. She needs to log it in the incident report book in case there are any repercussions.'

'She'll hit the roof.'

'Better for her to hear it from you than from one of the new volunteers,' Geoff had said, and I knew he was right.

Sitting in my kitchen with blasts of hot air warming my neck, I wonder if I can get away with not mentioning the knife. If Angela knows that's what Martin was asking for, she might realise I've let him use it before. She may be many things, but she's not stupid. When she clocks the fact that I've lent a penknife to someone with a severe mental health problem she will throw a major wobbly. But if she finds out I've lied to her she'll have my head on a stick. I sigh loudly.

Roz turns off the hairdryer. 'Everything OK?'

'Just worrying about work. Angela's going to lose the plot when she hears about this morning.'

'I know her type. All bark and bluster. Don't let her bully you.'

Roz is about to switch the hairdryer on again when she stops mid-air and cocks her head. 'What's that?'

The tinny notes of my ringtone can be heard from the hallway.

'My phone. It's probably Matt. I'd better get it. He's going out with the work crowd later.'

I push my chair back, the scrape of wood on tiles drowning out the sound of the phone for a second. Roz, still holding the hairdryer, steps towards the back door and out of my way. Impatient to hear Matt's voice, I don't notice the hairdryer's lead stretched across the gap between the kitchen units and the table, as taut as a tightrope.

I take a step forwards and feel a sharp tug on my shin like the jaws of a gin trap. I stick my hands out in front of me to steady myself but it's too late, I have already lost my balance. As I tumble forwards, my hands are not outstretched to break my fall. They're wrapped around my bump, protecting my baby. I scream and the world goes black.

CHAPTER TWENTY

NOW

When I come to, I'm propped up against a kitchen cupboard, a cushion behind my head and Roz's anxious face inches from mine.

'Sophie! Sophie, can you hear me?' Her voice is distorted, as if we're under water, and my head is throbbing like I have the mother of all hangovers. I run the tips of my fingers over my forehead. There's a bump over my right eye, as big as a quail's egg. I touch it and wince. 'What happened?'

'You tripped over the hairdryer lead. You must have caught your head on the back of the chair as you fell.'

I try to remember. 'You were drying my hair -'

She nods. 'And you went to answer your phone. I tried to grab your arm but I was too far away.'

A feeling of dread unfurls in my belly and for a second I think I'm going to vomit. I clutch Roz's arm. 'The baby!'

'Can you feel it move?'

I shake my head. It was so active this evening, virtually kicking on demand, and now it's completely still. I massage the side of my bump, which usually elicits a reaction, but there's nothing. My eyes grow wide. 'Oh my God, what have I done?'

'Nothing. You haven't done anything. I'm sure the baby's fine.'

But Roz's forced cheeriness doesn't fool me. I can tell she's as worried as I am. Her face is pale and she seems to be weighing something up in her mind.

'I tell you what, why don't I take you to A&E, just to be on the safe side?'

'Are you sure?'

'Of course. We'll get you and the baby checked over so you don't need to worry. Can you stand up if I help you?'

I take the hand she offers me and haul myself to my feet. A wave of dizziness grips me and I sway. Roz pulls out a chair and guides me to it.

'You stay there,' she orders. 'Have you packed a maternity bag yet?'

I shake my head again. 'Didn't want to tempt fate,' I mutter, hoping fate isn't about to have the last laugh.

'I'll grab some things for you. Stay put, OK?'

I blanche. 'You think they'll keep me in?'

'I'm sure they won't, but it's better to be safe than sorry, eh?'

I sit slumped at the kitchen table listening to the floorboards creaking overhead as Roz walks from our bedroom to the en suite and back again. As I listen I become aware of a warm sensation between my legs. Panic grips my chest and squeezes it like a vice. What if the baby is already dead, its lifeless body floating in its leaking amniotic sac like a heart suspended in formaldehyde? I could never forgive myself.

I stumble to the downstairs cloakroom and wrench down my maternity jeans and pants. I almost can't bear to look but when I do the relief is immense. It's urine. I must have wet myself as I hit the floor. I struggle out of my clothes, kick them into a corner, wrap a hand towel around my waist and stagger upstairs to find Roz.

She's in our bedroom with my Cath Kidston overnight bag open on the bed, studying the photo of me and Matt on his bedside table. It's a selfie, taken a couple of years ago during a weekend trip to Barcelona. Wrapped up against the cold, we're laughing like loons. She starts when she hears me, and quickly replaces it.

'What are you doing up here? I told you to stay put!'

'I need some clean jeans.' I gesture at the towel. 'Had a bit of an accident when I fell.'

She pulls a face and I don't blame her. Losing control of your bladder isn't exactly dignified.

'I've packed a clean set of clothes, some pyjamas and a wash bag. What else do you need?'

I glance around the room, my eyes falling on my phone charger curled on the floor by the bed. 'Just this,' I say, handing it to her. 'Are you sure you don't mind taking me?'

'We need to check the baby's OK. And there's no way you're driving yourself after whacking your head like that.' Roz zips the bag closed and hooks it over her shoulder. 'See you downstairs.'

We pass most of the journey to Ashford in silence. Roz seems agitated, flicking between radio stations incessantly and drumming her fingers on the steering wheel whenever we get stuck behind anyone doing less than fifty miles an hour. Is she regretting her offer to take me? If she is, I don't blame her. If I had a rare night off from toddler tantrums and demanding husbands, the last place I'd want to spend it would be in A&E. I stare out of the window, willing the baby to move, fretting when it doesn't.

As she pulls into a parking space in front of the sprawling William Harvey Hospital, Roz looks at me. 'Feel anything yet?'

I shake my head. I go to take my overnight bag from the back seat but she beats me to it. She strides off towards the main entrance and I scurry behind her, my hands supporting my belly and my head still pounding with the ferocity of a wrecking ball.

We follow the signs to A&E and walk up to the harassed-looking woman at the counter. As I feared, the place is heaving.

'Name?' she says, and for a second my mind goes blank. Roz nudges me in the ribs.

'Um, Sophie. Sophie Saunders.'

I give her my date of birth, address and the name of my GP. She types furiously, her eyes never leaving the screen.

'And what's the problem?'

'She had a fall. She's thirty-four weeks pregnant,' says Roz. 'The baby hasn't moved since.'

Hearing the words spoken so starkly sends me into a spin and I clutch the counter in desperation. The woman's expression softens and her voice is sympathetic when she says, 'Take a seat, dear. The triage nurse will be with you shortly.'

I follow Roz to a couple of empty seats tucked behind the door. Opposite us a small boy of about eight in grey school shorts and a white polo shirt is clutching a blood-stained cloth to his right index finger. He's waxwork pale. Beside him a woman in a pinstripe trouser suit and perfectly plucked eyebrows - his mum I presume - is ignoring the *No phone* signs that are dotted around the noticeboards and is scrolling down her iPhone.

To their right a dazed-looking woman with a frizz of white hair like candy floss is mumbling to herself, watched over by a care worker in an emerald-green tunic. A young woman in tennis whites cradles a limp wrist in her left hand and a man in his late fifties holds a bag of peas wrapped in a tartan tea towel to an impressive-looking bump on his forehead.

Roz sits neatly with her legs crossed and her hands clasped in her lap. I don't have the energy for conversation, so I pick up a tattered copy of *Hello!* and flick through it, feigning interest in the empty-headed celebrities and their tasteless homes.

After about ten minutes a cheerful nurse with a round face and even rounder hips approaches with a clipboard. 'Sophie Saunders?'

I nod.

'What's brought you here today, Sophie?'

She listens, making occasional notes, as I recount the fall.

'Did you lose consciousness?'

'I don't think -'

'She did,' Roz interjects. 'Only for a couple of minutes, but she was out stone cold.'

The nurse sucks the end of her ballpoint pen. 'And the baby hasn't moved since?'

'No,' says Roz. 'We've already told your colleague. We could do with seeing someone this side of Christmas.'

The nurse ignores Roz and smiles at me. 'We'll get you in to see a midwife as soon as we can.'

To my relief it's only a few minutes before my name is called again. As I heave myself out of the chair I think I feel a twinge in my abdomen. But it's so faint I can't be sure, and I don't mention it to Roz in case I've imagined it. Another nurse directs us to the maternity ward. We stop at the door to use the sanitising hand gel and head towards the waiting area. I give my details again and am assured someone will be with me shortly. Somewhere in the distance a newborn baby wails.

I reach for my phone. 'I should call Matt. Tell him what's happened.'

'There's no point worrying him for nothing,' Roz says. 'Wait until you know how things stand.'

She's right. There's nothing Matt can do, especially as he and a few others were heading out for a curry tonight to celebrate someone's impending wedding. He'll have had a couple of beers by now and won't be able to drive. And if he gets the train home his car will be stuck in Brighton. I'll phone him once I'm home.

'Sophie?' says a softly-spoken Irish woman wearing a blue tunic edged with white piping and a stethoscope around her neck. Her name badge informs us she is Siobhan Byrne and she is a senior midwife with the East Kent Hospitals University NHS Foundation Trust. She smiles at Roz. 'Are you the baby's -?'

'No, she's a friend,' I say. 'My husband works away.'

'Ah so. That'll teach me to assume. If you'd like to follow me.'

We traipse through the waiting room into a small side ward. Siobhan pulls back the curtains and pats the couch. 'You sit yourself there, my lovely, and tell me what happened.'

My throat throbs as I recount the fall yet again.

'Any blood? Any pain in your abdomen?'

'No.' I touch my forehead. 'Just my head.'

'Good. That should rule out a placental abruption. We'll have a look to make sure. But we'll listen to baby's heartbeat first, shall we?'

I roll up my top and peel down my jeans and she squirts a generous amount of gel onto my belly. She looks at me, holding the probe of the Sonicaid mid-air, and says, 'Remember to breathe please, Sophie.'

I hadn't even realised I'd been holding my breath.

Siobhan runs the probe over my bump, pressing here and there. Silence. My skin crawls with dread. She frowns, lifts the probe up and taps the end. Still no sound.

'Sorry. This one's been playing up. I'll try another.'

My hands are balled into fists at my sides. Roz is chewing a fingernail. The tension in the room is unbearable. Siobhan disappears, returning seconds later with another monitor.

'Right, we'll try again, shall we?'

I bite my bottom lip and will the monitor to work. And then... thumpthumpthump. The baby's heartbeat sounds loud and strong and *alive*.

'Thank God,' I mumble. Roz squeezes my hand. Siobhan, still holding the probe in place, beams at us both.

'That's one healthy baby. We'll do an ultrasound to check the placenta's OK and then I'd say you're fine to go home.'

She dims the lights, wheels over the ultrasound machine and angles the screen so we can see the grainy black and white picture.

'I never know which bit is which,' I admit, as she runs the larger probe over my bump.

Siobhan points at the screen. 'There's the head, and the knees, and the -'

'Balls!' cries Roz. 'Looks like you were right. You're having a boy!'

She must notice my sharp intake of breath because she says, 'Oh no, I forgot! You didn't want to find out, did you?'

I shake my head. 'We were going to wait until the baby was born.'

She claps her hand to her mouth. 'What an idiot. Hashtag awkward. Sorry, Soph. I was just so relieved it - he - was alright.'

'It's OK, you didn't mean to. And you're right. The important thing is that the baby's OK.' I turn to Siobhan. 'He *is* OK, isn't he?'

She wipes the gel off my stomach. 'I'd say he's absolutely fine. Babies are pretty resilient in utero. He's got all that amniotic fluid to keep him cushioned and your strong uterus muscles to protect him. And your placenta looks fine, too. My advice is to go home and get some rest. And,' she waggles her index finger at me, 'don't fall over again.'

CHAPTER TWENTY-ONE

NOW

R oz is reluctant to leave but I convince her I'll be fine. 'I'd rather be on my own,' I admit.

Hurt clouds her eyes and I feel a stab of guilt. I touch her arm. 'I'm so glad you were here when it happened.'

'If I hadn't been here you wouldn't have fallen in the first place,' she says in a terse voice.

'Maybe, maybe not. But you've been a superstar, driving me to Ashford, waiting with me at the hospital. Being there when I needed you. You're such a good friend to me.'

She appears mollified. 'Promise you'll phone if you're worried? Day or night. I'll be straight over,' she says.

'I promise.'

'And do me a favour and call in sick tomorrow, OK?'

'I'll think about it.'

'Which means you won't.'

'Probably not,' I agree.

We share a smile. She picks up her bags, presses her key fob and an echoing click from her car's central locking system sounds a few doors down. She holds her fist to her ear, her thumb and little finger outstretched. 'Remember, phone me if there's anything wrong with the baby, OK?'

It's only once her red tail lights have disappeared that I feel able to let go. Tears slide down my face as I close and double bolt the front door and retreat to the sitting room. The house is in darkness but I can't be bothered to switch on any lights. Today's been so draining I'm as empty as a husk, leached of emotion. I should be ecstatic, overjoyed the baby is safe. On one level I am, but mainly I'm just numb, and so bloody weary I could sleep for a week.

I curl up on the sofa and weep until the tears run dry. And then I remember with horror that I still haven't spoken to Matt. I check the time on my phone. It's almost ten. He should be home by now. I take the phone into the kitchen, pour myself a glass of water and blow my nose on a square of kitchen roll. The last thing I want to do is break down in tears while I'm talking to him, so I take a deep drink, clear my throat a few times and test my cried-out, swollen vocal chords, 'There's absolutely nothing to worry about.' My voice sounds nasally, as if I have a heavy cold. But I can pass that off as hay fever. 'You don't need to come home. We're both fine. I just thought you'd want to know.'

As I pick up my phone I'm reminded of something else. I now know the sex of our baby. Matt was adamant he didn't want to find out. So was I, but it's not Roz's fault she forgot. What do I do? Tell him we're having a boy and ruin the surprise, or don't tell him and pretend I don't know either? What if he meets Roz between now and the birth and she blurts it out? If Matt knew I'd kept such a big secret from him he'd be devastated. Perhaps I should tell him, even though he'll be gutted to find out. I go round and round in circles for another few minutes, then have an idea. I won't tell him tonight, but that doesn't mean I won't tell him at all. Instead I'll pick the right moment when he's home this weekend. If I explain that finding out is down to Roz, not me, he'll understand, of course he will. And deep down he'll be over the moon. After all, doesn't every new dad want a son and heir as their firstborn?

My mind made up, I call him but his phone goes straight to voicemail. I hang up, not wanting to leave a long, garbled message. He'll ring when he sees my missed call. But I also dash out a text as insurance.

Hey baby, hope you had a fun night. Give me a ring when you're in? x

Another wave of exhaustion washes over me and I stifle a yawn as I send a second text.

If it's before eleven anyway. Otherwise I'll spk to you tomorrow xx

I potter about in the kitchen, unloading the dishwasher and wiping down surfaces, keeping one eye on my phone all the while. The screen stays blank. Matt always phones or texts me straight back. Not hearing from him is unusual and I double check the phone's not on airplane mode. It isn't.

At a quarter to eleven I try phoning a second time but again it goes straight to voicemail. This time I do leave him a brief message to call me. He doesn't. By five past eleven I admit defeat and head upstairs. I take an age unpacking my overnight bag and getting ready for bed and when I crawl under the duvet it's gone half past. And there's *still* no message from Matt.

Worry is gnawing at my insides. Where is he? What if something's happened? The Fates might be feeling vindictive today, saving the life of our unborn son while ending the life of his father. I'm being melodramatic, I know, but I've felt their cruel hand before. He might have been knocked down by a drunk driver or robbed and beaten up by a gang of feral kids or...

'Get a grip, Sophie,' I mutter through clenched teeth. I grab my phone and ping off a text to Greg, the bank's assistant manager and Matt's closest friend in Brighton.

Hi Greg, sorry for the late text but I can't get hold of Matt. Are you still with him?

I don't have to wait long for a reply.

Sorry, Soph, he didn't come out in the end. Claimed he had a headache, the pussy! Everything OK?

Everything's fine. Sorry to trouble you. I expect he's turned his phone off. Don't worry, it'll keep till the morning. Thanks anyway.

No worries. I'll give him the heads up you need to speak to him tomorrow. You take care of yourself, OK?

I send a smiley emoji back, even though smiling is the last thing I feel like doing. Where was Matt tonight, if he wasn't with his mates at the Indian? I don't think he's had a headache in all the years we've been together. He's one of those lucky people who's never ill. And he loves having a beer with the boys.

For a second I consider calling his landlady, Moira. But she's getting on for seventy and will have long retired to bed. Instead I send one last text to my husband.

I'm worried about you. Call me NOW!!

He doesn't.

My phone finally pings at half past six in the morning. I grab it and squint at the screen.

Sorry babe, only just seen your messages. You awake?

I rub my eyes and sit up.

Yes.

Seconds later the phone rings.

'Hello, Mrs Saunders. How are you this fine morning?'

'I'm alright. But never mind me,' I say carefully. 'How's the head?'

He laughs. 'You know me so well. Truth is, I probably shouldn't have had that last pint. That lot are a bad influence.'

According to Greg he stayed at home last night with a headache, yet here he is telling me he was out on the piss and the only thing he's nursing is a hangover.

'Soph, are you still there?'

'Yes. So, you had a bit too much to drink, did you?'

'Just a bit.'

'But it was a good night?'

'Yeah, we had a right laugh. Greg was on top form.'

'Good,' I say, although nothing about this conversation is good. Truth is, I shouldn't have had that last pint, he said. But I'm not sure who's telling the truth right now.

'What did you have to eat?' I try to inject some warmth into my voice. I don't want him to think I'm suspicious, not until I've thought this through.

'Lamb dhansak. It was delicious. Pity our poor customers this morning, though. I must reek of garlic.'

Too many details. Everyone knows that if you're going to lie you keep it simple.

'Sorry I didn't pick up your texts,' he continues, 'my phone died halfway through the evening and I was out for the count last night. Is everything OK?'

'It is now. But it wasn't last night. I had a fall. I had to go to A&E to check the baby was OK. And when I phoned to tell you what happened you weren't there!'

'Oh Christ, I'm sorry. Is everything alright?'

'The baby's fine.'

'Thank God for that.' The relief in his voice is undeniable. 'And you, are you OK?'

'I've been better. I was so worried I'd lost the baby. And then when I couldn't get hold of you -'

'I'm sorry,' he says again.

'Luckily Roz was here. She drove me to hospital. I don't know what I'd have done otherwise. What if there had been something wrong? What if the baby had come early? You can't just disappear off grid like that.'

'I didn't disappear. I was with Greg and the boys. We were at the Indian Village.'

'I need to know I can contact you. I can't do this on my own!' I know my voice is rising but I don't care.

'I'm sorry,' he says a third time.

Sorry for what? Where was he last night?

'Look, I know it's not ideal, but you're the one who wanted me to take this job, remember. I was quite happy to...' He obviously decides not to go there because he exhales loudly and says instead, 'The main thing is you're both OK, isn't it?'

So many resentments, simmering under the surface. Ill feelings left unsaid. I take a deep breath and make myself smile. 'Of course it is.'

'You and the baby are the most important things in my life, you do know that, don't you? I would do anything, *anything* to protect you both.'

There's an intensity to his voice I've never heard before. Despite my anger I feel a need to reassure him.

'I know you would. We're fine. I'll see you tomorrow, OK?'

'OK. I'll try to knock off a bit early. I'll give you a ring when I leave. I love you, Soph.'

I end the call.

'I love you, too,' I whisper into the void.

———

Locking down the timeline is proving to be the trickiest element of the whole project. There are inherent risks involved if I implement my plan too early. Risks beyond my control, no matter how exhaustive my preparations. Act too late, however, and I would jeopardise everything. Nature will have taken its course.

Trouble is, I'm an impulsive person. I act before I think. I'm passionate and spontaneous, prone to grand gestures and over-the-top reactions.

But I can't afford to be spontaneous, not this time.

This time I must be measured, cautious, methodical and meticulous.

Softly, softly, catchee monkey.

CHAPTER TWENTY-TWO

NOW

It's as cold as a grave in the cellar at Cam and there are goosebumps on my bare arm as I reach for a couple of hand forks and a pair of secateurs. The overhead light flickers and I shiver. I've never liked it down here. It's as though the ghosts of the ill-fated Holborough family are lurking in the dark corners and cobwebby crevasses, waiting to come out and haunt the place when we leave for the day. I wish we had a purpose-built shed to store all our tools, but there isn't the money or the space, so for now we have no choice but to use this subterranean cavern.

I tuck the tools under my left arm, grip the handrail with my right and begin climbing. When I'm almost halfway the steps are thrown into shadow as something blocks the rectangle of sunlight at the top. My heart skips a beat and I stare up. Geoff was once trapped down here when the wind blew the door closed and the latch clicked shut. That can't happen anymore - he swapped the latch for a mortice lock, so you can only lock the door if you have a key - but the knowledge doesn't stop my pulse from racing.

'Hello?' I call.

There's a moment's silence, then Angela's reedy voice echoes down the stone steps.

'Sophie, I need a word.'

Great. Three days have passed since the induction day and thanks to Angela's never-ending schedule of networking events and business lunches I have managed to avoid her. I know Martin's meltdown needs recording, as much for his own interests as Cam's, but I could do without the aggro today.

I glance up at her. 'I just need to -'

'Now,' she barks, spinning on her heels and marching off. Once again the steps are bathed in light. I dawdle up as slowly as possible, putting off the inevitable bollocking as long as I can.

When I eventually trail into the office Angela is sitting at her desk with the incident log book open in front of her. She picks up a pen and taps it on a glass paperweight, as if she's calling a courthouse to order. Perhaps that's what this is, a kangaroo court.

'Shut the door behind you, please.'

I know the chair positioned in front of her desk is meant for me, but I can't resist the opportunity to wind her up so, once I've closed the door, I head over to my own desk. She narrows her eyes but says nothing. Round one to me.

She points her pen at the blank page in front of her and launches her attack. 'Can you please explain why you haven't logged Monday's incident with Martin?'

'It's on my radar. I just haven't got around to it yet.'

Angela sketches quote marks in the air. '*On your radar* isn't good enough. You know as well as I do that all incidents need to be logged as soon as they happen.'

'I know, but -'

'There's always a but with you, isn't there?' She regards

me, her lips pursed. 'Issues like this need to be flagged up to the board of trustees as soon as possible so they can decide what action, if any, needs to be taken.'

'Action?'

'I've spoken to Geoff at length but perhaps you'd like to give me your account of what happened?'

'Martin's behaviour has become increasingly erratic over the last few weeks. His mum says he's taking his meds but he's having problems sleeping. Rosie told me the other day he was talking to himself, so I think he might be hearing voices again.'

'And yet, knowing all this, you asked him to speak at the recruitment evening?'

My neck flushes with anger. 'I didn't know until afterwards that he hadn't been sleeping. Or about the hallucinations.'

'But you know anxiety can be a trigger for Martin.'

I rub a thumb over the scar on the underside of my right forearm. 'I do.'

Angela slams her pen on the desk in frustration. 'So why put unnecessary pressure on him?'

'He was nervous, I know, but Maureen said he was proud to have done it. Don't you think society continually sets limits for people like Martin when, actually, they can achieve far more than we ever give them credit for?'

'Even if it sends their behaviour in a downward spiral?'

I have no answer for that. She picks up her pen again.

'Take me through what happened.'

'We were in the greenhouse potting up plants for the open day.'

'We?' she queries.

'Me, Martin, and two of the new volunteers, Roz and Derek.'

She scribbles in the incident book. 'Go on.'

'Martin became agitated. I'm not sure what sparked it. I think he may have been hearing voices. I tried to calm him down, but he was getting more and more worked up. Roz was worried he was going to hurt himself and managed to restrain him. That's when Geoff arrived and we called Maureen.'

'I phoned Derek this morning to hear his version of events. He said Martin was asking for your knife.'

I lower my gaze. 'He may have done. I honestly can't remember. But I didn't give it to him. Obviously.'

Angela raises her eyebrows. 'Is it? Obvious, I mean. Derek had the impression you'd lent your knife to Martin before. Have you?'

For a second I consider lying, but that would call into question Derek's account, and I can't do that. I don't think Angela would believe me anyway.

'Yes, as a matter of fact I have. But only when the two of us have been working together and I have supervised him at all times. It means a great deal to him that I trust him with it.'

'Trust!' Angela explodes. 'Martin suffers from manic and psychotic symptoms. He's already stabbed you once. What if he'd killed you or one of the new volunteers with a knife you'd given him? Imagine the headlines!'

I pound my fist on the desk. 'Is that all you're worried about, the bad publicity?'

'Of course it isn't. There's a huge difference between treating our service users with dignity and respect and putting people's lives at risk through utter naivety and, I'm afraid, you have been terribly naive. I have no doubt you believe you were acting in Martin's best interests, but the fact is you weren't. I have grave concerns about your conduct. Consider this a verbal warning. Continued or repeated issues with your conduct may result in further disciplinary action including, in an extreme case, dismissal.'

'You've got to be kidding me!'

She fishes a letter out from under the incident book. 'The verbal warning will sit on your file for the next year. Here's a written record of it which I'd like you to sign to confirm this conversation took place.'

'But I was with him the whole time and he didn't hurt anyone!'

Angela strides over to my desk and places the letter in front of me. A muscle is twitching in her jaw.

'I would have been well within my rights to have called a disciplinary hearing. You're getting off lightly, believe me.'

I glare at her. 'That sounds like a threat.'

She shakes her head. 'It's nothing of the sort. Please sign the letter and we can move on.'

Frustration distorts my thinking and before I even realise what I'm doing I snatch up the letter, screw it into a ball and hurl it in the vague direction of the bin.

I haul myself to my feet. 'After everything I've done for Cam this is the thanks I get. Well, you can stick your verbal warning up your arse, you evil cow. I'm going home.'

Angela's hand flies to her mouth and she takes a step back. The shock in her eyes makes me feel immensely powerful and I grab my bag and storm out of the office, righteousness fuelling my anger.

'Sophie, wait!' she calls.

But I ignore her, slamming the door shut behind me.

It's only as I'm almost home that the doubts set in. Perhaps

Angela was within her rights to hold a disciplinary hearing. Perhaps I have been let off lightly with a verbal warning. Throwing a hissy fit wasn't the most sensible way to handle the situation. But she has an uncanny knack of winding me up and today I couldn't help but let rip.

I let myself into the house, wishing Matt was home so I could talk it through with him. I could use an objective view to work out if I've been out of order or if Angela's in the wrong. But Matt's ninety miles away in Brighton. I could phone Lou, but it's gone five so she's probably halfway to being pissed already. Instead I decide to see if Roz can meet me for a drink. She's the perfect person to talk it over with. She's met Angela, was there when Martin had his meltdown, and she's firmly on my side.

My phone pings seconds after I text her.

Sure. Phil and Cait are still at his mum's. What about the Beverlie? I can be there in half an hour. We can sit in the garden x

I'm smiling as I text a thumbs up emoji back. After the dramas we've survived this week, Roz and I have definitely moved from casual friendship to something more meaningful. I take a quick shower, slap on some foundation and mascara and change into my Vertbaudet teeshirt and white leggings.

It's not far to Ye Olde Beverlie and it's such a warm evening I decide to walk. Matt and I considered it our local when we first bought the house, and before he moved to Brighton we'd often pop in for a drink after work. We don't seem to do fun stuff like that anymore. He often brings work home with him at weekends and sits glued to his laptop while I catch up on chores. And money is tight after the IVF and he refuses to pay four quid for a pint when it costs him half the price at home.

As I mooch along the residential streets towards the pub I realise I still haven't tackled him about Monday night. I'm not sure why, to be honest. It's not like I haven't had plenty of opportunity. He sends me a dozen texts a day asking how the baby is. Thankfully it's been been as active as ever, kicking and wriggling like a whirling dervish. One less thing to worry about.

Is Matt genuinely concerned or is it a sign of guilt? The truth is I'm afraid to ask him where he really was. I can't bear it if he lies to me again. Greg's bound to have warned him that I know he wasn't with them. What if he spins me another yarn? It's pathetic, but I don't want to go there. Not when there's so much other crap to deal with.

The sound of my name makes me jump and I look up to see Roz crossing the street towards me. She's wearing a pretty print dress and her hair looks shiny and freshly blow-dried. Beside her I feel fat and frumpy. But the warmth of her smile as she slips her arm in mine is like salve on a wound and as we walk into the pub together my spirits rise.

CHAPTER TWENTY-THREE

NOW

Roz shimmies through the pub garden towards me, a drink in each hand. White wine spritzer for her, elderflower sparkling water for me. The garden is busy with people sipping craft beers and designer gins with Fever-Tree tonics while staring at their mobile phones. A couple of men look up and eye Roz appreciatively as she navigates her way around their picnic benches. It's endearing that she has no idea just how attractive she is. She looks like a single girl about town, not mumsy at all. I hope I still manage to turn heads once the baby's born.

'So,' she says, handing me my drink and sliding into the seat opposite me. 'What's up?'

'Angela found out I've been lending my penknife to Martin and went absolutely ballistic. She gave me a verbal warning.'

'She did *what?*'

'She said if there were any further issues with my conduct I'd be dismissed.'

'That's bang out of order. You ought to speak to your union rep.'

I shrug. 'I'm not in a union. Didn't think I needed to be.'

'Then make an official complaint about her to the trustees. Tell them she's been bullying you. That'll put the wind up her tail.'

'I don't think I could class it as bullying.'

'Who cares? It'd be your word against hers, and you've been there a lot longer. Workplace bullying and harassment is totally unacceptable these days. And no employer in their right mind is going to risk not taking you seriously while you're pregnant.'

'Even so...' I say, remembering my angry outburst. I can hardly claim Angela intimidated me. In fact, she'd probably be justified in making a complaint about my behaviour. I shift in my seat and fiddle with the straw in my drink.

'Don't let her walk all over you. You're always moaning about how annoying she is. She's a grade A bitch and she deserves everything she gets.'

'Perhaps she was worried because of what happened with Martin last time.'

Roz frowns. 'What do you mean?'

I hold up my arm and show her the three-inch-long scar, as serrated as the teeth of a pair of pinking shears, below my elbow.

'I assumed you did that when you were a kid, falling off a bike or something.'

'You noticed it?'

'Hard not to. What the hell happened?'

I hesitate. I still don't blame Martin. It wasn't his fault. 'About two years ago Martin had a psychotic episode at Cam. He was hearing voices. One of the voices told him the staff were zombies and if he wanted to protect the gardeners he had to kill us one by one. He snuck into the cellar and armed himself with one of Geoff's old handsaws. I realised he'd disappeared and went to look for him. I found him at the top of the steps to the cellar. It was weird. His eyes were totally blank. He was there but he wasn't there, if you know what I mean.'

Roz glances at me. 'I do.'

'I tried talking him down, but I couldn't get through to him. He lifted the saw high above his head. I thought he was going to slash me with it, so I held up my arms to defend myself. Then one of the other gardeners screamed and he whipped the saw back down. My arm was in the way.'

'Jesus.'

'He swore afterwards he hadn't meant to cut me. He'd told the voices he didn't want to hurt anyone. He was holding the saw out of their reach.'

'Easy to say,' Roz spits. She leans towards me and fingers the scar. 'You're lucky he didn't hit a main artery.'

'It wasn't as bad as it looks. I only needed a handful of stitches. The tetanus jab hurt more. Anyway, he soon stabilised once he was back on his meds and he's been fine ever since.'

'Until Monday.'

'Until Monday,' I agree.

'What are you going to do about Angela?'

I run a hand through my hair. 'Apologise, I suppose. I was out of order, yelling at her like that.'

Roz tuts. 'You need to stand up for yourself. You let people walk all over you.'

'You're probably right. Anyway, let's talk about something more cheerful. Are you looking forward to Caitlyn coming home?'

Roz takes a slug of her spritzer. 'Of course. The bedroom's all ready.'

'Oh, have you decorated it for her?'

'I've painted it cornflower-blue.'

'Not pink?'

Roz shakes her head. 'You know what a tomboy she is. I've made blue and white checked curtains and I've bought a Peter Rabbit frieze for the wall behind the cot.'

'She's still in a cot?'

'You know what I mean. One of those ones that converts into a bed.'

'It sounds great. I'm sure she'll love it.' I point to her empty glass. 'Want another?'

'Yeah, why not?'

I gather both glasses and head inside. The bar is dark after the glare of the summer sun and I push my sunglasses onto the top of my head. The barmaid is serving someone on the other side of the bar. I take the opportunity to pop to the ladies'. As I come out I reach into my bag for my purse and almost collide with a boy in a checked linen shirt and cargo shorts. He sidesteps me just in time, but not before the pint he's carrying slops over the rim of the glass and drenches his shirt.

I hold my hands up in apology. 'So sorry.'

'No worries,' he says in a Boston accent that's pure *Cheers*.

My heart lurches. It's Josh, looking more like Ed than ever as he smiles down at me.

'I'm an idiot. I wasn't looking where I was going. And now you've got beer all over your shirt. Let me buy you another. Beer, I mean.' I'm gabbling but I can't stop the words tumbling out of my mouth. 'You're Josh Sullivan, aren't you?'

Josh glances at the door to the beer garden.

'I know your mum,' I say before he has a chance to disappear. 'We were friends at school.'

His face creases into a smile. 'Hey wait, are you Sophie?'

I smile back. 'Got it in one.'

'Mom told me all about you. You were, like, best buds back in the day.'

'We were indeed.'

'Shame you guys lost touch. But I'm glad you invited her over the other night. She could use a friend right now.' A shadow darkens his face and I touch his arm.

'I'm so sorry about your dad. We were friends, too. Back in the day.'

'Yeah well, shit happens. Mom never mentioned you knew Dad.'

'It was a long time ago.'

Josh shoots another look at the door. 'I'd better go. I'm meeting some dudes from college.'

I realise my hand is still on his arm and I drop it to my side. 'Of course. Tell your mum I'll be in touch.'

He smiles again. 'That'd be cool. Hey, it was nice to meet you.'

'It was nice to meet you, too,' I say. But he's already turned his back on me and is waving to his friends.

'What took you so long?' says Roz as I deposit our glasses on the table.

I'm about to tell her about bumping into Josh but it's all too complicated. Instead I grimace.

'The baby's using my bladder as a trampoline so I needed the loo, then there was a queue at the bar.'

She narrows her eyes. 'You're not complaining, are you? You're lucky everything's OK.'

'I know.' I rub the side of my bump. My belly feels as tight as a drum.

Roz clasps her hands together. 'You need to be really careful now. This is a critical time for you and the baby. Are you and Matt still having sex?'

I am taken aback by her directness until I remind myself it's just her way and she has my best interests at heart. I cast my mind back to the last time Matt and I made love and then realise I can't remember. We're always too busy or too tired.

Roz, mistaking my silence for modesty, says, 'It's OK, you won't embarrass me. When I found out I was pregnant with Caitlyn, I wouldn't let Phil near me with a bargepole, let alone his dick. There was no way I was going to risk another miscarriage, not after all I'd been through.'

'I don't blame you,' I reply, thinking, Valentine's Day, that was the last time. A meal deal from Marks & Spencer and a bottle of Prosecco, not that I had much more than a couple of sips. I count surreptitiously on my fingers. Six months ago. Surely it can't be that long?

'So, are you?' Roz repeats, her green eyes fixed on mine.

'Not for ages, now you come to mention it.'

She gives an approving nod. 'Just as well. I know they say it doesn't hurt the baby, but you really can't be too careful.'

'I guess.'

'Although... ' She stops and gives a little shake of her head.

'Although what?'

She glances sidelong at me. 'It doesn't matter.'

'What doesn't matter? What were you going to say?'

She hesitates, then pulls a face. 'If he's not getting it at home, I hope he's not getting it somewhere else.'

Packages are arriving every day. Whenever the doorbell rings I skip along the hallway with the excited step of a five-year-old child impatient to see if Santa's on the doorstep. I snatch the parcels from the hands of startled delivery drivers before slamming the door in their faces and ripping open the packaging as I hurry upstairs to inspect my latest purchase.

Today's delivery was better than I could have hoped for. It was eye-wateringly expensive, but I'd been seduced by the marketing guff on the website. Unrivalled service, outstanding products, discretion guaranteed, you know the kind of thing.

I give the authentic, individually hand-crafted, medical-grade hypoallergenic silicone an experimental prod, pleased with the way it yields to my touch. I poke harder, just for fun, my forefinger disappearing in the folds of pink.

Suddenly excited, I pull my teeshirt over my head, toss it onto the bed and wriggle into my purchase. Take two steps across my tiny bedroom to the wall mirror and turn this way and that with my hands on my hips as I admire my new silhouette. I think of Juliana Sanchez, how frightened she must have felt when her contractions started, weeks too early.

I pick up the stainless steel scalpel on my dressing table and run it lightly along my new silicone belly from my breastbone to my pubic bone and sigh with pleasure.

CHAPTER TWENTY-FOUR

THEN

I'm sitting on the floor in the cramped bathroom at my house, staring at the plastic stick in my hand as if it holds the answers to the universe. Which, in a way, it does. The answers to my universe, anyway.

'Ready?' says Lou. She's perched on the closed loo seat, watching me.

I swallow. 'Not really.'

'Don't worry. I bet you my new Rimmel nail varnish it's negative.'

'It's Friday the thirteenth,' I wail. 'We should have waited until tomorrow.'

'Stop being superstitious. *And* jumping to conclusions. You might be fine and then you'll feel like a complete prat for making such a fuss.'

'What about the puking?'

'Morning sickness is called morning sickness for a reason. You've been puking halfway through the afternoon.' Lou speaks with authority, but she's talking out of her arse. Fact is, Mum had morning sickness in the afternoon. Some women do.

I hug my knees to my chest. 'How much longer?' My parents have popped into town and I'm not sure when they'll be back. I can't risk them arriving home in the middle of this... this catastrophe.

'Another two minutes, give or take.' Lou consults the box in her hand. 'And if you are, a thin blue line will appear in the window.'

I check. No blue lines yet, thin or otherwise. That's good news, surely? But deep down I know I'm pregnant. Up the duff. Knocked up. In the family way. Dress it how you like, I have well and truly cocked right up. Or Ed has, anyway. I clamp my hand to my mouth, stifling the gasp of hysterical laughter that's bubbling in my windpipe like indigestion. I have no idea why. This is so not funny. I have literally nothing to laugh about.

'Is it time?'

'One more minute.'

I take a deep breath. In just sixty seconds I'll know my fate. Lou is re-reading the instructions on the back of the box. She's been amazing, she really has. I expected her to completely freak out when I finally summoned the nerve to tell her I might be pregnant. But she didn't. She caught a bus to Herne Bay so she could buy the Clearblue One Step pregnancy test kit from a chemist where no-one knew her. And she held my hand and promised she would look after me, whatever the result.

She meets my eye. 'OK. Time's up.'

I'm too scared to look. I pass Lou the plastic stick and she takes it without a murmur, even though I was pissing all over it three minutes ago. She gasps and if I didn't know before, I do now.

'I'm pregnant, aren't I?'

Our eyes meet. Pity is etched across her face.

'We should do another test, in case this one's wrong.'

I shake my head. 'What's the point? You read the box, they're ninety-nine per cent accurate.'

'You might be that one in a hundred person. Let's at least try.' Lou tips the second plastic wand out of the box and hands it to me. I stand stiffly and wait for her to step out of the way so I can flip up the lid of the toilet and pee on the stick. This time I hand it straight to her.

The walls of our tiny bathroom are closing in on me. 'I need to get out of here. I'll be in my bedroom.'

A few minutes later Lou pads across the landing and my door swings open. She has the Clearblue box in one hand and a bottle of vampire-red nail polish in the other. She plonks them both on my dressing table and gathers me in her arms.

I cry until I can cry no more.

CHAPTER TWENTY-FIVE

NOW

I wake with a start when my alarm goes off. The duvet is tangled between my legs and my pillow is damp. I barely slept last night, and when I did my dreams were filled with images of Matt having porn star sex with a series of faceless women. It was just a dream, I tell myself. But I can't erase the images from my mind.

I groan, bury my head in the pillow and consider phoning in sick. But that would only give Angela ammunition for my next verbal warning, and I'm not giving her the satisfaction. Instead I force myself out of bed and into the en suite. Out of habit I scrutinise my face in the mirror. I look like crap, wan and hollow-eyed. My hair is dull and frizzy, and my roots need doing *again*.

'Fuck's sake. No wonder Matt's playing away,' I tell my woebegone reflection. 'I would if I woke up to you every morning.' I stab my finger at the mirror. 'You washed-up old hag.'

I feel more human once I've showered and drunk my first cup of tea. Especially when my phone pings with a text from Matt.

Morning gorgeous. Happy Friday! Can't wait to see you tonight. Love you x

He wouldn't be sending texts like that if he was having an affair, would he? Unless it's a cover. But I can't believe the man I married is capable of such duplicity. As I'm about to reply to his text I have an idea. I'll make an extra effort tonight. I'll pick up a couple of steaks from the farm shop on the way home from work and open the ludicrously expensive bottle of Chateauneuf Du Pape I bought him for Christmas. I'll put on a dress and a smile and see if I can't rekindle at least some of the heart-thudding passion we enjoyed when we first met.

Love you too, I type. *Don't be late home. I have something nice planned x*

Promises promises! I'll be home by seven at the latest, I promise. Have a good day x

By the time I arrive at Cam I'm almost cheerful. It's another glorious summer's day, and although it means I'll spend the last hour of the afternoon watering, it's a small price to pay. As I let myself into the garden I'm hit by the sweet scent of honeysuckle and roses. Mr Pickles darts out from behind an over-sized hebe and weaves through my legs. I bend over with difficulty and pick him up. He purrs when I tickle him under the chin. It's only cupboard love - he wants his breakfast, not me - but it makes me smile all the same.

'Come on, gutbucket. Let's find you something to eat.'

Geoff's already in the office, sitting at Angela's desk flicking through a seed catalogue. I deposit Mr Pickles on the floor and he stalks over to the fridge and miaows.

'In a minute,' I tell him. And then to Geoff, 'No Angela? Has she got a meeting?'

'She didn't mention one.' He folds the catalogue, running his soil-stained fingers along the crease. 'I hope she didn't give you too much grief yesterday.'

I shrug. 'Just a verbal warning.'

'I'm sorry.'

'To be honest it's the least of my worries. How's Martin? Have you spoken to Maureen?'

Geoff drops the catalogue in Angela's in tray. 'He saw the support worker yesterday and she's adjusted his meds. Maureen says he's already a lot calmer. She might bring him over for a cup of tea later if he's up to it.'

'Good idea. I don't want him thinking he's not welcome.'

I pick up my clipboard and skim-read the worksheets. Today Rosie and I are supposed to be weeding the long bed at the far end of the garden with Nancy, who at sixty-five is one of our oldest gardeners. But the ground's so hard I think we'll make a start on the bunting for the open day. Angela has decreed she wants the garden festooned with the bloody stuff, and what Angela wants, Angela gets.

Mr Pickles miaows again and butts my leg with his head.

'Did no-one ever tell you patience is a virtue?' I scold. The tip of his tail twitches. His narrowed green eyes remind me of someone, but I can't think who. It's only later I realise. He reminds me of Roz.

———

By ten o'clock I've set out everything we need for the bunting on a shady picnic table. One by one I tick them off on my fingers: the remnants of material I picked up for a song in town, a tape measure and a pen, a roll of brown garden twine, some pinking shears, a pair of eyelet pliers and a box of brass eyelets.

Angela's still not here. I'm surprised. She usually lets Geoff or me know if she's going to be this late. Although I suppose I didn't give her a chance to before I stormed out yesterday. A small kernel of anxiety is growing in the pit of my stomach. Surely she wasn't upset by my outburst? I tell myself I'm being ridiculous. She's as hard as nails.

The arrival of the minibus is a welcome distraction to my spiralling anxiety and soon Rosie, Nancy and I are sitting around the table, our heads bent together as we make the bunting. Rosie commandeers the pinking shears and the tip of her tongue protrudes from the corner of her mouth as she concentrates on cutting triangles from the many different coloured fabrics. Nancy is a dab hand with the eyelet pliers, grinning with satisfaction each time she stamps a hole in the top corners of Rosie's triangles. The fiddly job of inserting the eyelets into the fabric is left to me but it suits me fine. It takes my mind off everything else.

At eleven I heave my bulk out of the seat and head for the office to make tea for us all. As I'm dropping teabags into mugs the door clicks open. Expecting it to be Angela, I'm surprised to see Maureen shooing Martin into the office.

'Rosie said we'd find you in here. Martin has something to say, haven't you, Marty?'

He shuffles towards me, his head low and his hands in his pockets. 'I'm sorry for the other day,' he mumbles. 'I never meant to frighten anyone.'

'Of course you didn't. It's fine. Honestly. But thank you for apologising anyway.'

He gives a quick nod. I reach into the cupboard for two more mugs.

'You'll stay for a cup?'

'Just a quick one,' Maureen says.

'You go on out and I'll bring these over.'

While the kettle's boiling I check my phone to see if Angela has texted. She hasn't. I open our shared diary on my computer, but no meetings are scheduled. I contemplate phoning her, to check she's OK, but before I can Rosie bowls into the office, chivvying me up and rifling through my desk drawers for my secret stash of chocolate biscuits.

Martin and his mum are sitting either side of Nancy at the picnic table and I call Geoff and Mary over to join us. We chat about the weather and preparations for the open day and everyone admires our burgeoning lengths of bunting. I'm draining the last dregs from my mug when the gravel crunches and a car door slams. I check my watch. It's half past eleven.

'Angela?' Geoff says, his eyebrows raised.

I tut. 'About time. I'll remember this the next time she lectures me on my timekeeping.'

Busy brushing biscuit crumbs from the table, I don't notice how still Martin has become until Maureen says in a voice heavy with worry, 'Everything OK, Marty?'

He's staring at the entrance to the garden with a look of horror. The horror escalates to anger and he turns to me, his eyes blazing. 'You liar!'

'Martin!' cries Maureen.

'You promised you wouldn't call the police!'

'The *police*? I didn't.'

'Then who is *that*?' he shouts, pointing to the entrance with a trembling finger.

I turn and look. Sure enough, a uniformed officer is making his way towards us. He's over six-foot tall, with the muscular physique of someone who spends all their free time in the gym. With him is a woman with cropped, bleached blonde hair. She's wearing a severe black trouser suit and although she's almost a foot shorter than her colleague she still manages to match him stride for stride. As they approach the muffled static of a two-way radio cuts into the silence. The man says something to the woman, steps aside and starts talking into the handset in a low, urgent voice.

I glance at Martin. The anger has subsided as quickly as it arrived and he's clutching his head in his hands and rocking in his seat.

Maureen touches his shoulder and he looks up at her with pleading eyes. 'Not hospital. Please, Mum. I can get better, I promise. But not if you send me to hospital.'

I don't hear what Maureen says because the female officer is consulting her pocket notebook and saying something. It's only when Rosie gives me a nudge that I realise it's my name.

'Sophie Saunders?' the woman says again. There's a trace of exasperation in her voice but all I can think is, please God don't let it be Matt. Because that's why the police turn up on the doorsteps of law-abiding citizens, isn't it? To deliver bad news.

'That's me,' I say, barely above a whisper.

The officer's smile doesn't reach her eyes. 'Is there somewhere private we can talk?'

This is the bit where she asks if there's anyone I'd like with me. But she hasn't read the script because instead she points to the open door of the office. 'In there, perhaps?'

'Of course.'

Geoff makes as if to stand but she shakes her head and gestures him to stay before following me inside.

'I'm DC Sam Bennett from Kent Police. And this is PC Dillon Grant,' she says, as her musclebound colleague steps through the door. 'He's on secondment with CID.'

He holds out his hand and I shake it on autopilot.

I feel the detective's eyes burning into me. 'Are you alright,' she says. 'You look a little pale.'

'Has something happened to Matt?' I ask.

She frowns. 'Who?'

'My husband, Matt Saunders. Is that why you're here?'

Her face clears. 'You think we're here to deliver a death message? Not today. We're investigating a report of arson with intent to endanger life at a house in Union Road, Bridge, last night.'

'That's where Angela lives!'

DC Bennett flips open her notebook. 'Angela Platt. The manager of Camomile Community Garden. Your boss.'

I sit down in my chair with a bump. 'The arson was at her house? Is she alright?'

'Fortunately, Mrs Platt's neighbours were still up, heard her fire alarm and called the fire brigade. The fire damaged the carpet in the hallway and I understand there's some smoke and water damage. Mrs Platt was taken to hospital suffering from smoke inhalation but she's due to be discharged this afternoon. She's an extremely lucky lady. If the fire had been left undiscovered for even a few minutes longer I may well have been delivering that death message you appear to have been expecting.'

I don't like her tone, but there's no time to unpick why she's being so snippy with me.

'Why do you think it's arson?'

'Because a gallon of petrol was poured through her letterbox, closely followed by a lighted rag.'

My hand flies to my mouth. 'Oh my God, that's terrible. I should let our chairman know -'

DC Bennett cuts across me.

'I need to ask you a few questions. Is there anyone here who has a grudge against Mrs Platt?'

An image of Mary, the wronged wife, worms its way into my head. Angela's affair with Bob is the worst-kept secret at Cam. But it's ridiculous to think she'd set fire to Angela's house. I shake my head. 'Not that I know of.'

'No-one's had a falling out with her? An exchange of words, anything like that?'

I fiddle with the pen on my desk, hoping DC Bennett hasn't noticed the dark flush creeping up my neck. 'I can't think of anyone, no.'

'That's strange,' DC Bennett says, consulting her note-book. 'Because Mrs Platt told us this morning that you and she had words after she gave you a verbal warning yesterday. She said she'd never seen you so angry.'

'What, *that*? I force a laugh. 'I was just a bit hormonal.' I gesture at my bump. 'Blame it on the baby.'

She makes a non-committal noise and jots something down. Panic grips my insides. Surely she doesn't think I set fire to Angela's house?

'A neighbour's CCTV caught someone standing outside Mrs Platt's home last night, shortly before the fire started. Unfortunately they had their back to the camera, but you can see them pouring in the petrol and using a lighter to light the rag.' She looks me up and down. 'They were about your height.'

'You think I... ? That's crazy. I know Angela and I don't always see eye to eye, but I would never -'

DC Bennett clears her throat, cutting me short. We

both know she holds all the power. All I can do is watch and wait for her to pounce, and she doesn't disappoint me.

'Where were you between eleven o'clock and midnight last night?'

CHAPTER TWENTY-SIX

I've been avoiding Ed for days. Every time I see him in the distance I dip into an empty classroom or hide in the toilets until I'm sure the coast is clear. I know his timetable off by heart, and as we're doing different A-levels it's surprisingly easy to evade him. I know he's looking for me. Lou says he nabbed her in the canteen the other day and pleaded with her to tell him why I won't see him, what he's done wrong.

'You're going to have to talk to him,' she'd said afterwards, but I'd shaken my head. The only thing that's clear to me in this complete bloody fuck up is that Ed must not know I'm pregnant. I can't lay that on him. His heart's set on reading law at UCL. He's been offered a place, too. But he needs three As. What's going to happen if I tell him that in five months' time, on the day he's expecting to sit his first history paper, I could quite possibly be in Kent and Canterbury Hospital's labour ward giving birth to our baby?

Baby. There, I've said it. I've been avoiding going there, too. I can just about accept the fact that I'm pregnant, but I'm still in denial that pregnancy = baby.

Because here's the irony. I want children, I always have. When I picture my future I'm always surrounded by a brood of kids; three or four at least. Maybe it's because I'm an only child, but I want a big, noisy family of my own. But not until I'm in my thirties, happily married with a job I love, a nice house and two cars on the driveway. Having a baby at seventeen is not part of my life plan. Now when I picture my future, the farmhouse kitchen with the cream Aga and scrubbed pine table morphs into a grotty bedsit draped with damp washing. Instead of cooking mountains of spag bol for my happy tribe of kids, I'm trying to calm a wailing toddler before he wakes the druggie neighbours.

The other irony is this: if I told Ed I was expecting our baby he would stand by me, I know he would. He's the most loyal, decent person I've ever met. He'd give me a hug and say, 'Soph, you daft cow, everything will be alright. I'll look after you. We'll make it work.'

But the truth is, we can't make it work. Not really. Two naive seventeen-year-olds with their heads in the clouds and a tenuous grip on reality? We're barely able to look after ourselves. We wouldn't stand a chance.

I love Ed so much it physically hurts. It kills me that he thinks I'm giving him the cold shoulder, when all I really want to do is run into his arms and tell him everything. But he's better off without me. He has a golden future in front of him. I will not mess that up.

So, when he tracks me down in the library after lunch I channel my inner ice maiden.

'Sophie, why are you ignoring me?'

I shrug, my face blank.

He tries to take my hands but I snatch them away. His shoulders sag. His fringe is flopping over one eye. It's as much as I can do not to run my hand through it, straighten it out.

'What's the matter? Why won't you return my calls?'

There's a catch in his voice. My heart is shattering into a million tiny pieces.

'I think we should call it quits.' My voice sounds high and hard.

He flinches, as if I've struck him. Which, in a way, I suppose I have. But I plough on, showing no mercy. I'm pitiless, I have to be. 'It was fun, but now it's over.'

'But I don't understand. We love each other.'

I roll my eyes with practised scorn. 'We're seventeen. We should be out having fun, not tied down like an old married couple.'

His brow furrows. 'Have you met someone else?'

'No!' It bursts out of me before I can stop it. 'No, I haven't. But I don't want to go out with you anymore, OK? We're finished. Over.'

'You don't mean it.'

'Ed -'

'Whatever I've done wrong, I'm sorry, OK? I can make it right.'

'You haven't done anything wrong. It's not you, it's me.'

He shakes his head. 'Don't resort to clichés. Tell me the truth.'

I so very nearly give in and tell him everything. But I remember in the nick of time. Just because I've fucked up doesn't mean he has to. I can protect him and I will. I will not screw up his life.

I hold my head up and meet his eyes. 'You want the truth? I don't love you anymore.'

CHAPTER TWENTY-SEVEN

NOW

I take a step backwards. 'I'm sorry, are you accusing me of setting Angela's house on fire?'

The two police officers exchange a glance. PC Grant smiles. 'Of course not, Mrs Saunders. We're making routine enquiries so we can establish the circumstances.'

'Right.' I don't believe them, but I have nothing to hide. I take a moment to compose myself and smile back. 'I met a friend for a drink after work. I left her at about nine, walked home, watched some TV and went to bed. I was fast asleep by eleven. I'm afraid there's no-one who can vouch for me - my husband works away in the week so I was on my own. You'll have to take my word for it.'

'Of course,' says DC Bennett, her voice as smooth as chocolate. 'Who was the friend you met for a drink?'

'Roz Beaumont. I can give you her number if you want to check.'

'What can you tell us about Martin Miller?'

If I'm surprised by the change of tack I try not to show it. 'Martin? He's one of our gardeners. Why?'

'According to Mrs Platt he's been suffering from manic

episodes, the most recent of which happened on Monday when he threatened you.'

'That's not quite true. He was a bit agitated, but he didn't threaten me. Martin's harmless.'

'Mrs Platt is of the opinion that he should have been sectioned.'

'She's wrong. He's fine now he's had his meds adjusted. In fact, he's out there with the other gardeners now.' I point towards the window. 'Which is where I should be. Is there anything else?'

'No, that'll be all for now. We'll be in touch if we need to interview you under caution down at the station. In the meantime, let us know if you're taking any trips abroad. Just in case we need to check anything with you,' says DC Bennett.

I lay a hand on my bump. 'Do I look as though I'm planning to go anywhere other than the maternity unit anytime soon?'

She smiles thinly. 'Probably not.'

Martin and Maureen have disappeared when I rejoin the others. When I ask why they left so soon, Nancy drops the eyelet pliers with a clatter and Rosie turns to me, her eyes as wide as saucers.

'Martin thinks you told the police on him, even though his mum said he was being silly. He said she was the silly one for trusting you. Then he said he was going to... ' she pauses, screwing her face in concentration, 'scarper before the coppers nicked him. And he was gone,' she clicks her fingers, 'just like that.'

'What did they want?' Geoff asks.

'Someone tried to torch Angela's house last night. She's in hospital but she's fine.' Too late, I realise I shouldn't have said anything in front of Rosie and Nancy. Rosie's eyes grow even wider.

'Why would she be in hospital if someone shone a torch at her house?'

I give Rosie what I hope is a reassuring smile. 'She had a bit of a funny turn. She's fine. Now, this bunting isn't going to make itself. Shall we get on with it?'

Rosie nods and picks up the pinking shears. I pass Nancy a pile of flags and mouth to Geoff, 'Talk later.'

As I insert eyelets and thread twine through the holes I wonder who the hell hates Angela so much they would pour petrol through her letterbox and set light to it, knowing she was inside. What if her neighbours hadn't heard her smoke alarm? The whoosh of flames as the petrol caught light would have turned Angela's narrow hallway into a death trap. Acrid smoke curling up the stairs as she slept. Maybe the fire alarm would have woken her. More likely the smoke would have killed her first, burning a path through her respiratory system. I shiver. Someone wanted her dead, but who?

Angela has the kind of abrasive personality that must have rubbed a few people up the wrong way over the years, but that's not exactly grounds for murder. DC Bennett told me before they left that they were following a number of lines of enquiry. With a jolt I realise I'm one of them. But who else might the police think had a motive?

Not Mary, I can't believe that. She's one of the kindest, gentlest, most unassuming people I know. She's a volunteer at Age Concern when she's not here. She troops around the city selling poppies every November, for God's sake. But if the police hear about her husband's affair with Angela they might take a different view and treat her as a possible suspect. What is it they say? Hell hath no fury like a woman scorned. Even so, the thought of her creeping down Angela's road with a can of petrol is laughable.

Martin will be a 'line of enquiry', of course. So bloody predictable to point the finger of suspicion at the person with a mental illness. Especially someone with the prefix 'schizo' stamped on their medical notes. Martin has been unstable lately, but his anger was directed at me today. Why would he want to harm Angela? Yet he was really rattled when the two officers turned up. And then he ran away. If that's not a sign of guilt, what is? And he's small for a man. Not much taller than me...

'Sophie!' calls Rosie, waving her hand in front of my face as if she's hailing a taxi. 'I said I've finished. There's no material left.'

'Sorry, I was miles away. Great job. Do you know what I think this calls for?'

'Another cuppa and a choccie bicky?'

I smile at her, marvelling that she can stay so innocent in such a fucked-up world. If only all life's problems could be solved with tea and biscuits.

'Sure,' I say, and her round face lights up. 'Why not?'

I'm so preoccupied with the fire and the visit from the police that I clean forget to stop off at the farm shop on my way home. It's not until I let myself in the front door that I remember I was going to make an extra effort tonight. I can't face Sainsbury's so I rummage through the freezer to see what I can find. Lurking in the bottom drawer are a couple of steak and ale pies. I'll serve them with rosemary potatoes and the runner beans I brought home from Cam. I can still open the Chateauneuf Du Pape. It'll have to do.

After I've showered and put on my favourite maternity dress, soft jersey in patterned turquoise with a flared skirt and a tie under the bust, I wander into the garden to pick some sweet peas for the kitchen table. The dewy grass feels soothing on my bare feet and the sweet peas smell delicious. I snip away, shaking off the hordes of tiny black pollen beetles, feeling a stab of guilt as I interrupt their feast. As I walk back to the house I tread on something hard. With difficulty I bend down to see what it is.

A small rectangle of plastic is nestled in the grass.

At first it doesn't even occur to me that it might be a lighter, because neither Matt or I have ever smoked. However, when I look closer I realise that's exactly what it is. Perhaps Lou snuck out for a quick fag when she came over for dinner. But my sense of smell has been razor sharp since I fell pregnant. I would have smelt the smoke on her. So how did it get here? I'm about to pick it up and throw it in the bin when I pause, my arm outstretched. DC Bennett said whoever set the fire at Angela's used a lighter. What if they were coming for me, too, and were interrupted?

I straighten slowly, one hand on the small of my back, the other still curled around the rough stalks of the sweet peas. Should I call the police? But what would I tell them - that I'd found a lighter in my garden? Imagine the disbelief in the call taker's voice. It's hardly the crime of the century. DC Bennett might think it's relevant to her enquiries, but how do I get a message to her? She didn't leave a contact number.

It's probably nothing. Perhaps one of the teenage boys from next door hurled it over the fence to avoid being caught smoking by his parents. But the little voice inside my head disagrees. *What if it was meant for you? What if you're next?* My hand flies to my bump. It's not just me anymore, is it? I can't take the chance. I glance behind me, as if the culprit is hiding in the shadow of the flowering cherry. The hairs on the back of my neck stiffen as I peer into the gloom. But there's no-one there. I stoop down to pick up the lighter. Back in the kitchen I look for somewhere safe to keep it, settling on the untidy drawer where we horde spent batteries, old chargers and keys that no longer have locks to fit.

I don't usually pull the curtains downstairs but tonight I sweep through the house, dragging them closed, then check the smoke detectors on the hall and landing ceilings. They both emit an ear-piercing siren when I press the test button but I replace the batteries anyway and test them again, just to be sure.

I'm about to double lock the front door when I realise Matt will be home soon. Instead I busy myself putting the pies in the oven, peeling and chopping potatoes and topping, tailing and stringing the runner beans. The house feels eerily quiet, so I turn on the radio and half-listen to The Archers. When the familiar theme tune heralds the end of the show and Matt's still not home I call him.

'Hey babe, everything OK?' he says, his voice distorted by static.

I want to let rip, remind him that he promised he'd be home by seven *at the latest*. But I don't want to start a fight. Instead I keep my voice conciliatory. 'All good. How are you getting on?'

'OK. I was stuck on the M26 for ages after some twat ploughed into the central reservation. But the traffic's fine now. I should be home by half past. Can you wait that long?' he asks playfully, and I think, oh Christ, he's going to want sex tonight and I'm not in the mood. Not after everything that's happened today.

'I love you, Sophie Saunders. You know that, don't you?'

I'm surprised. Matt isn't given to declarations of love unless he's three sheets to the wind.

'I love you, too,' I say. 'Drive safely.'

Call over, I check on dinner, pour myself a glass of elderflower cordial and sit at the kitchen table with my phone. I scroll through my Facebook and Instagram feeds, then, on a whim, open Kent Online and type Canterbury into the search box.

The story about Angela's fire is the third news story down.

Fire crews tackle house blaze in Bridge

Fire crews were sent to the scene of a house fire in Bridge last night.

Kent Fire and Rescue Service was called to the blaze in Union Road shortly after midnight.

Two crews used breathing apparatus and a hose reel to tackle the fire, which started in the hallway of the terraced house.

A KFRS spokesman said one woman inside the address was taken to hospital suffering from smoke inhalation.

He confirmed fire investigators were currently treating the cause of the blaze as 'unexplained'.

The brief story is accompanied by a generic photo of a fire engine. I scroll back up to the top story. It's about a lorry which collided with the central reservation on the M2 just before the rush-hour causing 'misery' for commuters. It must be the traffic jam Matt was caught in. I click on the story and skim-read the report. Something is niggling me, though I can't work out what. And then I realise.

Matt said his crash was on the M26. This one happened on the M2 at the Bean interchange, yet both involved someone hitting the central reservation. Surely there can't have been two such similar collisions on major routes in Kent on the same evening?

Wondering if Kent Online has made an error I check the rival Kent Live website, but the crash was definitely on the M2. Matt's journey home takes him nowhere near it.

So why did he tell me he was stuck in it?

CHAPTER TWENTY-EIGHT

NOW

I pace the landing, watching for Matt's car. I'm about to give up and phone him again when I catch sight of it reversing into a space halfway down the road. It's at least five minutes before the driver's door opens and my husband's long legs swing out, followed by the rest of him. What was he doing in those five minutes? Calling his lover? Telling her how much he misses her, how he's dreading spending the weekend in the company of his fat, hormonal wife?

He reaches in the boot for his holdall. He looks hot and crumpled. Even from this distance I can sense the tightness in his shoulders. He glances up the street towards our house and I shrink back. It's grubby, spying on him like this. I head downstairs to the kitchen, picking up a magazine on the way so I can pretend I was reading that, not snooping on him.

In the moments before his key turns in the lock I decide against quizzing him about the accident. Not tonight. The front door clicks open and I force a smile.

'Hey baby,' he says as he dumps his holdall on the

kitchen table and gathers me in his arms. 'I've missed you so much.'

I bury my face in his neck and breathe in deeply, wondering if the tang of his aftershave is laced with another woman's perfume. If it is, I can't smell it. He pulls away from me and holds my bump in his hands. 'And you, Baby Saunders. I've missed you, too.'

Here's my opportunity to confess. To tell him we're having a boy. I duck the chance, loathing myself for being so weak. But I can't. Not yet.

I pour him a glass of red and set the table while he takes a shower. He comes back down, flushed and smelling of Head and Shoulders, and puts his phone face down on the table. Settling in his chair, his legs crossed under the table, he takes a sip of wine and sighs in appreciation.

'Tell me about your week.'

Where to start? Martin's meltdown? My verbal warning? The arson attack on Angela's house? The version of the last few days I give him is so diluted it's insipid, but even so he's open-mouthed once I've finished. And I haven't even mentioned the discarded lighter I found nestled in the grass in our back garden.

'Bloody hell. Arson?'

'That's what the police said.'

'Who would let someone burn in their bed? It's -' He shakes his head. 'I don't know. It's sadistic.'

'I think the police reckon it's Martin. Because of the manic episode.'

Matt pulls a face. He likes Martin. Though he's never seen him in the grip of his mental illness. 'I can't see that myself,' he says, draining his glass.

'Neither can I. Not really. It's all a bit of a mystery.'

I plunge the runner beans into boiling water and swirl

them around with a metal spoon. 'It's just pies I'm afraid,' I say over my shoulder.

'Fine by me.'

He sounds distracted and I glance across. He's picked up his mobile and is staring hard at the screen, his brow furrowed.

'Everything alright?' I ask, and he gives a little start.

'Fine. Just checking my emails. I'm expecting one from head office.'

'At eight o'clock on a Friday night?'

For a second our eyes meet. He looks down first and my heart lurches. It's like someone has plunged their fist through my ribcage and ripped it right out, coronary arteries still attached. He switches the phone off and slips it into the back pocket of his shorts.

'You're right. I shouldn't even be checking this time of night.' He shrugs an apology. 'Force of habit.'

I place his plate on the table with a thud.

'Perhaps it was Bob,' he says through a mouthful of flaky pastry a few minutes later.

'Bob?'

'Maybe Angela threatened to expose their affair.'

'What?'

Matt is warming to his theme. 'He was so worried his reputation would be ruined that he decided to put a stop to it. To her.'

I shake my head. 'Being banged up for murder would cause a greater slur to his reputation than a bit of extra-marital action. And anyway, Bob's six-foot tall and at least sixteen stone.'

'What's that got to do with it?'

'The detective said the figure caught on CCTV outside

Angela's house was small and slight. She seemed to insinuate it could have been me.'

I laugh to reinforce just how ridiculous this is, but Matt doesn't join in. His post-shower flush has paled and his face is pallid.

I touch his arm. 'Matt?'

'You haven't noticed anyone hanging around who shouldn't be?' he says.

My eyes slide over to the drawer behind him. I drag them back to my husband's face. 'No. Why?'

'It might be that someone has it in for Cam, not Angela. In which case...' he leaves the sentence hanging, but we both know where it was headed.

He grips my hand in his. 'Just be careful, OK? And if you see anyone acting suspiciously, here or at work, call the police.'

'The *police?* Isn't that over-reacting just a little bit?'

He squeezes my hand so tightly my knuckles crunch. I pull back and he lets go.

'Just promise me you will,' he says. 'I couldn't bear it if anything happened to you or the baby.'

I hold my hands up. 'OK, I promise.'

The intensity in his gaze makes my stomach flip. He pours himself another glass of wine. I place my knife and fork together and fish around for something else to say. I want to ask him where he really was this afternoon, who he spent the other evening with. No more lies, I want to say. Tell me the truth. Then I remember I don't want to know the truth. Not yet. Not until our son is born.

Instead I say in a rush, 'We're having a boy.'

Confusion darkens his pale features. 'We're what?'

'I found out at the scan.'

The confusion is quickly replaced by hurt. He looks like

a five-year-old who's just been told the tooth fairy doesn't exist.

'I thought we didn't want to find out until the birth.'

'We didn't.' This time I reach for his hand. It lies limply in mine. 'Roz let it slip.'

He frowns. 'Who the fuck is Roz?'

I drop his hand in frustration. 'Christ Matt, do you ever listen to a word I say? Roz is my hairdresser. She was here when I fell. She's the one who took me to hospital and she was there when I had the scan. I told you all this.'

'You didn't tell me you knew the sex of our baby.'

'I'm telling you now, aren't I? It was too big a thing to tell you on the phone.'

A muscle is twitching in his jaw. 'This Roz, what's she like?'

I raise my hands and let them fall to my sides. 'Is it important? She's my friend. She forgot we didn't want to know. I'm sorry, OK? It was an accident. But now we do know. So please let's not fight. Not about something as important as this. We're having a boy, Matt.' I massage my bump and smile at him. 'You're having a *son*.'

CHAPTER TWENTY-NINE

THEN

Lou squeezes into the seat next to mine, takes a leaflet out of her bag and slides it across the desk to me. I don't have to read it to know what it says. It's the third abortion pamphlet she's given me this week.

'Not now,' I say, tapping my English exercise book in which I've been trying and failing to write an insightful essay on the part played by jealousy in Othello's downfall. 'I need to finish this for third period.'

She raises her eyebrows at my unfortunate choice of words. I shoot her a withering look and slide the pamphlet back.

'You can't keep burying your head in the sand. You're nearly ten weeks.'

I lay my pen on the desk. I can tell from the determined jut of her jaw that she's not going to leave me in peace. I'd hoped that by hiding away at the back of the library I might have been able to evade her. No such luck.

'Have you read the others?' she says, unfolding the leaflet and smoothing it open with the palm of her hand. I try not to glance down but I can't help it and gross phrases like 'gentle suction', 'dilatation and evacuation' and 'bleeding and cramping' creep into my field of vision.

'Nope.'

'Sophie!' she scolds. 'Are you telling me you want to have this baby?'

'Shush!' I cry, looking around me in horror, but no-one appears to be listening. 'No. Yes. Look, I don't know, alright?'

'You can't go through with it. You're seventeen, for Christ's sake. It'll totally screw up your life.'

'Other girls my age have babies and seem to manage.' My voice sounds sulky even to my own ears. 'Are you saying I wouldn't cope?'

'Of course not. But you want to go to uni, get a degree. Since when was being a teenage mum part of your life plan?'

'It wasn't.' My hands creep around my still-flat belly. 'But some girls take their babies to university and get first class degrees. I read about one in the paper the other day. She ended up doing a master's.'

'I know, but think about all the fun you'd miss out on. Freshers' week, nights out at the students' union, hooking up with guys for casual sex.' She says this with a gleam in her eye. Knowing Lou, she's only half joking.

'As if I'm not in enough trouble as it is.' I pause, frowning. 'Why is it so important to you that I get rid of it anyway?'

She runs her hands through her hair. 'This isn't about me. It's about you, your future. Look at this,' she says, stabbing the pamphlet with her index finger. 'If you have it before twelve weeks it only takes five to ten minutes. But if you leave it longer they have to give you a general anaesthetic and they dilate the cervix and everything. You'll virtually be giving birth!'

'Don't be ridiculous.' I snatch the leaflet from her and skim-read it. 'It says it's a safe and simple procedure right up to twenty-three weeks and six days. I've plenty of time to make up my mind.'

'Like I said, you're burying your head in the sand.'

I give her an icy smile, but under the desk my hands are trembling. 'It's my decision.'

'I'll come with you, if that's what you're worried about.'

'Thanks, I know you would, but it's not that.'

'What is it then? Help me understand.'

I shrug. Trouble is, I don't even know myself. Practical me knows this is the wrong time in my life to have a baby. Practical me says I should follow Lou's advice and go ahead with the abortion. That years into the future I'll look back on it as a blip that couldn't be helped. But there's a tiny voice in my head urging me to keep the baby. To make a go of it. And the tiny voice won't shut up. Tears pricking my eyes, I drop my head in my hands.

Lou tucks a wisp of hair behind my ear and watches my shoulders shudder in silence. Eventually she says, 'What about Ed? You said you didn't want to ruin his life.'

I look up and we lock eyes. 'I don't. But he doesn't have to know.'

'You might be able to hide an abortion from him, but there's no way you're going to be able to hide a baby.'

'I could tell him it's not his. Pretend I had a drunken one-night stand.'

'He's not stupid. He'll work out the dates.'

'I'll say it's premature.'

'It won't work.'

'Then I'll move away. Get a place at Edinburgh or St Andrew's.'

'I don't want you to move away. You're my best friend. I want things to go back to normal. How they were before. And they can. If you'd only have an abortion.'

'But -'

Lou shakes her head. 'You're living in cloud cuckoo land.'

I chew on the ragged skin around my thumbnail. 'What would *you* do? In my shoes?'

She pushes her chair back and jumps to her feet. 'I'd get rid of it,' she says. 'In the blink of an eye.'

CHAPTER THIRTY

NOW

I wake to the smell of bacon drifting up the stairs. A quick look at my phone tells me it's half past eight. I haven't slept in this long for months. I stretch like a cat, toes pointed and back arched, smiling as I remember last night. Matt was so tender with me, made me feel so desirable, so precious, that afterwards I felt all my anxieties float away like dandelion seeds on the wind.

I'm propping myself up on my pillows when he appears, carrying a tray laden with a thick-cut bacon sandwich, a glass of orange juice and a pot of Earl Grey.

'Am I forgiven?' I ask, sitting up and balancing the tray on my bump.

He raises an eyebrow. 'Forgiven?'

'For finding out we're having a boy.'

He sits on the end of the bed. 'I over-reacted last night. Tactless of this Roz woman to let the cat out of the bag, but it wasn't your fault.' He lays a hand on my bump. 'I know I never said, but I always hoped it would be a boy.'

'He'll eat us out of house and home and leave sweaty socks lying all over the place.'

'But he'll be straight-forward and uncomplicated and we can talk football over a pint at the pub. I'm not sure I could have coped with another hormonal woman in the house.'

'Oi,' I say, prodding him with my foot. 'Girls can talk football and drink pints, too.'

He's wearing his favourite sapphire-blue polo shirt and navy golf trousers.

'What time are you playing?'

'We're teeing off at ten. I'd better get cracking. Will you be alright?'

'I'm sure I'll survive without you for a few hours.' I take a bite of bacon sandwich, rubbing the fat that oozes down my chin with the sleeve of my pyjama top. 'I'm meeting Lou at twelve.'

'How is the Merry Widow? No more *incidents*?' He makes as if he's tying a noose around his neck and pulling the cord.

'Matt! You're incorrigible.'

He grins. 'Sorry. Inappropriate, I know. But is she OK?'

'Hard to tell. Lou's very good at putting on a front. But she seems much more positive. We're having lunch at that new Italian place by the cathedral. She said I might as well make the most of eating for two while I still can.'

'I'll probably have a quick pint in the clubhouse afterwards if that's OK?'

'You don't need to ask.'

He pecks me on the cheek. 'Give my love to Lou.'

I shake my head. 'Like she needs any encouragement.'

I pick a table in the window and take a menu from a waitress with hair as dark as molasses and a pleasingly Italian Roman nose.

Lou's texted to say she's running late, but I don't mind. The street is bustling and I'm happy to people watch, making up back stories for the elderly couples, tourists and families mooching past on their way to the cathedral.

She rocks up at a quarter past twelve, wearing an office-smart navy trouser suit and shades. She kisses me on both cheeks, rubs my bump and takes the menu I offer her with trembling fingers.

'You'll have a glass if I order a bottle, won't you?' she asks, beckoning the waitress over. She gives the wine menu the briefest glance. 'The Merlot, I think. Two glasses,' she adds, even though I'm shaking my head.

'This is nice.' She perches her sunglasses on the top of her head, her eyes following the waitress as she weaves through the tables to a floor-to-ceiling wine rack at the back of the restaurant. 'How's work?'

'Oh, you know. The usual. One of the gardeners had a psychotic episode and someone tried to set my boss's house on fire. The police think it was me. Oh, and I've been given a verbal warning. But other than that, all good.'

Her attention, which was still on the waitress, snaps back to me. 'You are joking, right?'

'I wish I was. And to top off the week I had a pregnancy scare.'

Her forehead rumples with worry. 'What happened?'

I pull a face. 'I fell arse over tit and landed on the bump.'

'Pissed again?'

'Very funny. No, I tripped over the cable of a hairdryer. But we went to hospital to get the baby checked over and it's fine.'

'Thank Christ for that.'

'I know.' I fiddle with the menu as the waitress appears with the wine, shows us the bottle and pours an inch into Lou's glass. Lou takes a sip, nods and her glass is filled. I place a hand over mine.

The waitress fishes a notepad and pen out of the back pocket of her trousers and takes our order. Seafood linguine for Lou and salmon ravioli in a creamy dill sauce for me. Once she's gone Lou looks at me squarely.

'Are these things connected?'

'What do you mean?'

'Did the psycho gardener start the fire at your boss's house?'

'I don't think so. Martin's harmless.'

'Why do the police think it's you?'

'Because I'd lost my temper with her the day before.'

'Blimey,' says Lou, looking impressed. 'It's always the quiet ones you have to watch.' She takes a slug of wine. 'But you didn't -'

'Of course not!' Keen to change the subject, I ask how's she's getting home.

'I'm not driving, if that's what you're worried about.'

It occurs to me that I don't even know if she ever passed her test. She'd only just started having lessons when I went travelling. There's so much we don't know about each other. I know the teenage Lou inside out, but the adult version is a stranger to me, and I to her. There are vast chasms in our common history and I'm not sure they can ever be crossed.

As if she's reading my mind, Lou leans forwards and says, 'Tell me about your gap year that turned into a decade. I want to know everything. Where you went, who you met, whether you missed me.'

I give her the well-rehearsed version, which I have

edited and re-edited over the years like a zealous teacher with a red pen. This version is designed to make my time abroad seem fun and adventurous, when the truth is it wasn't adventurous at all. I was just running away.

Lou listens and drinks and drinks and listens, and by the time our pasta arrives she's sunk half the bottle. The ravioli smells delicious and I spear a piece greedily. My fork is halfway to my mouth when a shadow falls on the white tablecloth and I look up to see Roz staring through the window at us.

'Who the hell is that?' says Lou.

'My friend Roz. I'll see if she wants to join us. She's great fun. You'll love her.'

I push my chair back and beckon Roz inside. She gives a little shake of her head but I'm not going to be dissuaded. I want Roz and Lou to be mates. I'm already picturing the three of us on girlie nights together, as tight as thieves.

'Come on, just for a quick drink,' I mouth, motioning the half-empty bottle of Merlot. Roz glances at Lou, who's watching with interest, her fingers tapping a tattoo on the starched white tablecloth.

Roz shrugs her shoulders. 'Five minutes,' she mouths back, and I am smiling as she deposits a couple of shopping bags on the floor and sits next to me.

'So, you're the famous Lou Sullivan nee Stapleton,' she says. 'I've heard all about you.'

Lou leans back in her chair and studies Roz. 'That's funny, because I haven't heard anything about you.'

There's a stony silence. The image of girlie nights is fading fast. I'm reminded of a bull fight I once watched in Spain, the magnificent black bull and the valiant matador circling each other warily, waiting to see who would strike first. I clear my throat and inject some cheeriness into my voice. 'Are you sure you don't want something to eat, Roz?'

'No, I haven't got long. I have a client at two.'

'What do you do?' Lou asks.

Roz smooths her hair self-consciously. 'I'm a mobile hairdresser.'

'That's how we met,' I explain. 'I was looking for a new hairdresser when Roz posted a flyer through my letterbox. I don't usually believe in fate, but it was as though we were preordained to meet.'

Lou twists linguine around her fork. 'Was it your hairdryer lead Sophie tripped over?'

There's an uncomfortable pause and Roz's hand flutters to her neck. 'Yes, why?'

'Bit careless to leave it where she could trip over it, wasn't it? What if something had happened to the baby?'

Roz inhales sharply and I jump in to defend her. 'I told you, it was my fault. I wasn't looking where I was going, klutz that I am. And anyway, everything's fine.'

'The last thing I want is to hurt the baby,' Roz mutters.

'Roz is the one who insisted on taking me to hospital. If she hadn't been there I don't know what I'd have done.'

'If she hadn't been there you wouldn't have tripped over the lead in the first place,' Lou says, her eyes narrowed.

I fork ravioli into my mouth, but my appetite has disappeared and the pasta and its rich filling is claggy and hard to swallow.

Lou is still twirling linguine, but her eyes aren't on her lunch. 'Are you expecting?' she asks Roz.

Roz frowns. 'Expecting what?'

'A baby, what else?' Lou mocks.

When Roz still looks nonplussed, Lou points to the bags beside her feet. 'The pregnancy mag.'

I peer over. A copy of *Mother & Baby* magazine is poking out of the top of one of the carrier bags.

'I bought it for Sophie. There's an interesting feature on home births I thought she'd like.'

'That's sweet of you,' I say, touched.

'There's no way I'd even contemplate having a baby at home. Think of the mess! And no pethidine or epidural.' Lou shudders.

'Roz had a natural birth, didn't you?' I touch her arm.

'Bully for Roz,' says Lou, downing the last of her wine. 'Give me drugs every time.'

Roz pushes back her chair. 'I'd better be off. Nice to see you, Sophie. I'll see you at Cam.' She slaps the magazine down on the table and, without a backward glance, stalks out of the restaurant.

'Who rattled her cage?' Lou says, gazing after her.

I huff in exasperation. 'Perhaps she didn't take kindly to the fact that you virtually accused her of tripping me over. It wasn't her fault.'

'Sure, whatever. She's a bit uptight, though.' Lou pushes her plate to one side, picks up the magazine and starts flicking through it. 'I suppose her baby slept through at four weeks and is a model child. Oo, look, Joshie had one of those.'

She points to a photo of the most beautiful pram I have ever seen. Navy and silver, it's both sleek and elegant. It's also over a thousand pounds. I give a low whistle.

Lou's eyes have taken on a faraway look. 'We were the envy of our mother and toddler group. I know it's not cheap, but you know what they say, you get what you pay for.'

'Which in our case will be a Mothercare own brand, which will do the job just fine.' I smile at the waitress, who glides over to clear the table.

'It was delicious, thanks,' I say, even though I've only managed half of mine and Lou's is virtually untouched.

'You're such a people pleaser,' Lou says, once she's out of earshot.

I'm puzzled. 'You say it like it's a bad thing.'

She tilts her head to one side. 'Listen honey, sometimes it is.'

I thought I was in control, but Sophie's emergency dash to hospital reminded me how easily even the best-laid plans can turn to shit.

I'm seething.

One careless mistake that could have altered the trajectory of my entire future. A sliding doors moment I was powerless to stop.

It was stupid. So stupid.

What if Sophie had gone into labour six weeks early?

What would have happened to the baby?

His kidneys would have been fully functioning and his nervous system and brain fully developed. He would have been the size of a honeydew melon.

But some babies need help breathing if they're born before thirty-six weeks. They need specialist care from properly-trained doctors and nurses.

That wouldn't do.

That wouldn't do at all.

CHAPTER THIRTY-ONE

NOW

The day before the open day I wake at half five, my head buzzing. It's the most important date in Cam's calendar. A chance to show everyone the work we do, day in, day out, nurturing and supporting both plants and people. An opportunity to invite the public into Canterbury's own secret garden to see the magic happening behind our high brick walls.

I turn over and try to empty my mind so I can drift back to sleep, but it's no good. Instead I make a mental list of all the jobs that need tackling. When the baby wakes up and starts dancing an Irish jig on my bladder I admit defeat and haul myself out of bed.

By seven I'm in the car, driving through the quiet streets to work. After weeks of sun the weather has broken and a fine drizzle blurs the windscreen until I flick on the wipers. The rain is due to clear by nine, which is just as well as I have so much to do. All gardeners are fixated by the weather, but lately I've become obsessed, glued to the long-range forecast and checking and re-checking the three weather apps on my phone.

A journey that can take forty minutes in the rush hour takes a little under ten this morning, and soon I'm pulling into my usual spot in the car park. I grab my bag from the passenger seat, pull up the hood of my waterproof jacket and cross to the oak door. It's only when I'm holding the key to the lock that I realise it's already ajar. Puzzled, I push the door open with the tips of my fingers and step inside.

I know straight away that something's terribly wrong. The two lavender-filled terracotta pots that usually stand sentry just inside the door have been upended, the plants spewing out onto the gravel path. Beyond them, the picnic table where Rosie, Nancy and I made the bunting only a few days ago, has been flipped on its side. I take a hesitant step forwards. Forks, spades and rakes are strewn across the lawn. Tyres on the overturned wheelbarrows have been slashed. I break into a run, my heart in my mouth, skidding to a horrified halt by the vegetable garden. It's a scene of devastation. The neat rows of lettuce, radish, spring onions and beetroot have been pulled up and hurled indiscriminately across the garden. Rosie's runner beans, the seedlings she so carefully planted, have been ripped from the soil, the bamboo sticks she coaxed them up snapped in two.

I run further into the garden. Someone has attacked the herbaceous border with a pair of shears, snipping dusky pink rudbeckia and cosmos in half. The roses have been beheaded, too, and petals lie sodden on the ground like long-forgotten confetti.

I push my hood back and stumble past the greenhouse to the corner we had earmarked for tomorrow's plant sale. Every single pot has been tipped out in a pile by the greenhouse door. Hours of work wrecked. The wanton destruction takes my breath away. It's as if a tornado has swept through the garden, destroying everything in its path. But a freak weather event I could understand. Even forgive. Not this... this man-made *mayhem*.

I turn, my eyes sweeping the garden, assessing the extent of the damage. Everywhere I look there is ruin. Hatred oozes from every shattered pot, crushed plant and broken tool. I rub a hand across my face. My cheeks are wet, with rain or tears I can't tell. A creak behind me makes me cry out in fear, but it's only the door to the cellar swinging open, caught by a sudden gust of wind. Whoever caused this has long gone.

I make my way to the office. There are things I need to do. Phone the police. Call Angela and Geoff. Cancel the gardeners and volunteers. Cancel the open day. A surge of anger floods my veins, the sheer force of it taking me by surprise. Who would do this to a charity like Cam, which does only good? What kind of screwed up individual would take pleasure in destroying something so carefully, so lovingly created?

The anger seeps away as quickly as it arrived and I'm left feeling numb. As I climb the steps to the office I take one last look behind me. On the brick wall beside the oak-studded door someone has articulated their rage in red spray paint. The thirteen seething letters are each a metre tall.

Fuck you Sophie.

If DC Bennett is shocked by the damage, she doesn't show it. The expression on her face is inscrutable as she takes it all in.

I bend down to pick up a rake that has been abandoned on the path in front of us, prongs facing skywards, and can't stop myself flinching when she barks, 'Don't touch anything!'

She follows me into the office where Geoff is sitting with his head in his hands, and Mary is working her way through our contacts book, phoning gardeners and volunteers to tell them not to come in. The officer's police radio crackles and she holds up a hand to silence me, even though I haven't said a word. She listens to the distorted sound of the dispatcher and nods twice in quick succession.

She turns to me. 'CSI are on their way. Should be here in half an hour or so. Once they've been you can start clearing up.'

'Thanks,' I mumble.

She must notice I'm close to tears because her features soften for a second as she reaches in her pocket for a notebook and gestures me to sit down. 'Do you mind running through what happened this morning one more time?'

'Of course not. I arrived at ten past seven -'

'Why so early?'

'Couldn't sleep. And I had so much to do before tomorrow's open day I thought I might as well make a start.'

'Did you see anyone on your way in? Any strange vehicles?'

I shake my head.

'Did anyone else know you'd be first in this morning?'

'No. It was a spur of the moment decision. Geoff's normally here first.'

DC Bennett glances over at Geoff, who nods.

'Who has keys to the garden?'

'Me, Geoff, Angela and the chairman of our trustees, Bob Wittershaw.'

'Do you have his contact details?'

'He's Mary's husband.' I tip my head towards Mary,

who has the phone pressed to her ear and is deep in conversation with one of the volunteers.

DC Bennett jots something in her notebook. 'Are there any spares?'

'Just one set. We keep them in the filing cabinet.'

'Are they there now?'

Geoff runs his hands through his hair. He's aged ten years since he arrived this morning. 'No. It was the first thing I checked.'

'Who has access to the office?' asks DC Bennett, with the air of someone who thinks they may be finally getting somewhere.

'Just the staff and Bob. But the office is left unlocked when the garden's open,' I say.

'So, anyone could have come in and helped themselves without you noticing?'

'I suppose so.'

The detective gives a little shake of her head as if she finds our security measures sadly lacking. But we've never had to worry before. No-one has ever taken anything. It's not that kind of place.

'I'll need a list of every single volunteer and client who attends the community garden,' she says.

'Of course,' says Geoff. 'I'll get right onto it.'

'I also need to know if anyone has a grudge against the charity, but more specifically you, Sophie.'

Blood pounds in my ears. 'Me? You were only asking a couple of days ago whether anyone had a grudge against Angela!'

DC Bennett points her thumb through the open door towards the graffiti. 'This seems to have been a targeted attack, wouldn't you say? Maybe the arson at Mrs Platt's home was a case of mistaken identity. It's a line of enquiry we need to consider. Can you think of anyone who would want to cause you harm?'

I picture the lighter, hidden in the kitchen drawer at home. Maybe she's right. But who on earth would want to set fire to our house?

Then I remember how rattled Martin had seemed when DC Bennett and her musclebound colleague turned up at Cam the morning after the fire. Rosie said he thought I'd called the police to arrest him. And he disappeared before anyone had a chance to explain why they were really here. Perhaps he still thinks that's what happened. That I, to use Rosie's words, told the police on him.

Anger is a powerful emotion, especially when it's magnified by mania. But I can't believe Martin would ever cause so much destruction, even in the grip of psychosis. He loves Cam. It's the one place that gives him head space. The one place he feels safe.

I'm at a crossroads. Tell DC Bennett how aggrieved Martin was when he thought I'd reported him and she'd have him under caution in a stuffy interview room at the police station before you could blink. Don't tell her and I could be hindering the investigation. Because when all's said and done, someone out there wants to frighten me, maybe even hurt me. I curl my hands around my stomach. And it's not just me to think about, is it?

'Sophie, can you think of anyone who might want to harm you?' DC Bennett says again, failing to hide the impatience in her voice.

I hesitate, just for a second. Then shake my head. 'No-one I can think of, no.'

'I thought that might be the case.' She nods to Geoff and Mary and marches out of the office. The interview clearly over, I'm left feeling as though I've failed some sort of test. She stops in front of the red-daubed wall.

'If you do, please get in touch immediately.' She hands me a card with her contact details on. 'Here's my number. I probably should be reassuring you that people who commit acts of vandalism like this are usually cowards who would never actually assault anyone. But this is a frenzied, vicious attack. Whoever did it could be capable of anything.'

CHAPTER THIRTY-TWO

NOW

D C Bennett's words ring in my ears as I work alongside Geoff and Mary, sweeping up shards of broken terracotta, throwing wilted lettuce and runner bean plants on the compost heap and returning tools to their rightful places in the cellar.

The smiley crime scene investigator girl was here for just over an hour, dusting the handles of wheelbarrows, forks and door knobs for fingerprints and taking photos of the graffiti.

'Someone really isn't very happy with you,' she'd observed, as she hefted her bag onto her shoulder and prepared to leave.

'No shit, Sherlock,' I'd felt like saying. Instead I mustered a smile and said, 'Apparently not.' And then, out of curiosity, asked, 'How often do you get a match? With the fingerprints, I mean?'

'If their prints are on the system we'll get a hit straight away. But if they've never been in trouble with the police the prints are about as much use as a chocolate teapot.' She gave an apologetic shrug. 'Unless they're brought in for questioning and their prints are taken then, of course.'

'So, I need to have faith in DC Bennett's investigating skills.'

The CSI girl raised her eyebrows. 'I wouldn't underestimate Sam Bennett if I were you. She's one of the best detectives we have. As tenacious as a terrier. I'm surprised Major Crime haven't snapped her up, to be honest. Once she gets her teeth into an investigation she doesn't let go.'

As I wheel yet another load of dead plants to the compost heap I ask myself who hates me enough to destroy the garden. *Fuck you Sophie.* So much loathing in three short words.

There's no doubt Martin feels betrayed. Would betrayal prompt such an extreme reaction? Even though he's bound to be top of the tenacious DC Bennett's list of suspects I still can't believe it. I draw an imaginary cross through his name.

What about Angela? She's never liked me. Matt says she's jealous because I'm more popular with both Cam's gardeners and volunteers. DC Bennett said earlier that Angela had been discharged from hospital. She has a key. She knows where I live. Perhaps she staged the arson at her house as a double bluff to deflect any police attention. Was she the figure caught on CCTV pouring petrol through her own letterbox?

Who am I trying to kid? Angela needs the open day to be a success as much as I do. She'd be horrified if there was even the faintest whiff of a scandal. And she'd have to have a screw loose to set her own house on fire. I discount her, too.

A name pops into my head unbidden. Lou. Under that veneer of gushing affection runs a seam of seething resentment. I know that now. She begrudges me both Matt and the baby. While I'm building my little family, hers has splintered. And that's made her bitter. There was hatred in her eyes when she came over for dinner. So, she was pissed. But you know what they say. *In vino veritas*. In wine there is truth. Quite how she managed to steal the spare keys when, as far as I'm aware, she's never set foot in Cam I don't know, but...

A heavy hand on my shoulder makes me jump out of my skin.

'Geoff! Don't creep up on me like that!'

He pinches the bridge of his nose. 'Sorry, love. I didn't mean to scare the Bejasus out of you. I just wanted to say I think we should go ahead with the open day. Don't let the buggers defeat us.'

I wave my arms around. 'How can we? It's such a mess.'

'It looks worse than it is. I have some young lettuce and cabbage plants at home. I'll bring them over after lunch and we'll plant them up in the vegetable garden. Mary's going to pop to her nephew's garden centre to buy a few trays of bedding plants. She says he'll sell them to her at cost. We'll plant them up, too. Fill all the empty spaces. No-one will even realise anything was wrong.'

'It'll take hours.'

'Not if we drum up a couple of spare hands. Mary says her friend Margaret will help, and I'll ring Derek and Mike. We'll have the garden looking shipshape in no time.'

I shake my head. 'I don't know.'

Geoff fixes me with a look. 'What's up? It's not like you to give up so easily.'

'I suppose it would save the aggravation of cancelling. Oh alright, let's do it.'

He beams at me and pats my shoulder again. 'That's my

girl. You sit down while I make a drink and we can talk through our plan of action. We'll show the bastards they haven't won.'

We manage it - just. Mike was out but Derek was here within minutes of Geoff's SOS call. Mary's nephew Tim was so horrified by what had happened that he refused to take any money for the trays of geraniums, begonias and busy lizzies he unloaded from his van and insisted on staying for the rest of the afternoon to help plant them up.

Geoff climbed a ladder with a bucket and scrubbing brush and scrubbed the graffiti off the wall. Mary and Margaret swept paths and tidied borders. I fetched and carried, strung up the bunting and made endless cups of tea.

It's now five o'clock and I'm shattered, but the garden has been transformed. We sit around a picnic table and clink mugs.

'Told you we could do it,' Geoff says with satisfaction.

'Many hands,' agrees Margaret.

'Where's Mr Pickles?' says Mary. 'It's not like him to miss a tea break.'

She's right. He normally appears as if by magic at the slightest rustle of a biscuit wrapper.

'Who is Mr Pickles?' asks Tim.

'The garden cat,' she tells him. 'A tabby. On the chubby side.'

'Nope, haven't seen him.'

The others shake their heads.

'I expect he's in the office,' I say. 'He's taken a liking to Angela's chair. I think he sits there just to wind her up.'

But Angela's large, black swivel chair is empty, and

there's no sign of Mr Pickles on top of the filing cabinet, either. I stand in the doorway and rattle his box of biscuits, which is usually guaranteed to flush him out, but he still doesn't appear.

'He was probably scared off by all the kerfuffle.' Geoff gestures at the garden. 'He'll turn up soon enough.'

'Remember that time he disappeared and we all thought he'd been run over?' Mary says. She turns to the others. 'He was gone for over a fortnight. We'd given up hope of ever seeing him again, but he turned up eventually. Must have had a touch of wanderlust.'

'Or been accidentally locked in someone's shed,' says Geoff.

'I'll leave some food out for him anyway.' I tip some biscuits into his bowl, refill his water and give the cat flap a poke to check it isn't stuck. It isn't. I stifle a yawn. 'I might make a move if that's alright?'

'Of course, love. You go home and put your feet up. We'll finish up here,' says Mary.

I flash her a grateful smile. 'You'll text me if Mr P turns up?'

'We will,' says Geoff, taking my elbow and steering me towards the car park. 'Now do as Mary says and give yourself the evening off.'

A terrible thought occurs to me and I stop in my tracks. 'You don't think whoever did this will come back tonight?'

'They wouldn't be so stupid. And if they do, we'll deal with it like we dealt with it today. Don't worry, everything's going to be alright.'

I give him a wan smile. He means well and I wish I could believe him. But I can't.

CHAPTER THIRTY-THREE

NOW

It's no surprise that the nearest parking space is right at the end of the road. It's been one of those days. I curse under my breath as I reverse into the bumper of the car behind me. Luckily when I get out and examine it there's no damage. I trudge up the road, stepping aside to let a leggy blonde jogger with wraparound shades and earphones past. She doesn't bother thanking me.

It's not until I push our gate open that I notice the cardboard box on the front step. It's a big box with the Amazon logo on. Wondering if Matt has ordered something for the nursery, I open the door, drop my keys and bag on the sideboard and go back for the box. The baby kicks me in the ribs as I bend over to pick it up.

The address label and brown tape have been ripped off the top of the box although the flaps are still tucked in. I shift it onto my right hip and as I do the contents lurch sideways. I struggle through the door and along the hallway and drop the box with a thud on the kitchen table.

Perhaps it's the baby sling Matt said he was going to

order, although the box feels too heavy for that. I insert a finger underneath the flaps so I can prise the lid open. A sharp pain like the sting of a bee makes me pull my hand back and exclaim out loud. A line of blood runs the length of my index finger. As paper cuts go it's a humdinger.

Blood drips onto the kitchen floor. I suck my finger and pull a face at the metallic taste. It reminds me of the first few weeks of my pregnancy, when I felt as though I was chewing coins. Even Matt could smell the metallic odour on my breath. I hold my finger under the cold tap until the water runs from crimson through pale pink to clear. I'm wrapping a folded square of kitchen roll around it when the phone rings.

'What now?' I mutter, marching back into the hall and snatching the handset.

'Hey baby.' Matt's voice is crackly. He's obviously in the car. 'I left early. Should be back in an hour or so.'

'OK.' I hold my finger up and watch blood seep through my make-do bandage. Tucking the phone under my ear, I wrap the kitchen roll tighter. 'What have you ordered from Amazon?'

'Amazon?'

'Was it something for the baby?' I ask, but the line goes fuzzy and then breaks up and I'm talking to myself. When I phone him back it switches straight to voicemail. I replace the handset without leaving a message and head back into the kitchen.

This time I use the bread knife to prise open the box. There's another box inside, a red Nike shoe box big enough to fit a pair of size elevens in. Whatever it is, it's patently not for the baby.

'Not more running shoes, Matt. We're supposed to be

saving,' I say to the empty room, pushing the box into the middle of the table in disgust before remembering with alarm that new shoes on the table is bad luck.

I swipe the box off and as I do the lid flies open to reveal not the brightly-coloured pair of running shoes I was expecting but Mr Pickles, curled up like a Cumberland sausage ring. At first my brain doesn't compute and I say, 'What on earth are you doing in there, you silly cat?'

I'm about to give him a gentle prod when I notice his half-closed eyes are glassy and there's a dullness to his normally shiny coat. As the realisation hits me I stifle a scream.

My heart hammering in my chest, I shrink backwards until the edge of the worktop bites into my back. I can't take my eyes off the box. From here the cat looks as if he's asleep, but I know if I touch him his body will be stiff and as cold as stone. I stay like this as the minutes tick past and the room grows darker. Adrenalin is pulsing through my body, sending my blood pressure rocketing, yet I'm paralysed with shock.

The phone rings again, bringing me to my senses. I bolt out of the kitchen and grab it like a lifeline.

'Sorry about that. Bad signal.' The sound of my husband's voice makes my legs go weak with relief.

'Oh Matt, Mr Pickles -' I gabble.

He cuts through me. 'What were you saying about an Amazon parcel?'

'Matt, listen -'

'I haven't ordered anything, I promise.'

'Matt, just listen, please. Someone trashed the garden last night.'

'Our garden?'

'No, Cam.'

'Trashed as in vandalised?'

I nod, forgetting he can't see me. 'We've spent all day clearing up. And we couldn't find Mr Pickles. Geoff said he'd turn up. And he was right. He turned up at our house -'

'What, like that film, *The Incredible Journey*? You ought to phone the Gazette.'

'No, he turned up dead. He was in the Amazon box.'

'*What?*'

'Someone killed him and left him on our doorstep.'

'Sophie, don't joke. It's not funny.'

'I'm not joking. It's a message for me. A threat. But I don't know what I've done wrong.' I dissolve into tears.

'Did you see anyone at the house?'

'No. The parcel was on the doorstep when I got home.'

'And there's no-one there now, hanging around?'

'I don't think so.' My voice sounds strangled and I gulp back the tears.

'Good. Look, I'm just coming up Detling Hill. Stay in the house and lock the doors. Make sure your phone is with you. I'll be twenty minutes max, OK?'

'Matt, you're scaring me.'

'Sorry, I don't mean to.' He is quiet for a second. 'Just be careful. I'll be as quick as I can.'

I replace the handset in the receiver, reach in my bag for my mobile and slip it into my back pocket. Once I've double locked the front door I take a deep breath and head back into the kitchen.

This time I keep my eyes averted from the shoe box as I check the bolts on the back door are closed. My heart's still leaping about in my chest as if I've downed a dozen expressos. I expected Matt to calm me down, tell me not to worry, that it was probably some stupid kid playing a prank. But he sounded so serious, so worried, that he's ramped up my own anxiety levels. What did he mean, *be careful*? Does he think I'm in danger, too?

Who would kill Mr Pickles? Everyone at Cam has loved that cat since the day he wandered into the garden and decided to stay. He was our lucky mascot. Rosie doted on him, sneaking him pieces of chicken from her lunch even though she knew he was supposed to be on a diet. Martin and Maureen used to take him to the vet for his annual injections. Even Nancy bought him a cat toy every Christmas. Angela was the only one who hadn't fallen under his spell. But she wouldn't have... would she?

My head's spinning with conjecture and hypotheses when Matt's key turns in the door. I meet him in the hall and sink into his arms.

'You OK?'

'Not really,' I mumble into his chest.

He holds me at arms' length, studying my tear-streaked face. 'I'm not surprised. You'd better show me where he is.'

I dip my head towards the kitchen. Matt thumbs a tear from my cheek and gives me a brief smile. It's supposed to be reassuring, but there's anxiety behind his blue eyes. Anxiety and another emotion I can't quite put my finger on.

'Jesus,' he says, when he sees the lifeless form of Mr Pickles squashed into the shoe box. He picks up the empty Amazon box. 'Where's the address label?'

'It'd been ripped off. The shoe box was inside.'

Matt drops the box onto the table and goes to lift Mr Pickles out of the Nike box. I grab his arm. 'Don't touch him!'

He glances at me. 'It's OK. I'm not squeamish like you.'

'What about fingerprints?'

'Too late. Mine are already all over the box. I want to see if someone left a note.'

Matt eases the dead cat out of the box. Mr Pickles' body is rigid. He looks like a life-sized version of one of those fake cats people keep on the parcel shelves of their cars. I grimace and stare at the ceiling.

'No note. He's been strangled. Look.'

Matt turns the cat's body upside down and parts the fur at the base of Mr Pickles' white neck to reveal an angry red weal as wide as a thumb.

I gasp. 'What kind of person strangles a cat?'

'A dangerous one,' he says, replacing the cat in the box. 'Have Geoff or Angela had anything like this happen to them?'

'Angela had the arson attack, but Geoff hasn't had anything.'

'Why you and Angela?'

'I wish I knew. There's something I need to tell you about the vandalism at Cam.'

I describe the message of hate scrawled on the wall. Matt drops the box on the table and it lands with a dull thud.

'Christ,' he mutters. 'What next?'

'DC Bennett said the arson at Angela's may have been a case of mistaken identity and it was me they were targeting all along. I've been going over and over it, trying to get things straight in my head. But I can't think of anyone who'd want to frighten me like this, can you?'

Silence.

'Matt, are you listening to me?' I gesture at Mr Pickles. 'Can you think of anyone who'd do this?'

His eyes dart to mine. 'Sorry, no, I can't.'

I reach for my mobile. 'I should call DC Bennett.'

Matt pauses, his hands on the Amazon box. 'Who?'

'The detective who came to Cam this morning.'

'Is that really necessary?'

I give him an 'are you mad?' look. 'Someone's murdered a cat and left it on our doorstep. What if I'm next?'

'I'm sure she wouldn't -'

'She won't mind. She told me to phone if anything else happened. Anyway, how do you know DC Bennett's a woman? I never said.'

'What?' says Matt, his forehead wrinkling. 'Oh, the copper? You did. You must've forgotten.'

I stare at him. 'I don't think I did.'

He pats my bump. 'I expect it's your baby brain. Either that, or early onset dementia.'

'That's not even remotely funny. I'll phone her from the sitting room while you get rid of the cat.'

I fish DC Bennett's number from the pocket of my jeans and dial, but it goes straight to voicemail, so I leave a long, garbled message that sounds unintelligible, even to my own ears. Matt wanders in and stares out of the window with his hands in his pockets. When I've finished the call, he turns to face me.

'I've put him in the shed.'

'Thanks.' I sink into the sofa, exhausted.

'I know this is probably the last thing on your mind but I'm starving. What's for dinner?'

I bite my lip. 'I'm sorry. I haven't even made a start on it.'

'It's OK. I'll rustle up something.'

He holds out a hand and pulls me to my feet and I follow him back into the kitchen. He opens the fridge and peers inside. 'What do you fancy?'

The thought of eating makes my stomach roil. He

thrusts a packet of flaccid ham under my nose. 'Ham, egg and chips?'

I make it to the sink just in time.

'What's up?' he says.

But I'm too busy vomiting the entire contents of my stomach to reply.

CHAPTER THIRTY-FOUR

NOW

To my surprise I plummet into a deep and dreamless sleep the moment my head touches the pillow. I wake just after seven to find Matt propped up on one elbow, staring at me.

'Why are you looking at me?' I mumble, running a hand through my tangled hair.

'Because you're beautiful. And you and our baby are the most precious things in the world to me.'

I groan. 'Even at this time in the morning?'

'Especially at this time in the morning.' He runs a finger along my cheekbone. 'I don't suppose...'

I glance at the alarm clock. 'I promised I'd be at work by eight. Maybe tonight?'

He rolls over and reaches for his phone. 'Maybe,' he grunts.

I feel a flicker of irritation. After the couple of days I've had, wouldn't it be obvious sex is the last thing on my mind? I swing my legs over the side of the bed, trying to ignore my puffy ankles. 'So, I'll see you at ten?'

He's too engrossed in his emails to answer.

As the doors open to the public for Cam's tenth annual open day I feel a surge of pride laced with a hefty helping of gratitude to Geoff, Mary and the others. Only the sharpest-eyed visitor would notice anything was amiss. There's still a smudge of red paint on the wall and the flower beds are emptier than normal, but otherwise the garden looks amazing considering it was a scene of devastation only twenty-four hours ago.

To my surprise Lou is one of the first people through the door. She spies me, rushes over and we hug.

'Still blooming, darling. Everything OK?'

I eye her skinny jeans and fitted top with envy. 'I'm the size of a house, I have constant heartburn and some nights I'm getting up three times to pee, but yes, other than that I'm fine.'

She laughs. 'Simple. Don't look in the mirror, take plenty of Gaviscon and remember it's your body's way of preparing you for sleep deprivation on a grand scale. It'll be worth it, I promise.'

'I know. And I shouldn't complain. But I'll be glad when the baby arrives. I seem to have been pregnant forever.'

'You're doing brilliantly.' She rubs my arm and looks around. 'Is Matt coming?'

'He's supposed to be here now.' I scan the heads of the people milling around by the entrance but there's no sign of him. 'I expect he got sidetracked.'

'And your NBF? Is she coming, too?'

'My what?'

'New Best Friend. That awful Roz woman.'

'Don't be mean. Roz is lovely. You must have rubbed her up the wrong way.'

'If you say so.' Lou glances over her shoulder. 'Is she here?'

'I haven't spoken to her for a couple of days. I think she might be away.'

'Right.' Lou pauses. 'She's married with a kid, right?'

'Yes. Caitlyn's almost two. Why?'

'It's probably nothing, but it struck me as a bit weird, you know?'

'Not really. What are you wittering about?'

'I was in Waitrose the other day and she was in the checkout queue ahead of me. She had no idea I was there.'

I frown. 'People go shopping. It's hardly news. If this is because you're surprised a lowly hairdresser can afford to shop in Waitrose you're a bigger snob than I thought.'

'Of course not! It's what she was buying that caught my attention. Meals for one, one of those tiny loaves, a small pack of cheese and two pints of skimmed milk. Two pints!'

'And your point is?'

'There were no nappies or wipes, no rice crackers or boxes of raisins. No bananas or Sudocrem. No big six-pint cartons of full fat milk. No beer or shaving gel, for that matter. It was your archetypal singleton's food shop. I should know,' she adds with a twisted smile.

'Phil and Caitlyn have been staying with his mum for a few days,' I say, even though I'm pretty sure they must be home by now.

But Lou is like a dog with a bone. 'Even if they were, there's always something to pick up for your kid when you go shopping, isn't there? If wipes are on special offer or you know you've run out of baby shampoo. But there was nothing for a husband or child in her shopping. Nothing. Don't you think that's odd?'

'I -'

'Have you ever met Phil or Caitlyn?'

'No, but Phil's at work and Caitlyn's at nursery when Roz comes to do my hair or we meet for a coffee. There's no reason for me to have seen them.'

'You haven't been to her house?'

I don't want to explain to Lou that Roz has never invited me. It's none of her bloody business. I straighten my back. 'Not yet, no.'

Lou arches her eyebrows.

'I've seen their photos,' I say, remembering the picture of a slightly overweight man with a cherubic toddler riding on his shoulders that Roz showed me with undisguised pride the first time she cut my hair.

'Doesn't mean anything. She could have downloaded them from someone's Facebook page.'

'What exactly are you trying to say?'

She puffs out her cheeks. 'You've known her all of five minutes and she acts like she's your best friend, but you know nothing about her. She could be anyone.'

Something clicks into place and I shake my head. 'You're jealous!'

Her eyebrows concertina. 'I'm *what*?'

'You expected to waltz back into my life after all these years and it would be just like the old days. Sophie and Lou against the world, especially now Ed's gone. Two's company and all that.'

Lou recoils as though I've slapped her, but I continue regardless. She's really pissed me off. 'It was never going to happen. I'm not that girl anymore. I have more in common with Roz than I do with you. I'm sorry if you feel sidelined, but there it is. I can't change how I feel.'

She is silent during my outburst and when she does speak she addresses the sky above my right shoulder. 'I hear what you say, but hear me out. You've always been too trusting. Take it from me, people aren't always who they seem. Be careful, Sophie. That's all I ask. I'll see you around, OK?'

I'm left staring at her open-mouthed as she hoists her bag over her shoulder, turns on her heels and disappears through the throng of people. An elderly woman with half-moon glasses asks me the way to the toilets. By the time I've given her directions Lou has gone.

I'm too busy for the next couple of hours to spare a thought for Lou. Instead I show people around the garden and talk about Cam's work on autopilot.

My jaw is aching from smiling so much when Rosie tracks me down just before noon. She's hand in hand with Matt.

'Look who I found,' she says, beaming. 'Matt said my dress was pretty!'

'Your dress is pretty,' agrees Matt, his eyes twinkling. 'But you, my sweet Rose, are beautiful.'

'You old rogue.' Rosie nudges him with her shoulder and we laugh. Her grin widens until it threatens to split her face in two.

'Come on,' I say. 'Let's grab a table and have a drink. I haven't stopped since eight. I reckon I'm due a break.'

We find an empty table and I take a seat while Matt and Rosie make a beeline for the cakes. The garden's still busy. With the bunting, stalls and the gentle hum of conversation

I'm reminded of the summer fetes my parents used to take me to when I was a kid. Lou would have enjoyed it if she hadn't stormed off in a huff.

She's the third person to tell me to be careful in as many days. But why are the warnings directed at me and not Angela or Geoff? I rack my brains yet again to figure out what I might have done, knowingly or inadvertently, to rile someone to such an extent that they would trash a garden in retaliation.

Be careful, Lou said. But she couldn't even look me in the eye. Was it a piece of friendly advice... or a threat? Before I can dissect that particular thought any further, Rosie appears with Matt on her heels.

'Matt said you'd want coffee and walnut, but I said you liked lemon drizzle best of all. I was right, wasn't I?' She hands me a paper plate and a polystyrene cup of a weak brown liquid that faintly resembles tea.

'You were. Lemon drizzle every time.'

'Told you!' Rosie breaks off a piece of her Victoria sponge and looks around her. 'Mr P! Mr P!' she calls.

My eyes meet Matt's and I mouth 'Should I tell her?'

He nods.

I take a deep breath. 'Mr P's not here, Rosie.'

'Where is he?'

'He's -' I hesitate.

'Gone walkabout again?' she asks. 'I'm not surprised with all these people hanging around.'

'No, not walkabout. He... look, there's no easy way to say this. I'm afraid Mr Pickles died.'

Rosie's eyes widen and the piece of cake she's holding falls from her hand. 'I don't understand.'

'He must have been poorly and we didn't realise. He

died yesterday. I'm so sorry, Rosie. I know how much you loved him.'

Tears cloud her eyes. 'Was he very old?'

'We don't know, do we? He just turned up one day and decided to stay, do you remember?'

'I do.' She sniffs. 'He was the most beautifulest cat in the world.'

Tears well up in my own eyes as I picture the tabby cat curled up in a shoe box in our shed. I nod, unable to speak.

'He had a good life,' Matt says.

'He did,' agrees Rosie, absentmindedly taking a mouthful of cake. 'Will we have a funeral? I could say a few words.'

'I don't think Sophie's had a chance to tell anyone yet, so it might have to wait a few days, but I'm sure we can give Mr P the send-off he deserves,' Matt says.

'That woman will be pleased. She told me she hates cats. They're a dirty vermin, she said. What's a vermin?'

'It's an animal that spreads disease.' A piece of cake is lodged in my throat and I take a swig of tea to wash it down. 'What woman said she hates cats?'

Rosie looks uncomfortable, as if she's already said too much.

'I can't remember.'

CHAPTER THIRTY-FIVE

NOW

No matter how much I press her, Rosie won't tell me which woman she was talking about.

'Do you think she means Angela?' I whisper to Matt as she disappears in search of a second slice of cake.

He shrugs. 'She'd say if it was, wouldn't she? Where is Angela, anyway? I thought you said she was supposed to be showing her face?'

'She was. I'll go and ask our venerable chairman. He's bound to know.'

Bob Wittershaw is holding court by the vegetable garden, telling a handful of bored-looking city and county councillors what a vital role the garden plays in local mental health service provision. I loiter on the fringes until he's finished, then ask after Angela.

'She's still wobbly. She wanted to come but decided this morning she wasn't up to it. The fire's affected her badly.' His face hardens. 'Give me five minutes in a room with the bastard who started it and he'll never light a match again, let alone a fire.'

'You think it was a man?'

'I know exactly who it was. That waste of a space ex-husband of hers.'

I try to remember what Angela has told me about her ex, Pete. 'Doesn't he live in Manchester?'

'Why would that stop him coming to Kent? Angie always said he never came to terms with the divorce.'

I thought Angela said Pete had recently bought a house with his new partner. In which case, why would he want to set his ex-wife's house on fire? Unless she still has life assurance. Burn the house down with Angela in it and Pete could cash in. If that's not a credible motive I don't know what is. Hope flares in the pit of my stomach.

'I've told the police what I think,' Bob continues. 'Not that they seemed very interested.'

'I'm sure they'll check it out. They said they had a number of lines of enquiry.'

He harrumphs.

'Do you think Pete might be responsible for the vandalism, too?' I ask.

He fixes his pale grey eyes on mine. 'Not from what the police said, no. That seems to have been targeted at you, wouldn't you say?'

The tiny spark of hope is snuffed out in an instant.

'Who have you pissed off?'

I meet his gaze. 'That's the problem. I have no idea.'

By half past three the last few visitors have drifted away and the garden is ours again. Paper plates and plastic cups litter the picnic tables and the grass paths are worn bare by shuffling feet. Cam has the air of a village hall after a particularly riotous children's party. But the day has been a great success, and when I check in with Mary she says over two hundred and fifty people passed through our doors.

I'm dropping abandoned cups, plates and napkins into a black sack when someone clears her throat behind me. I spin around to see DC Bennett at my shoulder.

'I picked up your message. Can you talk?'

'Of course. There's a bench by the greenhouse. It's quiet there.'

I sit down and she follows suit, taking her notebook out of her jacket pocket.

'Any news on the arson?'

'We're still following a number of lines of enquiry.' She shakes her head. 'That's the official version. Between you and me we've hit a brick wall. We've identified the brand of petrol can used and have rung around local garages to see if anyone matching our offender's description has used a can to buy fuel in the last couple of weeks, but so far that's drawn a blank. We'll issue a media appeal, but I don't hold out much hope to be honest. The CCTV images are too fuzzy to be much use at all. But that's not why I'm here. I want you to tell me about this cat.'

She listens with her head cocked to one side as I describe finding the parcel on the front doorstep and opening it to reveal the tabby cat crammed into a Nike shoe box inside.

'You still have the cat and the boxes?'

I nod. 'Although they'll have my fingerprints all over them. And Matt's.'

'Your husband?'

'That's right. He put them in the shed.'

'I'll send someone round in the morning to pick them up. And you're sure the cat didn't die of natural causes?'

'There was a red mark around his neck.'

'Right.' DC Bennett closes her notebook. 'I don't know if you're aware, but there's a well-established link between cruelty to animals and violence to people.'

'What are you trying to say?'

'That those who torture or kill animals are often perpetrators of violent crimes against people. It's been proven time and again. I need you to be careful, Sophie. Whoever killed that cat could hurt you next.'

She leaves after I've promised to call 999 if I have any concerns. As her unmarked car sweeps out of the car park I try to reassure myself she's over-reacting, but I'm kidding myself. If an experienced copper is warning me to be worried, I probably should be.

My phone rings. When I see the name on the screen I let out a little sob of relief. 'Roz!'

'You alright?'

'Not really.'

'What's the matter? Is the baby OK?'

'The baby's fine. It's everything else that's shot to shit.'

'You're talking about the garden?'

'How did you know about that?'

There's a crackle of static in my ear and I grip the phone tightly.

'I bumped into Bev in town. She told me the place had been trashed. Someone's got it in for you.'

'I know.' I swallow. The need to off-load to her is overwhelming. I could use a bit of her don't-mess-with-me attitude to life right now. 'Where are you?' I ask in a small voice.

'Portsmouth.'

'*Portsmouth?*'

'Visiting an old friend. Why?'

'I was hoping to see you, that's all.'

She laughs. I'm holding the phone so close to my head I can feel the sound waves travelling along my ear canal and vibrating my ear drum.

'Don't worry, Sophie.' She laughs again. 'You'll see me soon enough.'

CHAPTER THIRTY-SIX

NOW

I thought I'd hate being on maternity leave, but I was wrong. My last week at work was exhausting, both physically and emotionally, and I was ready to go. It was only once I'd left that I realised what a strain I'd been under, organising the recruitment evening and open day, coping with the vandalism and wondering, always wondering, who might be behind it.

Cocooned within the four walls of my home, I've been able to relax. I've slept, pottered, and nested. I've painted the walls of the nursery cornflower-blue, and hung pencil sketches of Winnie the Pooh and Christopher Robin on the walls. Matt and I took a trip to Bluewater the day after I finished work and blew a month's wages on all the things we've been too superstitious to buy: cot, changing table, moses basket, baby bath, bouncy chair, baby monitor, and car seat. I spend hours in the baby's room rearranging the furniture, fingering the cotton-wool soft blankets and sorting the sleepsuits and bodysuits into colour co-ordinated piles.

I know the baby could come at any moment and

although I can't wait to meet him, I'm enjoying this brief interlude between one life and another.

Matt is harder to read. When I have his full attention he's as excited as me, chattering about the playlist he's putting together for the birth and looking up trikes on the internet. But every now and then his expression shuts down and he withdraws completely. I don't know where his thoughts have taken him, but it's far away from here. It's as though the baby and I don't exist.

Tick tock tick tock. Time is racing by, like sand through my fingers.

Not long now.

For the first time in months I'm clearheaded and purposeful. I spend my days running through my plan, checking everything's in place, ready to move into the execution phase the minute I need to.

Sophie, poor, sweet, unsuspecting Sophie, is ready, too. I can tell by the cardboard boxes left out for the recycling, the smell of paint wafting into the street from the nursery and the newly-washed sleepsuits hanging from her washing line.

The warm summer air is heavy with expectancy. Our excitement is palpable.

Tick tock tick tock.

Not long now.

CHAPTER THIRTY-SEVEN

NOW

I'm dozing on the sofa when the doorbell rings one Friday afternoon, two weeks before my due date. Expecting a parcel, I'm surprised to see Lou standing on the doorstep. I haven't seen her since the open day and we didn't part on the best of terms.

'Hello, Sophie. How's things?'

'Fine.'

'You look well.'

'Thanks.'

She clears her throat. 'I hope you don't mind but I've got something for you. It's in the car. I'll get it, shall I?'

I shrug. I don't care if I'm being as bolshy as a teenager. I'm not going to make this easy for her.

She looks discomfited. 'Right. Good. I won't be a minute.'

I watch from the doorway as she crosses the street to her car. My eyes widen as she lifts a pale grey pram out of the boot. I recognise it at once - it's the top-of-the-range model I admired in *Mother & Baby* magazine. She wheels it across the road and through our gate.

She stops in front of me and holds up a hand. 'Before you say anything, it's not a guilt gift. I told you Josh had one and I wanted you to have one, too. Accept it in the spirit with which I give it. Friendship. Please?'

For a moment I'm torn. It's such a beautiful pram and there's no way Matt and I could justify spending so much on one. Lou always was as generous as she was gregarious. I believe her good intentions. She sticks out her bottom lip like she used to when we were kids and I can't help but laugh. 'Oh alright, you silly moo. Thank you. I suppose you want a coffee while you're here?'

'That would be nice.' She abandons the pram and virtually skips through the door. Rolling my eyes, I manoeuvre it over the doorstep and follow her inside.

I study her as I wait for the kettle to boil. Her face looks less puffy and her eyes are clear. She looks... glowing.

As if reading my thoughts, she smiles self-consciously. 'I've given up the booze.'

'Completely?'

'Yup. Even I realised it was getting out of hand when I started craving a glass of red at ten in the morning. I've found a local AA group. They meet on a Saturday night at the Baptist church opposite Waitrose. While most people are at the pub I'm sharing drinking stories with my alky mates. Actually, we have a laugh. And it's a cliché I know, but taking one day at a time does seem to do the trick.'

'Good for you.' I'm genuinely impressed.

'Yes, well,' she says, glancing at her nails. 'Something had to change.'

As I carry Lou's coffee to the table my stomach muscles contract sharply and I let out a small gasp.

'Hey, are you alright?'

'The midwife promises me they're just Braxton Hicks.'

I rub my bump, which is as hard as a rock, and grimace. 'It'll be over in a minute.'

'Brings back memories. I remember when Josh was born. I was in labour for thirty-six hours. You know that old wives' tale about shitting a melon? Take it from me, they weren't far wrong.'

I arch my eyebrows. 'And that's supposed to make me feel better how exactly?'

Lou bursts into peals of laughter. 'What goes in must come out.'

'At least I'm going to have a natural birth. I'm not too posh to push.'

Lou laughs harder. 'There's nothing natural about it, believe me. It really, really, *really* hurts.'

'OK, enough already. Can we please change the subject?'

'But I wanted to fill you in on my episiotomy. The doctor who stitched me up was *dreamy*.'

'Lou, you're hopeless,' I giggle. The muscles in my stomach finally relax and I pull up a chair opposite her.

She catches my hand across the table and holds it tightly. 'I've missed this. Us. Just having a laugh together like we used to.'

Without thinking, I squeeze back, smiling. 'Me, too.'

'I know you blame me for the abortion.'

'Let's not do this now.' I try to pull my hand away, but she tightens her hold.

'I think we should. So many things were left unsaid. I tried talking to you at the time, but you didn't want to know. I thought having an abortion was the right thing to do. I didn't want you messing up your life. Not at seventeen! You had such big hopes and dreams. And you were so bright. You had the world at your feet, if only you knew it. That's why I pushed for you to get rid of the baby. I wanted the best for you. You were my best friend, for God's sake. I loved you better than I loved my own sister.'

She hangs her head. 'When I saw how it tore you apart I realised how wrong I'd been. You were broken. Which was totally understandable. But not just that. Your personality changed overnight. My Sophie, my kind, funny, affectionate best friend, was gone. New Sophie was as hard as nails. I couldn't get through to you. It was as if they sucked your heart out when they sucked out the baby.'

A sob catches in the back of my throat and I gulp for air. Lou massages the inside of my wrist with her thumb.

'I should never have convinced you to go through with the abortion. You would have coped, with or without Ed, although he adored you so much he would have stuck by you, I know he would.' Her voice thickens. 'I've carried the guilt around with me for the last twenty years. But I'm not asking for forgiveness, I'm really not. I'm not sure I'd forgive you if the boot was on the other foot. I just want you to understand that I know I was wrong, and that I feel sorry every single day.'

She lets my hand go and sits back in her chair. Tears are streaming down her cheeks. I, too, am crying. I fish around in my pocket for a tissue and blow my nose.

'I developed pelvic inflammatory disease after the termination,' I say. 'It's an infection of the uterus that can spread to the fallopian tubes and ovaries if you're really unlucky. I was. Mine were as battle-scarred as a Tommy on the Somme.'

It's a poor excuse for a joke but Lou gives me a limp smile through her tears.

'I had no idea, of course. After the abortion I had terrible abdominal pain and a raging temperature, but I thought it was a side-effect and no more than I deserved for killing my baby. I had a week off school, do you remember? I told Mum and Dad I had the flu.'

Lou nods. 'I brought you flowers but you refused to see me.'

'Did you? It's all a bit of a blur to be honest.' I pick at the hem of my top. 'When Matt and I started trying for a baby I couldn't understand why I didn't fall straight away. I knew it couldn't be my fault. Ed and I only had unprotected sex once and I was up the duff. I thought I was the original Miss Fertile.'

I give a hollow laugh. 'I assumed the problem lay with Matt, so I nagged and nagged him until he agreed to get tested. Of course, he was over the moon when he found out he wasn't shooting blanks. When I went in for tests they found severe scarring on my fallopian tubes and told me the only way we stood a chance of having a baby was through IVF. It took four rounds and nearly killed us, emotionally and financially.'

'Oh, Sophie, I'm so sorry.'

'It's OK. I saw it as my punishment.' I pause. 'I used to think you wanted me and Ed to split up, so you could have him all to yourself.'

Her eyes widen. 'That's not true!'

'I know. I see that now.'

She reaches for my hand again. 'I'm so sorry.'

'Don't be. It was my decision. I was my own person. I could have said no. I loved that baby with all my heart, even though I knew it wasn't much more than a mass of cells. But I was too scared to go through with the pregnancy. Too worried what people would say. I didn't want to be one of those teenage mums you read about in magazines. It wasn't your fault.'

Lou lets go of my hand and shakes her head. 'Christ, what idiots we've been.'

'We were kids, doing what we thought was right at the time.'

She gestures at my bump. 'You deserve your happy ending, Sophie darling.'

I give her a weak smile. I want to believe her, I really do. I want to think that I'm finally absolved from the guilt I've carried around for the last twenty years. But it's too ingrained, too entrenched. Deep down I know the guilt won't go until I forgive myself. And I'm not sure I ever can.

CHAPTER THIRTY-EIGHT

NOW

'I'd better go,' Lou says. 'I'm supposed to be picking Josh up from the station at five.' She eyes me rubbing my belly. 'Are you going to be alright?'

'I'll be fine. Matt's promised to be home by seven. I'm still only thirty-eight weeks. It could be another month yet, knowing my luck.'

'You're probably right. Josh was ten days late.' She hugs me tight. 'I'm so glad we've sorted things out.'

'Me too. And thanks so much for the pram.'

'It's my pleasure.' She pats her jeans pocket and frowns. 'Have you seen my phone?'

I shake my head.

'No worries. I must have left it in the car while I was faffing about with the pram. Make sure you call me if you need anything, OK? Otherwise I'll pop by on Monday to see how you're doing.'

I smile. I'm glad Lou's back in my life. 'You'd better go or you'll be late,' I chide.

She gives me another hug. 'Take care of yourself,' she says fiercely.

'I will. Now go!'

I close the door behind her and wander into the sitting room. The pram is parked between the window and the back of the sofa and I pull it out to have a proper look. It is a thing of beauty. Sleek aluminium chassis, a hood lining as soft as butter and a thick fur seat liner. There's even a matching silver-grey changing bag. It is, as Matt would say, the dog's bollocks.

'Lucky baby,' I murmur. My stomach muscles contract again and I groan out loud and massage the small of my back until the pain fades. An unwelcome thought hits me square between the eyes - if Braxton Hicks hurt this much, what the hell are contractions going to be like? My carefully-constructed birthing plan includes soft lights, chill-out music and a TENS machine. Pain relief does not figure. I've read too many horror stories about epidurals that have ended in forceps deliveries and Pethidine making mums vomit and babies too sleepy to breastfeed to want to go down that route. I want to do it naturally, like women before me have for millennia. After all, how hard can it be?

Jackie, my midwife, was silent as she read my birthing plan, but I saw her mouth twitch.

'You think it's all a bit sanctimonious, the "I want a natural birth" thing, don't you?'

'Not at all. Just keep an open mind. If you go into this thinking it'll be intervention-free, you might be bitterly disappointed if it doesn't go to plan. And babies have a habit of doing things their own way.'

I smiled and nodded, but inside I thought, *she's wrong*. I've wanted this baby for so long I'll be able to withstand any pain to hold him in my arms.

Now, as another Braxton Hicks sweeps through my body, doubt edges into my mind. Have I been too prescriptive? Surely a little gas and air wouldn't harm? And if an epidural is on offer...

My musings are interrupted by my phone bleeping with a text. It's Roz. I haven't seen her since I left work, but she texts me every day to see how I'm doing, regular as clockwork.

How's things?

OK, I tap back. *Getting a few twinges but I'm sure it's nothing to worry about.*

What kind of twinges?

Braxton Hicks... I think.

Is Matt home?

No, he won't be back 'til seven.

I can see from the three dots in the speech bubble that she's typing a reply, but I've wandered back into the kitchen and am staring inside the half-empty fridge wondering what to cook for dinner when my phone pings again.

I've been in two minds whether to tell you this because I don't want to worry you, especially at the moment. But I know who's behind everything.

I sink on a chair and stare at the screen.

What do you mean?

The arson, the vandalism and the cat. I know who did it.

My fingers feel rubbery, as though they aren't attached to my arms, as I type a response.

WHO???

There's something I need to show you first. Can you meet me now?

I glance at the kitchen clock. It's just gone half five. I could always pick up a curry while I'm out. Something spicy that might get the baby moving.

OK, as long as I'm no more than an hour. Where shall we meet?

Her reply is back in a blink.

Cam.

I dash out a note to Matt, which I leave propped against the fruit bowl on the kitchen table.

Had to pop to work.
Don't worry about dinner.
I'll treat us to a lamb dhansak on my way home.
Be back about 7.15pm x

At the front door I pause. My navy hospital bag is under the console table, packed and ready to go. It wouldn't do any harm to take it. As I bend over to pick it up another twinge grips my body and I hold onto the table for support until the pain subsides.

I'm locking the front door, the strap of the hospital bag digging into my shoulder, when my mobile rings. Assuming it's Matt letting me know he's on his way home, I fish around in the bag for my phone.

'Sophie, it's Lou.'

'Everything OK?'

'You know I couldn't find my mobile? I've hunted high and low for the bloody thing then remembered I put it in the pram when I carried it to the car. I must have left it in there. Can you have a quick look?'

'Sure.' I tuck the phone between my chin and shoulder, let myself back into the house and peer inside the pram. 'I can't see it. Oh wait, there it is. It's slipped under the padding. Do you want me to drop it round?'

'Don't worry. I'll come over in the morning. I'm sure I can live without Facebook and Instagram until then.'

'It's no trouble, honestly. I'm popping to Cam now anyway. I can swing by your house on my way home.'

'Cam? It's a quarter to six on a Friday night and you're on maternity leave. Why are you going to *work*?'

'Roz has worked out who's been causing all the problems. I'm meeting her there. She's got something to show me.'

'Roz?' Lou's voice is sharp.

'I know you two haven't exactly hit it off, but she's been a good friend to me.'

'Can't it wait until the morning? I could come with you.'

'I can't wait that long. I need answers now. Look, I've got to go. I'm already running late. I'll drop by yours on the way home, alright?'

She's still chuntering away in the background when I end the call and slip both phones into my hospital bag.

Pulling out of our road, I realise too late that I'm heading straight into rush hour traffic. It's going to take an age to cross the city. What if Roz thinks I've changed my mind and leaves before I arrive? I wasn't exaggerating when I told Lou I had to find out who's behind all this. The need to know is insidious, infiltrating every dark crevice of my mind. It's not curiosity, it's far more deep-rooted, more primeval than that. It's my survival instinct kicking in. I *have* to know who hates me enough to harm me. Not for me. For my baby.

I swerve onto the pavement, ignoring the angry blast of a horn from the white van behind me, and try to call Roz to warn her I'll be late, but her phone goes straight to voicemail.

'Roz, it's me, Sophie. I'm on my way, OK? I should be with you in about twenty minutes. Don't leave before I get there. Please?'

I pull back onto the carriageway and soon I'm inching forwards on the ring road. As I drive past the police station I wonder if I should swing in and leave a message for DC Bennett telling her I'm close to finding the answers. I glance at the dashboard. It's already gone six. I don't have time.

The traffic is lighter as I head up Old Dover Road and soon I'm passing Kent Cricket Ground and indicating right onto Stone Street.

I check my mirror for police cars and, seeing none, put my foot down.

CHAPTER THIRTY-NINE

NOW

I'm expecting to see Roz's little hatchback, so I'm surprised when I reach Cam and the car park is empty. I pull into my usual space and try phoning her, but it goes straight to voicemail again and I don't bother leaving a message. She must have tired of waiting and gone home.

Shit. I run my hands through my hair. I would drive to her house, but it occurs to me that I have no idea where she lives. I turn the keys in the ignition. As I slip the car into reverse I'm racked by another Braxton Hicks. *Shit.* This one literally takes my breath away and I grab the steering wheel like a drowning man grasps a lifebuoy. A vice-like pain grips my stomach. I count out loud to take my mind off the agony, reaching forty before it subsides.

I try to remember what Jackie told me about Braxton Hicks. She described them as the body's way of getting ready for labour, lasting less than a minute and happening a few times a day. She said they were irregular and didn't increase in intensity.

Are you kidding me? These are getting worse and worse. What if they're not Braxton Hicks? What if they're contractions? The last was just before Lou rang, at a quarter to six. Twenty-five minutes ago. Could I be in the early stages of labour? All thoughts of Roz forgotten, I snatch my phone and dial Matt's number.

'Hello, this is Matt Saunders. I'm afraid I can't come to the phone right now -'

'Fuck's sake! What's the point of having a mobile phone if you don't bloody answer it?' I howl. The urge to be at home is overwhelming and I slam the car into reverse and stamp my foot on the accelerator. The car skids on the loose gravel and I throw it into first gear. Out of habit I glance in the rear-view mirror before I pull away. The old wooden door is swinging wide open. I hit the brakes. The seatbelt presses into my belly and the baby squirms in protest.

I'm torn. I need to get home. But it's a quarter past six. The door should be locked at this time of night. Roz doesn't have a key. I was going to meet her in the car park. If Geoff was working late his battered Land Rover Discovery would be here. What if he forgot to lock the door when he left for the day?

I'm desperate to go home, have a bath and count my contractions until Matt gets back. But I can't bring myself to leave. What if the person who wrecked the garden has come back for another go? What if Roz was here when he arrived and she's lying somewhere, hurt?

One quick look, I decide, reversing the car as close to the open door as I can. If the crunch of gravel hasn't already alerted any intruder to my presence it will have now. I peer through the driver's window into the garden. There are no broken pots or overturned wheelbarrows. Everything looks exactly as it should. I switch off the engine and slip the keys and my phone into the front pocket of my maternity dunga-rees and heave myself out of the car.

I inch my way over to the door, feeling like an intruder myself. There are no signs of forced entry. My heart in my mouth, I step into the garden.

At first glance it looks deserted, but I stand inside the door and scan every inch, to be sure. Satisfied the only sign of life is a robin, watching me with bright eyes from the branch of a pear tree, I walk in.

'Hello!' My voice sounds scratchy, as if I haven't used it for weeks. 'Hello! It's me, Sophie. Is anyone here?'

Nothing.

I cross the garden to the office door and try the handle. It's locked. I walk around to the window and look inside. All's in order. My breathing returns to normal. Everything's fine. I wrap my fingers around the clutch of keys in my pocket, thankful Angela didn't insist I returned Cam's keys when I went on maternity leave. I can lock the outer door, drive home and wait for my baby to arrive with a clear conscience. I'll have done my duty. Whoever was last out must've forgotten to lock up.

No harm done.

End of story.

Except as I turn to leave I hear a faint cry. The hairs on the back of my neck stand to attention. I stop, cock my head and listen. And there it is again. My name.

'Sofee!'

It's a woman's voice, weak and reedy, but I recognise it instantly.

'Roz, is that you?'

'I'm in the cellar.'

I stumble forwards, trying to ignore the tightening of the muscles in my abdomen that presages a contraction. But it's futile. The pain comes in waves like an incoming tide, fast and furious and absolute bloody agony. I cry out involuntarily and hold onto the edge of the cellar door.

'Are you alright?' calls Roz from the dark depths.

I wait until my breathing has steadied before I answer. 'I'm fine. But never mind me. Are you OK? What happened?'

'Someone had left a spade out. I was putting it away when I slipped on the steps. I think I've broken my ankle.'

'Shit!' I feel in my pocket for my phone. 'I'm phoning for an ambulance.'

'No, wait!' she cries. 'It might just be a sprain. I can make it back up with your help.'

'OK, if you're sure. I'm coming down.'

I feel behind the door for the light switch, grimacing when my hand comes in contact with the filmy mesh of a spider's web. I flick the switch, but nothing happens. I try it again, just to make sure, but the cellar remains inky black.

'Bloody light's not working,' I shout.

'I know. I couldn't see the steps. That's why I lost my footing. Be careful, OK?'

'I will,' I mutter, grabbing hold of the handrail. The darkness grows denser as I descend until I have to feel with my toes for the edge of each step. The temperature drops, too, and I shiver in the damp, musty air.

'Where are you?' I call into the shadows. It's so dark I may as well have my eyes closed.

'In the corner by the hand tools.'

I turn my head towards the sound of Roz's voice. By my calculation I must be two-thirds of the way down.

'Almost there,' I puff, as much for my reassurance as hers.

She groans and I quicken my pace, almost stumbling over the last two steps. I give the ground an exploratory sweep with my toe and, satisfied I have reached the bottom, take a couple of steps forwards, my arms outstretched.

Afterwards, I can't help but wonder why I didn't use the torch app on my phone. But in the cold, dark cellar it doesn't even occur to me. Baby brain.

I take a tentative step to my right, towards Geoff's neat shelves. Without sight, my other senses have taken over. I can almost taste the dank cellar air. A movement to my left makes me stop for a moment, but I press on. The sooner I find Roz and we both get the hell out of here the better.

I hear a sharp intake of breath and stand stock still, trying to work out where it's coming from. I sense a whoosh of air and feel a searing pain at the back of my head. The last thing I remember is a rushing sound in my ears and strong arms under my armpits as my legs buckle beneath me.

CHAPTER FORTY

NOW

When I come to, the cellar is still in darkness and I'm sitting slumped against an old potting bench. The base of my head is throbbing like crazy but when I try to lift a hand to assess the damage I realise my wrists are tied to one of the bench legs. Even worse, I'm not wearing my dungarees. Fear turns my stomach to liquid.

'Roz,' I whisper urgently. 'Are you OK?'

Laughter ricochets off the walls. There's a click and light floods the room. Flinching, I squeeze my eyes shut before the powerful wattage burns my retinas.

Roz steps in front of the light. 'Never better. Thanks for asking.' Her face is in darkness.

I blink. 'You're OK,' I say, surprised.

'Of course I'm OK. More than OK, in fact.'

'What the hell's going on?'

She laughs again, the sound as deadly as shattered glass, and flexes each ankle in turn, inches from my face. 'As you can see, there's no broken ankle.'

'So why did you -'

'Lure you down here? Because it's almost time.'

'Time for what?'

'For someone who's supposed to be intelligent you're surprisingly stupid. Time for the *baby*.'

As if on cue I'm racked by another contraction even stronger than the last. Shudders convulse my body and I long to curl up in a corner and cradle my bump in my hands. I struggle against the ties, but they don't shift an inch. The pain gradually subsides and my muscles relax.

Roz squats on her haunches so I can see her properly for the first time. Her hair is scraped back in a pony tail and her face is devoid of make-up, but it's her eyes that transfix me. They're blazing with a terrifying intensity.

'Another contraction?' she asks.

I'm silent, watching her warily.

She prods me on the shoulder. 'I said, was that another contraction?'

'I think so,' I mumble.

'When did you have the last one?'

I shrug.

'No matter. We'll just have to time it, won't we?' she chirps, tapping at the screen of her mobile. I glance at my pocket.

'Don't worry, your phone and keys are safe. Safely out of reach, anyway,' she chuckles, jerking her head back-wards. Metal glints from the highest shelf.

'What do you want?' I croak.

She sits cross-legged opposite me and claps her hands together. 'I've been looking forward to this for months. It's been so hard to keep the secret.' She hugs herself and for the first time I notice she's wearing a lavender-blue wraparound maternity dress.

'I've got a dress like that.'

'It is your dress. I found it in your wardrobe and borrowed it. You don't mind, do you?'

My head is muzzy and it takes a second for her words to sink in. 'Are you pregnant, too?'

'My neighbours think so,' she trills. 'Thanks to my fake baby bump. It's made from silicone. It's so lifelike I almost convinced myself I was up the duff.' She laughs again.

'Why would you -'

'Christ, you really are slow today. I'm faking a pregnancy so that when I bring a baby home no-one'll be suspicious. They'll assume he's mine. Which, of course, he is.'

Fingers of dread squeeze my heart. 'You mean my baby?'

'Of course I mean your baby.' She makes a show of looking over her shoulder. 'I don't see any other pregnant women here, do you?'

'But you can't,' I say, stifling a sob. 'He's not yours to take.'

'I'm afraid that's where you're wrong,' she says, jumping to her feet and rifling about in her handbag. She takes something out and examines it in the light. At first I think it's a Biro, but with mounting horror I realise it's a syringe. She taps the end of it a couple of times and bears down on me, her face a mask of concentration.

'What are you doing?' I shriek, shrinking back.

She stabs the syringe into the muscle in my thigh and I cry out, more in shock than pain. 'What have you given me?'

Roz tosses the empty syringe over her shoulder and it rolls under an old shelving unit. 'Syntocinon,' she says, as if that explains everything.

I'm expecting to slide into unconsciousness, but nothing happens.

'It's the synthetic form of oxytocin, used to speed up labour. It stimulates the uterus, making it contract.' She peers at me. 'Matt promised me a baby, and a baby's what I'm going to have.'

'Matt *what*?'

'You heard.'

'But you've never even met him!'

She leans over, her face inches from mine. Her breath is hot on my cheek. 'Is that what you think? If so, I'm afraid you're wrong.'

What is she talking about? I try to marshal my thoughts, remembering the missed calls, the mystery card and the flowers. Roz is just his type. Dark, slim and pretty. Like I used to be before pregnancy bloated my face and thickened my ankles.

'Are you the one he's having an affair with?'

For a second, doubt flickers across her face. Her eyes search mine. 'He's having an affair?'

Even though I'm shackled to a bench and Roz is looming over me, anger makes me brave. 'Don't play the innocent with me. I know he's been playing away. No wonder you always check he's at work before you come over. Too worried you wouldn't be able to resist falling into each other's arms in front of me like star-crossed lovers?'

'You're wrong -'

'I don't give a monkey's what you say. I'm not completely stupid. But tell me this, Roz, how many men actually leave their wives, their *heavily-pregnant* wives, for their mistresses?'

'He was mine before he was ever yours,' she hisses.

'*What*?'

'I met Matt twelve years ago when I was twenty and he was twenty-three.'

'You went out with each other?'

'We lived with each other, Sophie. We had our lives mapped out. A house, wedding, kids, the lot. Even a fucking golden retriever. That's what he promised me.'

'I don't believe you.'

Crack! Roz's hand snakes through the air so fast I don't have time to twist my head out of the way. Her palm connects with my cheekbone with blistering force.

'Bitch!' I cry, straining at the ties around my wrists.

'Shut up then,' she says in a low voice. 'Do you want to hear this or not? I was the love of his life. He was about to propose, I know he was. Then that slapper Tess arrived at the bank and started making cow eyes at him.' Roz adopts a coquettish tone that's so exaggerated it's grotesque. '"Oh Matt, you're so clever. Can you please run your eye over my figures?" He was weak, like all men, and he fell for it.'

I'm curious despite myself. Perhaps she is telling the truth. I know so little about Matt's past. 'He left you for her?'

She throws her head back and laughs, exposing the translucent white skin of her neck. My hands twitch in their bindings and for a second I wonder what I'd be capable of given the chance.

'Technically she left him. Very silly of her to go running along country lanes at dusk. She was asking for trouble.'

'Why? What happened?'

Roz re-arranges her features so her face is a picture of concern. 'It was all terribly sad. She was knocked over by a hit and run driver and left for dead. The funny thing was, when they found her she was. Dead, I mean.'

I gasp.

'I know. Terrible, right?'

'Was it you who ran her over?'

She smirks. 'I couldn't possibly comment.'

My God, she's actually insane. I'm used to dealing with people having psychotic episodes, but this is something else entirely. Keep her talking, says a voice in my head. So I do.

'Did you and Matt get back together after Tess... died?'

Her face hardens. 'They sent me away. I wasn't displaying 'normal' behaviour.'

'Define normal,' I say, trying to inject warmth into my voice.

'My point exactly!' she cries. 'I only followed Matt because I wanted to speak to him. He ended it so suddenly. I needed to understand why.'

A new wave of pain rolls in and I let out a guttural grunt.

'Oh goody, another one!' Roz exclaims, rubbing her hands in anticipation. 'Let's count together.'

My chin is on my chest as I try to breathe through the contraction, doing my best to ignore Roz as she counts to fifty-two. She pats my knee and I force myself not to flinch.

'Not long now!' she says.

I give her a wan smile. Beads of sweat are trickling down my brow despite the chill dampness of the cellar.

'Where did they send you?'

'Oh, back to the asylum. Only they don't call them that anymore, do they? A locked ward on a psychiatric unit. Bastards. And by the time they let me out Matt had disappeared.'

'What do you mean, disappeared?'

'He'd left the bank, sold our house, left Portsmouth. I tracked him down in Chester, but he moved again. He kept bloody moving. And then I lost him completely.'

'But you found him in the end,' I say in a dull voice.

Her eyes gleam. 'I created a fake profile on Linked In -'

'Matt's not on Linked In.' Or Facebook, or Twitter, or Instagram for that matter. I always assumed it was because he couldn't be bothered with social media. More likely he didn't want Roz using it to track him down.

'If you'll let me *finish*,' she says, glaring at me, 'I used my fake profile to connect with a few people we used to work with and pretended I was recruiting for a bank in London. When I asked them if they knew any branch managers looking to further their careers, one suggested a certain Matt Saunders, who managed the Brighton branch of a high street bank. I made some more enquiries and realised it was him. Bingo.'

'Wouldn't it have been easier just to Google him?'

'He'd changed his name. So no, it wouldn't.'

'Changed his name?' I repeat stupidly. *Why didn't he tell me?*

'He used to be Matthew French.'

French and Saunders. Matt's always loved them. Christ almighty, I owe my last name to a comedy act. What else don't I know about my husband?

'I knew he might be a bit... wary if I turned up without any warning, so I changed my name, too. Clever eh?' She winks at me.

'Very clever,' I agree tonelessly.

'My real name is Leanne.'

'So, when I told Matt a woman called Roz was cutting my hair he had no idea it was you. Have you actually spoken to him?'

'Not in so many words. I've tried calling and texting. But he's very loyal to you, Sophie. He's a good man, I can see that. He doesn't want to hurt you. Unfortunately for you, I do.'

CHAPTER FORTY-ONE

NOW

'He'll come looking for me the minute he gets home and realises I'm not there,' I tell Roz.

She picks up my mobile and waves it at me. 'Afraid not. I sent him a text from your phone while you were out cold. He thinks you've had a change of plan and have come to mine for supper. You told him not to wait up. He won't start worrying until at least midnight.'

'And when he does he'll call the police and you'll be arrested for kidnap and assault.'

This time I see her hand in time and I jerk my head away, catching a glancing blow. *Keep her talking.* 'What is it you want from me?'

'Just your baby.' She disappears into the shadows. Her voice is muffled as she talks over her shoulder. 'We're going to have the baby here. Everything's ready.'

She reappears, holding two large Waitrose bags. One contains towels. A packet of newborn Pampers is sticking out of the top of the second.

'Are you mad? I can't have my baby in a cellar!'

'You'll be fine. You're fit and healthy. It's amazing what

you can learn on YouTube. I prepared for every eventuality. C-section was my first choice.'

I gape at her.

'I wanted to dictate where and when the birth was going to take place, but I knew I had to read up on natural delivery too, in case you suddenly went into labour.'

'I need to go to hospital! I'm forty-one and this is my first baby. What if something goes wrong?'

'Have a bit of faith. I've spent months watching birthing videos. I'll be your very own doula.'

I shake my head in disbelief. Roz rummages around in the second bag and pulls out a cornflower-blue fleece blanket. To my astonishment she puts her thumb in her mouth and rubs the blanket against her top lip. She looks at once absurd and intensely vulnerable. She takes her thumb out and eyes me with a steely gaze. 'Once he's born I need you out of the picture.'

Fear prickles my skin as if a thousand ants are crawling over me. 'What do you mean?'

'Matt, the baby and I can hardly be a happy family if you're still on the scene, like the spectre at the feast. Which would you prefer - an overdose, a broken neck from falling down the cellar steps or electrocution from Geoff's old electric fire?' She doesn't wait for an answer. 'Electrocution would be fitting. Not unlike ECT.'

She puts her thumb in her mouth again, cradles the blanket and rocks back and forth, her eyes fixed on a point in the ceiling.

ECT. Electroconvulsive therapy. Used to treat serious mental health problems such as schizophrenia or psychosis.

'Did you have ECT in the psychiatric ward?'

She shakes her head without looking at me, then takes

her thumb out to say, 'Not that time.' The thumb goes back in and she continues rocking.

'When did you have it, Roz? You can tell me.'

'When I was seventeen.'

The same age I had the abortion.

Her thumb drops from her mouth and she draws her knees to her chest and hugs them tightly. 'Procedure. That's what they call it. Such an inoffensive word for such an invasive act, don't you think? Four hundred volts of electricity pumped into my brain and they call it a *procedure*?' She spits the words out.

'I had to have a general anaesthetic and a muscle relaxant to stop the physical convulsions. I was strapped on my back to a table, for fuck's sake. "Don't worry,"' she mimics in a falsetto voice, '"the table can be pivoted if you're sick". Oh well, that's alright then.' She gives a short bark of laughter. 'It was only later I realised I should never have had it. ECT might help manic depressives and schizophrenics, but it doesn't help people like me.'

'What do you mean, people like you?'

Roz rakes her nails across her forehead, leaving a row of red weals. 'People with borderline personality disorder. So, it does fuck all to improve my BPD and instead I'm left with memory loss, anxiety and difficulty concentrating, just to add insult to injury. And do you know the funny thing?'

I shake my head.

'It was my decision to go through with it. I thought it would give me a fresh start, a new beginning. I truly believed it would wipe the slate clean and I would be all sparkly and new. I thought it was *the right thing to do*. You have no idea how fucking angry that makes me.'

She jumps to her feet again and paces from one side of the cellar to the other, her hands balled in fists at her sides.

As she passes me the scent of stale sweat fills my nostrils and I turn my head to avoid it.

'The system swallowed me up and spat me out. I didn't deserve it. But I'm going to have my happy ending. Thanks to you and the baby.'

I feel another contraction coming and brace my legs. Roz drops to the floor like a stone and counts the seconds until it passes.

'Over a minute,' she says with satisfaction. 'Not long now.'

'One thing I don't understand,' I say slowly. 'You've already got your own little family. What about Pete and Caitlyn?'

Laughter, shrill and piercing, echoes around the cellar.

'They don't exist, you silly bitch. I made them up so we'd have something in common. I needed to win your trust.'

Lou was right after all. Why didn't I believe her, my oldest friend, over someone I barely knew?

'You were very convincing.'

She smiles. 'I was, wasn't I? But you made it so easy. Poor, gullible Sophie. You fell for it hook, line and sinker.'

'How did you know Matt lived in Canterbury?'

'I followed him home from work one Friday night. And once he was back in Brighton the following week I posted my flyer through your door. I retrained as a hairdresser when I was released from hospital.'

All of a sudden everything is clear. 'It was you who set Angela's house on fire, wasn't it?'

'I did it for you. Angela's a bully, and you should always stand up to bullies,' she chants in a sing-song voice.

'Stand up to them, not burn their bloody house down!'

'She was sending your blood pressure through the roof.

Who knows what risk that could have caused to the pregnancy. I was looking after you.'

So you could concoct a crazy plan to steal my baby. What kind of warped mind must Roz have to be able to justify setting someone's house on fire while they are asleep upstairs? Angela could so easily have died. And it would have been my fault. If I hadn't sounded off to Roz about my boss it would never have happened.

I remember the lighter I found on our dew-soaked lawn. 'Were you planning to burn our house down as well?'

She snorts. 'Why would I do that? I needed to keep the baby safe, ergo I needed to keep you safe, too. Until he was born anyway.'

'But I found a lighter in the garden.'

'Not just any lighter, Sophie. *The* lighter. That really was inspired, even though I say so myself. Because I knew I needed to cover all bases.'

'What do you mean?'

Roz sits back on her heels. 'It was the lighter I used to start the fire at Angela's. I wanted a contingency plan in case I missed the birth.'

My mind is whirring. 'You were framing me for arson?'

'Only as a last resort. You had motive and opportunity, after all. An anonymous tip-off to the police should have been enough to have you arrested and then, when they found the lighter at your house, charged. You'd have been banged up for five years for arson with intent.'

'And I suppose you were planning to worm your way back into Matt's life while I was in prison.' I shake my head in disbelief.

'As I said, it was a last resort. I needed to think of everything. That's why the cat had to go.'

My jaw clenches as I remember DC Bennett's warning

that people who torture or kill animals are often perpetrators of violent crimes against people. Of course Roz killed him. Who else?

'What did Mr Pickles ever do to you?'

'Nothing. It's what he could have done to the baby that mattered. I had no idea how much shit there was in the garden. Disgusting. Didn't you know cat faeces can contain a parasite that causes toxoplasmosis? If you get infected while you're pregnant it can cause miscarriage or stillbirth and damage your unborn baby.'

She sounds as though she's reciting straight from a medical textbook.

'I always wear gardening gloves.'

She shakes her head sorrowfully. 'Not good enough. Sometimes I think you don't even want this baby. You show a wanton disregard for his safety. It's a good job you're giving him to me. We both know I'll do a better job looking after him.'

I gulp down the tears that are forming a hard mass at the back of my throat. *Keep her talking.* 'Was it you who trashed the garden?'

She looks sidelong at me. 'Might have been.'

'You can't pretend that was to protect me. I'd spent weeks working towards the open day. Why did you do it?'

She looks up at the ceiling as if finding the strength to deal with a particularly tiresome toddler. 'Because you'd really pissed me off. So cosy, having lunch with your best friend Lou. You've never invited me to lunch, have you? Yet I'm a better friend to you than she ever was.'

'You're keeping me prisoner so you can steal my baby, yet you're a better friend than Lou? You're insane! She warned me about you. I should have listened to her.' My thoughts track back over the last few weeks. 'I suppose you left the cord of the hairdryer out on purpose, too.'

'Of course I didn't. I would never, ever harm the baby. Don't you see? Everything I've done has been to protect him. I only started volunteering at the bloody garden so I could keep an eye on you.' She shudders. 'It was like being back on the ward, surrounded by nutters. But it's just as well I did, isn't it? That psycho Martin could have killed you.'

'How did you know how to restrain him?'

She throws me a look of utter contempt. 'I've been on the receiving end enough times to learn how it's done.'

'What about my presentation? Was that you?'

'Guilty as charged, m'lud.'

'Why?'

'Just for fun. I wanted to unsettle your perfect, safe little life. I wanted to see you squirm.'

She watches me dispassionately while another contraction takes hold.

'Please undo my hands,' I beg once the pain has subsided. 'My arms are killing me. I promise I won't try to escape.'

Her mouth twists into a cruel sneer. 'Not a fucking chance.'

I slide my hands up and down the table leg and wiggle my fingers, trying to coax some feeling back. Roz unpacks the two bags. I watch her in silence.

'Plastic sheeting and towels to clear up the mess, sterile gloves, scalpels, medical scissors and umbilical cord clamps, a head torch and maternity pads. Oh, and a bowl for your placenta.' She looks at me. 'I won't be eating it, in case you're wondering. I may be BPD but I'm not a complete nutjob.'

As she arranges her home birthing kit, exhaustion hits me like a steamroller and my eyelids grow heavy. I don't fight sleep. Even a few minutes' respite from this nightmare would be a relief. I twist around so I can rest my head against the leg of the potting bench, close my eyes, slow my breathing and wait for oblivion.

CHAPTER FORTY-TWO

NOW

I'm asleep on the blow-up bed in Lou's lurid pink bedroom. She's doing her best to rouse me, but I don't want to wake up. It's the morning after the night before, and it must have been a heavy night because my head is throbbing. That'll teach me to knock back her stash of cheap vodka.

'Go away,' I mutter. I squeeze my eyes shut and try to edge my way back into oblivion.

But she's insistent, though her voice is faint, almost inaudible. She is either very, very far away or whispering oh so softly in my ear.

I try to flap my hands in front of my face to send her away, but my arms won't work. I know I mustn't wake. It's a reverse nightmare. If I wake, I'll be plunged back into hell. *I must stay asleep. I must stay asleep. I must...*

'Sophie, it's me, Lou. Where are you?' she calls again.

I'm in your bedroom, you twit. I long for sleep to return, but it oozes away, like rainwater down a gutter, and I prise open my eyes. Expecting to see my seventeen-year-old best friend grinning at me I'm shocked to be greeted by the sight of a woman towering over me with narrowed eyes and a finger to her lips. In an instant the horror of my predicament slaps me in the face. I'm being held prisoner in a cellar by a deranged woman intent on stealing my baby and killing me.

Roz darts towards me with a length of duct tape. I throw my head from side to side, but she grips my chin with one hand and presses the tape to my mouth with the other. She backs away, her eyes never leaving me, picks up a spade, flicks off the light and steps into the shadows at the bottom of the steps.

'Sophie! Are you in there?' shouts Lou.

Every nerve in my body is tingling with the effort of not calling out. All I can do is wait and listen while blood pounds through my veins. She'll have seen my car and know I'm here somewhere. Be careful Lou, I silently will her. Don't take any chances or we're both dead.

Minutes pass and I hear nothing. No crunch of gravel, no warning cry from the robin in the pear tree, no creak of rusty hinges. The silence is all-encompassing and seems to suck the air from the damp cellar until I'm struggling for breath. I force myself to breathe in through my nostrils until my heart rate steadies. I can't afford to pass out. Not now, with Lou so close.

Still there is nothing. I slump in despair and my cramping biceps scream in response. But the pain is nothing compared to the bitter disappointment that Lou has given up on me and gone home.

I sense rather than see Roz's body stiffen. I watch her out of the corner of my eye. She crouches down, her gaze fixed on the door at the top of the steps. I hold my breath as it swings open, casting a glimmer of palest moonlight into the cellar.

For a second the light fades and I picture Lou's silhouette in the doorway.

'Sophie!' she calls.

I breathe in, ready to cry out as best I can with duct tape across my mouth. At the last second something stops me. If Lou realises I'm here she'll come hurtling down the steps into this nightmare. She won't stand a chance against Roz, armed as she is with both a spade and the element of surprise. If I stay quiet Lou will think I'm not here and will go. Maybe she'll call the police, maybe she won't, but she'll be safe, and that, at this precise moment, is all that matters.

But I underestimate her. The slap of leather sole against stone echoes around the cellar's four walls. I crane my neck to watch as her feet appear, followed by her legs as she descends the steps. Roz is crouched low, ready to pounce. Surreptitiously I slide as far down the bench leg as I can, hoping I can bring Roz down with my feet. But it's no good. Even when I'm almost horizontal she's a foot too far away.

Lou pauses on the bottom step and stares into the gloom.

'Sophie!' she calls again. There's a tremor in her voice and I will her to turn around and retrace her steps out of the cellar to safety. But she takes one more tentative step forwards and Roz strikes with the ferocity of a cobra.

CHAPTER FORTY-THREE

NOW

It happens so fast it's over in seconds. Roz lunges forwards, wielding the spade high above her head. Lou's head snaps around and she steps backwards. But it's too late. The spade connects with her temple with a sickening thud. Time stands still, as though someone has pressed the pause button on a video nasty. My eyes flicker over the scene. Lou's eyes are bulging and her nostrils are flared. Roz is holding the spade aloft, about to take another swing. Then Lou's knees buckle and she crumples to the ground like a puppet whose strings have been slashed with a carving knife.

Although my scream is muffled by the duct tape it doesn't stop Roz from spinning around and aiming a desultory kick at me. Her foot connects with my thigh, but the pain is nothing compared to the agony of the next contraction, which takes over my whole body. I close my eyes and count in my head, reaching sixty before the spasms pass.

When I open my eyes, Roz has switched the light back on and is winding duct tape around Lou's wrists and ankles. Lou's head is drawn back at an awkward angle and her cheek is pressed against the filthy cellar floor. I hope to God her neck isn't broken. I stare and stare, willing her to show some sign of life - a shallow intake of breath or a rise and fall of her chest - but she's as lifeless as a doll.

I turn on Roz in fury. 'What have you done?' I bellow. It comes out as an incoherent mumble and Roz gives me an amused look.

'Sorry, I didn't quite catch that.'

She advances towards me, the spade still in her hand, and although all I want to do is cringe, I force myself to raise my chin and stare her out. She bends down, takes a corner of the duct tape and rips it off. 'What were you saying?'

'You need to check Lou's breathing!'

'You think I've killed her? What do you take me for? She's going to wake up with one hell of a headache, but she'll be fine.' Roz kneels in front of me. 'I'm going to take a look to see how we're getting on, alright?'

I tense as she peels off my pants and plucks two latex gloves from a box.

'For fuck's sake just relax, Sophie.'

I bite my lip and look away, trying not to cry and wondering where it all went wrong. When I think I can bear it no more she pulls away. 'Obviously this is the first baby I've delivered, so don't hold me to it, but I'd say you're almost fully dilated. I can feel the baby's head, anyway.'

I pull myself straighter. 'You can?'

She smiles and her face is transformed. 'I can. You must be thirsty. Would you like a drink?'

I nod. She scrabbles around in one of the shopping bags and pulls out a bottle of water, which she holds to my lips so I can drink. When I've finished she wipes my chin and screws the lid back on the bottle. She fishes something else out of the bag. To my horror it's a thick leather strap. What new torture is she going to inflict on me?

She must sense where my thoughts are spiralling because she gives me a best buddy grin. 'It's for you to bite down on, silly billy. Do you really think I'd hurt you?'

The sudden shift in her demeanour is bewildering.

'I don't suppose this is how you imagined labour to be.'

I glance at the dank brick walls of the cellar, the rows of garden tools and the prone body of Lou half-hidden in the shadows.

'It's not exactly the William Harvey Hospital's maternity unit, is it?'

She laughs, and then the smile slips from her face. 'I'm sorry it has to be this way. When I found out Matt was married I made up my mind I'd hate you. I don't. You're alright. But I have no choice. Matt might not want me, you see. I'm not stupid. At least this way I'll have his baby. You're a means to an end. Collateral damage, if you like.'

'There must be another way,' I plead. 'Maybe we could share the baby. I could be his birth mum and you could be his stepmum and we could do alternate weeks or something.' It sounds ridiculous, but I press on regardless. 'We can make it work if we want it hard enough.'

For a minute she appears to consider the idea, then her mouth curls down and I brace myself.

'Thing is, I don't want to share the baby. I want him to love me unconditionally. All the time you're still in the picture he'll never be able to give me all his heart. You have to go.'

'You can have Matt. Just let me keep my baby, please? I can't bear to lose another one.'

She frowns. 'What do you mean, another one?'

I can't answer. I'm in the grip of another contraction.

But this one feels different and I have an uncontrollable urge to bear down and push.

Roz jumps to her feet as a belly-roar escapes my lips.

'Action stations,' she cries, grabbing a handful of towels and spreading them around me. She takes a pair of scissors from the nearest bag and holds them inches from my face. 'I'm going to cut your arms free now, Sophie. But you need to remember that if you try any funny business there'll be consequences.'

She draws the open-bladed scissors across her neck in such an exaggerated fashion it's almost comedic. But it's clear from the fervour in her eyes that she wouldn't think twice about slashing my neck.

With a flick of the wrist she slices through the duct tape and I rub feeling back into my deadened arms. She hands me the leather strap and, sensing another contraction is on its way, I place it between my teeth.

The next half an hour is a blur as I retreat into myself and concentrate on managing the pain.

'I can't do it,' I sob at one point.

'Of course you can. Women in comas have babies. Your body knows what it's doing. Don't fight the contractions. Go with them.'

Then she is beside me, wiping my forehead with a damp flannel. Another wave of pain flows through me and I grab her so tightly my fingers leave red welts on her arms and she doesn't even notice.

Suddenly I feel a burning sensation.

'He's crowning!' she cries.

I stop pushing and let the contractions take over. The baby slithers into Roz's hands. Minutes later the placenta follows him. Relief that it's over is so all-consuming I barely register the fact that he's silent. I could quite happily turn over, forget all about him and go to sleep. But I remember all the advice about skin to skin contact being so important for bonding. I sit up and unbutton my shirt. 'Can I hold him?'

Roz shakes her head, refusing to meet my eye.

'Roz, please!'

'It's not that,' she mutters. 'I don't think he's breathing.'

'*What?*'

'Shut up! I need to concentrate.' Working quickly and efficiently, Roz wipes the baby with a towel and gently massages his back. I can't take my eyes off his scrunched-up, vernix-covered face. Come on, little man, you can do it, I will him. Just when I'm giving up hope, he takes one shallow breath, then another. And then his mouth gapes open and he wails.

CHAPTER FORTY-FOUR

NOW

Roz wraps a towel around my son, kisses his fuzzy black hair and hands him to me.

'Five minutes while I clear up. There's no point getting attached,' she says, but I don't pay any heed. I am drinking in his new baby smell and watching in wonder as his tiny hand closes around my little finger. He's warm against my skin and my breasts tingle. I shift and he nuzzles closer.

Roz stops shoving towels into a black sack and narrows her eyes. 'What are you doing?'

I look at her beseechingly. 'He should have one feed. He's two weeks early, don't forget. The colostrum's good for him.'

She pinches the bridge of her nose. 'Alright, but that's it, OK?'

I nod and watch as he latches on with rosebud lips. I feel a welter of emotions. Love, pride, and an animal instinct to protect this tiny scrap of life at all costs.

'You're good with babies,' I tell Roz as he suckles.

'You have to be, don't you, when your mum's a smack-head and your dad's fucked off with the woman next door and you have a baby sister and there's literally no-one else to look after her.'

'Is that what happened?'

'No, I made it up for the sympathy vote.' She tosses another towel into the black sack. 'Yes, that's what happened.'

'How old were you?'

'Ten. I think so, anyway. Our mother wasn't big on birthdays.'

'That's awful.'

She stares at the baby hungrily. 'That's where you're wrong. Katy being born was the best thing that ever happened to me. She was perfect. Unlike the rest of my life which, frankly, was shit.'

'I can imagine,' I murmur. Only I can't. I had a sheltered, happy childhood with a clean, warm home and parents who loved me. I have a hazy picture in my mind of a fetid council house with grubby mattresses on bedroom floors, nicotine-stained walls and a rotting sofa in the front garden. It's a clichéd image gleaned from gritty television dramas and I'm ashamed at my naivety.

'I did everything for her. Fed her, changed her nappies, bathed her and read her stories. If our mother was ever off the smack long enough to take an interest Katy didn't want to know. I was the one she wanted.'

'Are you still close?'

Roz's expression darkens as she turns on me. 'I don't know, do I? Our stupid bitch of a mother overdosed and we were taken into foster care. I begged them to keep us together, but they said she was more likely to be adopted without an older sister in tow. Especially one with behavioural issues.'

She laughs without humour and holds her hands out for the baby. 'It's time. Give him to me.'

'He's still feeding. Just a couple more minutes,' I plead.

Roz tuts, ties the black sack up and starts packing away her home birth kit. While her back is turned I eye the distance between me and the steps. It's at least five metres. Even if I make it to the bottom of the flight without her noticing there's no way I'll beat her to the top. My legs are as weak as pipe cleaners. I'm not convinced they'll support me, let alone the baby, and there's no way on earth I'm leaving him. I could lay him on the floor behind me, try to wrestle Roz to the ground and either knock her out or tie her up. I need an element of surprise if I stand a chance of succeeding. As if she's reading my mind she turns her head and watches me over her shoulder. I try a smile, but she doesn't smile back.

Keep her talking.

'What happened to you both?'

'They were right. Katy was adopted and I was sent to a children's home because no-one wanted me. I stayed there until I was eighteen when I started work at the bank and moved into my own flat.'

She says this without a trace of self-pity and, despite everything, I admire her for it.

'I could help you find her.'

She raises an eyebrow. 'Why would you want to do that?'

I shrug. 'Because I -'

'Feel sorry for me?' she spits, her face twisted in anger. 'Fuck you.'

' - want to help,' I finish. 'It's not your fault she was taken away. But you can't replace her with my baby. Two wrongs don't make a right.'

She laughs again. 'Spare me the platitudes. Katy wouldn't want to know me, not now. An older sister with borderline personality disorder? I'd only be an unwelcome reminder of her shitty start in life and her arsehole parents. No, Katy's dead to me, I've known that for a long time. I need to start again with a clean slate and a new baby. So, shut the fuck up and let me get on with this, alright?'

She gathers the new sleepsuits, nappies and cartons of milk and packs them away. I scan the cellar looking for something I can use against her. My eyes rest on Lou. Is it my imagination, or has her head moved a fraction? I stare harder, but her eyes are still closed. At least I can see her chest rising and falling.

Roz disappears into a shadowy corner. My heart plummets when she reappears with a car seat. She really means to go through with this. I suck in air and cup my hand around the baby's head. I can't let her take him. *I won't.*

'What will you do?' I say dully.

'Get as far away from here as possible. Don't worry, I have a plan. And I'll look after him, you can be sure of that.'

'They'll find you in the end.'

'Who will?'

'The police. They'll find you and arrest you and you'll go to prison for murder and snatching a child and grievous bodily harm. You'll lose him then anyway.'

'Are you still talking?' She glares at me. 'Anyway, I won't. They'll have to send me to a mother and baby unit until he's eighteen months old.'

'But he's not your baby!' I cry. 'And if I'm dead and Matt can't cope he'll be taken into foster care and sent for adoption like Katy. You don't want that to happen, do you?'

She hesitates for a second and I seize my chance. 'If you let us go I promise you can be part of our lives. I'll help you get treatment for your BPD. You can be his godmother. Please Roz, at least think about it.'

'Thought about it, decided against it. But thanks for the offer.'

She delves into her handbag and produces a second syringe.

'What's that?' I whisper.

'I've decided an overdose is the way to go. Heroin and fentanyl. Spike says it should be enough.'

Tightness grips my chest. 'Spike?'

'My mother's dealer. Christ knows how he's still alive. He owed me big time for giving her the batch of skag that killed her.' She holds the syringe up to the light and studies its contents. 'Don't worry, it'll be like drifting away on a cloud.'

My heart pounds as adrenalin races around my bloodstream. She's going to kill me. Here and now in this dank, dark cellar a few feet under my beloved Cam. If it wasn't so sick it would be funny. The baby has fallen asleep, his mouth open. A snail trail of colostrum is trickling down his chin but I daren't wipe it away in case Roz realises he's stopped feeding.

'Are you going to inject Lou, too?'

She shakes her head. 'You're the only one I need to get rid of. The authorities will stop looking for us eventually. We'll be two more in a long line of missing person reports. But mothers - mothers who give a shit, anyway - never give up looking for their children. I can't risk you finding us.' She stares at me with dead eyes. 'You need to die.'

She lays the syringe on the shelf next to my phone and car keys. There's a roaring in my ears and I hold my precious cargo tighter and rock from side to side.

Roz holds out her hands again. 'Give him to me.'

I shake my head. Tears are streaming down my face. 'I can't, Roz. Please don't make me. *Please*. Take anything. Take my house, take Matt. But not my baby. Not my little boy.'

I hold him as tightly as I dare and swivel away from her grasping fingers. But she's too quick, too strong, springing forwards and wrestling him from my grip.

I scream, the piteous sound magnifying as it bounces off the walls, and lunge forwards to take him back. Roz kicks me in the stomach with such force that I'm thrown back onto the floor. The pain is so intense I must pass out, because when I come around a few seconds later my wrists are bound again and my baby, now dressed in a white sleep-suit, is strapped in the car seat at the bottom of the stairs, the blue fleece blanket wrapped around him.

I don't know what makes me look at Lou. Intuition, perhaps. Her eyes are open. I blink and look again just to make sure. I glance at Roz. She's stacking her bags next to the car seat. I turn back to Lou. She is mouthing something to me and nodding towards Roz. I can't hear what she's saying but I have a pretty good idea.

On my own, there's no hope of overcoming Roz, but with two of us we stand a chance.

CHAPTER FORTY-FIVE

NOW

I rack my brains, wondering what we can use to overpower Roz. I dismiss Geoff's neat rows of gardening tools because they are on the far side of the cellar with Roz playing piggy in the middle. I look at Lou. She's still mouthing something and pointing to the floor beside me. I pull a what-are-you-talking-about face and glance around wildly. At that moment Roz switches off the light and the cellar is plunged into darkness.

I feel around on the floor. Lou must have seen something. The bricks, laid in a herringbone pattern all those years ago, feel rough against my hands. I'm about to give up when my fingers alight on something smooth. It's the leather strap Roz gave me to bite down on during labour. I pick it up. From memory it's about two-foot long and has holes at one end. It was probably once a belt, although the buckle has long gone.

When Roz turns on the torch app on her phone I almost drop the strap in shock. She walks over to the shelf where my phone and keys lay next to the syringe she is going to kill me with. I shoot another desperate look at Lou. She nods and I drop the strap and shift my weight so I'm sitting on it.

Roz advances towards me, the needle in one hand and her phone in the other. 'Ready for oblivion?' she coos. 'I need to find a vein. Where's that old belt?'

She sweeps the beam of the phone's torch on the floor beside me and I mentally cross my fingers, hoping she doesn't shine it over Lou.

'No matter. I'll make do without. Christ knows I've seen it done enough times.'

She kneels beside me, places the needle on the floor and reaches in her pocket for a small knife which she uses to saw through the duct tape around my wrists. She grabs my left hand, shines the torch at the pale skin on the inside of my arm and slaps it several times until the vein is raised.

She's still gripping my hand when Lou groans. I hold my breath, wondering how she'll react. Lou groans again and begins to struggle to all fours.

Roz is on her feet in an instant, her arm raised high in the air. She swipes at the back of Lou's head but Lou swerves just in time. My hands close around the leather strap and I stagger to my feet, conscious of the fact that I'm wearing nothing below my shirt. But there's no time for modesty. As Roz raises her hand to strike Lou again there's a plaintive whimper from the car seat.

My baby.

My baby.

Rage zips through my body with the speed of a bush fire and I bounce on the balls of my feet, ready to strike. With one fluid movement I whip the strap around Roz's neck before she even realises I'm behind her.

Fury makes me strong and I pull as tightly as I can. Roz struggles, her arms flailing as she tries to loosen the strap, but the more she thrashes the angrier I become, until the red mist descends and I lose it completely.

'You bitch!' I howl, pulling tighter still. Roz's movements become weaker as the blood supply to her brain is slowly cut off. She sways on her feet and for a second I loosen my grip, only to tighten it again when she starts plucking at the strap. Her body goes limp and she slides to the floor, unconscious.

Lou appears by my side. She's wiggled free of the duct tape and is waving something in my face. It's only when she grabs Roz's arm and starts looking for a vein that I realise what she's planning.

'No!' I yell.

'But she was going to kill you!'

'Do you want to spend the rest of your life in prison? Because I sure as hell don't.'

'It's self-defence. Reasonable force. Us or her.' Lou brings the syringe closer to Roz's arm.

'Giving someone an overdose isn't reasonable force.'

'And strangling someone is?' she explodes.

'I'm not strangling her. She's still breathing. Look.'

Roz's eyes are closed but her chest is rising and falling. The baby whimpers again and Roz's eyelashes flutter. I tighten my grip on the strap.

'Call the police before she wakes up,' I beg.

Lou's brown eyes are locked on mine. 'If you let her live she'll come looking for you, you know that, don't you? You'll always be looking over your shoulder, worried she's there. She's obsessed by you. You, Matt and the baby.'

I glance at the car seat but all I can see is the blue blanket. I pray the baby is alright. Unshed tears thicken my voice. 'She won't be able to hurt us. She'll be in prison.'

'You hope.' Lou still hasn't released her grip on Roz's

hand. 'We could finish this here and now. You can be free of her. You need never look over your shoulder again.'

'You're probably right. But I can't live with the guilt.'

'You don't have to. I'll do it. It'll be on my conscience, not yours.'

My eyes are wide. 'You'd do that?'

'You're my best friend. I'd do anything for you. Call it a long overdue payback for the abortion. I know it almost broke you. Let me make amends.'

'I can't. It's not right. Let the police deal with her and she'll get the help she needs.'

Lou shakes her head. 'You always were too soft.' She lets go of Roz's hand and it drops limply by her side. 'You win. I'll call the police.'

She takes my phone from the shelf and I tell her my passcode. She peers at the screen. 'No bloody signal. I won't be a minute, OK?'

She bounds up the cellar steps to the door. Roz still feels like a dead weight in my arms but even so I know I should tie her hands and feet in case she comes to before the police arrive. I lay her on the floor and study her face. Her breathing is shallow, but her eyes are still closed. She looks strangely at peace.

Before I go in search of the duct tape I check the baby is OK. He's asleep, his tiny fists above his head and his face turned towards me. I gaze at his features greedily. His perfect snub nose. Lashes as thick and curly as Matt's. Lips pursed in an Instagram-worthy pout. He's so beautiful I can't drag my eyes away.

At the top of the steps Lou is barking instructions to the police call taker. The police station is only a couple of miles away. Soon they will be here, Roz will be arrested and this nightmare will be over. Lou was looking for redemption when she offered to kill Roz, but she was wrong. Two wrongs *don't* make a right.

Save a life, however, and you might be in a position to seek redemption for a past wrong. I killed one baby, now I've saved one, too. Maybe, once this is all over, I'll be able to forgive myself for the abortion. I run a finger down the baby's cheek and smile as his lips twitch in response.

I shall call him Edward. Teddy for short. I hope Lou won't mind. I don't think she will. It's clear now that by shutting her out of my life I hurt her as much as she hurt me. We wasted so many years. I'll never make that mistake again.

'You OK?' Lou calls.

'We're fine.' I smile up at her.

'I'm going to make sure the door is open so the police can get in, alright? I won't be long.'

I pull a towel from one of the black sacks, wrap it around my waist and make myself comfortable on the bottom step so I can keep stroking the cheek of my sleeping baby.

My back is to Roz as I sing the opening lines of the first lullaby that pops into my head. My voice is shaky so I clear my throat and start again. 'Rock a bye baby on the tree top, when the wind blows the cradle will rock.' I shiver in the chill cellar air and tuck Teddy's blanket around his narrow shoulders. 'When the bough breaks the cradle will fall, and down will come baby, cradle and all.'

I stop to take a breath. That's when I hear it. A shuffling sound, like a sack of potatoes being dragged across the floor. My head snaps round. Roz has vanished. As I grip the handle of the car seat a cold hand wraps around my mouth and the sharp blade of a knife is pressed against my throat. Roz's breath is fetid as she rasps in my ear.

'Give me the baby, Sophie. He's mine now.'

CHAPTER FORTY-SIX

NOW

I scream and, though my voice is muffled by her hand, Teddy's eyes flutter open. I'm glad his sight is still fuzzy and he'll never remember the next few minutes.

Roz is muttering incoherently in my ear and I feel drops of spittle on my earlobe. She presses the knife into my neck with one hand while the other snakes around me and grabs the handle of the car seat. Once again anger consumes me. I will not let her take him. Silently I count to three, summoning all my strength. I only have one chance.

I stamp on her foot and swing my right elbow between her ribs with as much force as I can. She gasps and hunches over, the knife falling to the floor. I swing my elbow again, breathing heavily as she crumples to the ground. Grabbing the car seat, I run up the steps as fast as my legs will carry me.

The garden is in darkness apart from the weak light cast by the solar fairy lanterns strung over the wrought iron gazebo and the wooden archway into the rose garden.

I call Lou but am met with silence. I hobble towards the oak door. She must have walked down the drive to meet the police at the bottom. I set off to find her. I need to put as much distance as possible between me and the cellar. It's only four hundred metres to the road but it feels like four kilometres as the combined weight of Teddy and the car seat grows heavier with every step.

'You weigh a ton,' I tell him softly, shifting the seat onto my other arm.

It occurs to me that I have no idea how much he weighs and how long he is. He has missed his vitamin K injection and I don't know what his Apgar score would have been. Roz had denied us the things other people take for granted and I will never forgive her for that. Bitterness strengthens my resolve and I pick up my pace.

The orange glow of a street light grows brighter and I make out Lou standing at the end of the drive, her hand shading her eyes from the glare of car headlights as they rumble along Stone Street.

'Lou,' I call again. I'm light-headed, as if I've drunk a double gin on an empty stomach, and I sway. Lou sprints over and takes the car seat in one hand and my elbow in the other.

'What are you doing here?' she cries.

I suck in lungfuls of air. 'Roz woke up. She was going to take Teddy. I had to stop her.'

'What did you do?' she whispers. 'Tell me, Sophie. We need to get our story straight.'

'She threatened me with a knife, so I elbowed her in the ribs. I must have winded her.'

'Did you lock her in the cellar?'

The look on my face tells Lou everything she needs to know, because she gives me what she obviously thinks is a reassuring smile and pats my arm. 'Don't worry. Even if she gets out the police will find her. They'll be here any minute.'

The wait seems interminable, but it can only be a couple of minutes before the familiar sound of sirens fills the air. Lou hands me back the car seat and steps into the carriageway, waving her arms like an air traffic controller. A marked Skoda Octavia with its blue lights flashing screams to a stop a few feet in front of her.

Lou rushes around to the driver's door and gesticulates wildly. She steps back and the officer throws the car into gear and speeds up the drive, sending gravel flying in its wake. Seconds later a second patrol car arrives and follows the first, and a couple of minutes later a third joins them.

'What are you doing?' I ask Lou, who is staring myopically at the screen of my phone.

'Calling Matt. Do you want to speak to him?'

I shake my head. I'm emotionally and physically spent. I'm not sure I can deal with anyone right now, even my husband.

As it is, he doesn't answer anyway. Lou leaves a curt voicemail ordering him to call the minute he picks up the message.

'We should go back,' she says, jerking her head towards Cam. 'They're sending an ambulance for you and the baby, but they'll want to speak to you first. Can you face it?'

'Not really.' I give an apologetic shrug. 'I'd rather go home. But I don't suppose that's an option.'

'I don't suppose it is. Shall I take the baby?'

I nod, and hand her the car seat again. Lou links her other arm with me and we trudge back up the drive towards the flashing blue lights.

'You're calling him Teddy?'

I glance sidelong at her. Her expression is unreadable and I feel a flicker of anxiety. 'Is that alright?'

Her face breaks into a smile. 'Are you kidding? Of course it's alright. It's better than alright. It's bloody brilliant!' She swallows. 'Ed would have been made up.'

'Did you ever tell him about the other baby?'

She shakes her head. 'It wasn't my secret to tell. He never knew.'

I bite my lip. 'I wish I had told him. He had a right to know.'

'You were seventeen,' Lou says. 'You did what you thought was right. It all worked out in the end, didn't it? Ed and I had Josh, and now you and Matt have little Teddy.'

We are both quiet for a minute, lost in our own thoughts. Then she squeezes my arm.

'Thank you,' she says quietly.

'What for?' I ask, puzzled. I'm the one who should be thanking her. She was prepared to go to prison for me tonight.

'For forgiving me. Because I think you have, haven't you?'

'Don't be silly.'

Her face falls.

I smile and squeeze her back. 'There's nothing to forgive.'

An earnest-looking officer introduces himself as Sergeant James Holland.

'Have you arrested her?' Lou demands.

He can't meet our eyes and my heart skips a beat.

'She's gone, hasn't she?'

'We've searched the cellar and are conducting a search of the garden, but yes, it seems she has.'

'Shit.' Lou runs a hand through her hair. 'What about sniffer dogs or helicopters?'

'All the available dogs and the police helicopter are looking for an elderly gent with dementia who's gone missing on the Isle of Sheppey.'

'But Roz is dangerous. She was going to kill Sophie and take her baby. You need to find her!'

'We're doing our best with limited resources, Mrs -'

'Sullivan,' supplies Lou curtly.

He turns to me. 'This woman who threatened you, what's her name?'

'Roz Beaumont. Although her real name is Leanne. She may have changed her last name, too.'

He scribbles in his pocket notebook. 'Where does she live?'

I give a helpless shrug. 'I don't know. But I have her mobile number if that's any use?'

He jots down her number. 'We found a Sony Xperia in the cellar. Is that yours?'

'No, Lou has my phone. It's Roz's.'

'In that case we can't track her phone. Does she have a car?'

'A red Clio. Old shape.'

'Registration plate?'

'I'm sorry, I don't know it. But it wasn't in the car park when I arrived this evening.'

'She may have parked it nearby. I'll alert the control room and we'll see if we can get any hits on ANPR. Ah, here's the ambulance. I'll let them check you and the baby over.'

Two paramedics jump out of the ambulance, introduce

themselves and usher me, Lou and Teddy inside. I feel myself relax as they regale us with stories of the strange places women have given birth on their shift, from a village post office to the car park of a Chinese restaurant. They check us over with friendly efficiency and declare us in good shape considering our ordeal, although they want to take us to the William Harvey Hospital in Ashford, so Teddy can be checked over by an obstetrician just to be sure.

There's a cough at the door and Sergeant Holland appears. 'Mrs Saunders, do you feel able to give me a brief idea what happened here this evening?'

'Sure,' I say, although re-living the last few hours is the last thing I feel like doing. I wrap the blue cotton blanket one of the paramedics gave me tighter around myself and he perches on the bed beside me.

He listens in silence as I relate the events of the last few hours, from the moment I received Roz's text to the arrival of the police. His eyes widen as I describe Roz's makeshift C-section and home birthing kit and the needle filled with a deadly cocktail of heroin and fentanyl.

'We found two hypodermic needles. One full, one empty.'

'The other one was Syntocinon. It's used to bring on labour.'

'Yes, my wife had it for our twins.'

'Roz injected me in the leg with it. It wasn't long before Teddy arrived.' I pause to run a finger down the sleeping baby's cheek. 'She also admitted the arson at Angela Platt's home in Bridge a few weeks ago, and the criminal damage here last week. DC Sam Bennett was investigating them.'

'Righto.' He barks something unintelligible into his

radio. Another officer, an older man with the suggestion of a paunch under his uniform, appears in the doorway.

'No sign of anyone, Sarg. You want us to check the fields and outbuildings?'

'It wouldn't do any harm, Reg.' Sergeant Holland smiles at me. 'That's all for now. You and the little 'un get yourselves to hospital. We'll be in touch.'

As we watch his retreating back I remember my hospital bag stowed in my locked car containing everything Teddy and I need.

'My bag's in the car but I don't suppose they'll let me into the cellar to pick up the keys,' I say.

'They don't need to.' Lou plunges her hand into the pocket of her jeans and produces the keys with a flourish. 'I grabbed them when I picked up your phone. Didn't want Psycho Bitch using your car to get away. Won't be a sec,' she calls over her shoulder.

I clutch the handle of Teddy's car seat and stare at my phone. It's two thirty in the morning, almost an hour since Lou left a message for Matt, and he still hasn't phoned back. Where is he? Doesn't he care that his heavily pregnant wife has disappeared off the face of the earth?

My imagination running overtime, I picture our empty house, my note screwed up on the kitchen table and a second propped against the fruit bowl in its place. But this one is in Matt's messy scrawl. He's sorry, he says. He didn't mean for it to happen. It's not me, it's him. He tried so hard not to fall in love. He just couldn't help himself. He's leaving. He can't live a lie any longer.

Who stole his heart?

Not Lou. I chastise myself for the thought ever crossing my mind. I know now Lou would never betray me. Not

Roz, either. She couldn't disguise her shock when I told her Matt was having an affair.

Perhaps it's Susie from head office, who is always tipping him off when the regional manager is about to make a surprise visit. Or Kelly, the pretty redhead from accounts, who seemed to hang on to his every word at the awards night we went to a couple of years ago.

Lou returns, my hospital bag on her shoulder. One of the paramedics slams the door closed and his colleague turns on the ignition. As the ambulance trundles down the driveway Lou takes my hand in hers.

'Has he phoned?'

I shake my head.

'Everything's going to be OK, Soph. I promise.'

I blink back tears. Roz is on the run and my husband doesn't give a toss if I'm alive or dead.

'I love you for saying so. But it's not really, is it? Everything is not going to be OK.'

CHAPTER FORTY-SEVEN

NOW

The bright lights of the hospital hurt my eyes after the gloom of the cellar and I blink as one of the paramedics wheels me into A&E. Lou resembles a pack horse, with Teddy's car seat in one hand and my hospital bag over her shoulder. Every few minutes he stirs, the snuffles and whimpers becoming louder each time, and once we are shown into a cubicle he begins testing out his lungs properly for the first time. His wails reverberate around the ward and his face is red and angry.

'He needs a feed,' Lou says, unclipping him from the car seat and handing him to me. At first, he's too worked up to latch on, which sends me into a panic, but then he remembers what to do and the cubicle falls silent as he feeds.

Lou pours me a glass of water from the plastic jug on the bedside cabinet. 'Christ knows how long it's sat there but you need to drink something.' She looks at me critically. 'You look very pale. Are you alright?'

I don't know if it's the relief of being in hospital or the fact that the adrenalin that has seen me through the last few hours is wearing off, but I feel terrible. Nauseous from the ride in the back of the ambulance and light-headed with exhaustion. 'I'll be fine,' I say, taking a sip of water. It tastes so fusty I almost gag.

Lou places a hand on my forehead. 'You feel very cold.' She takes the blue baby fleece from the car seat and drapes it over my shoulders.

I shudder. 'Not that one.'

'Sorry.'

She gives me her cardigan instead and ferrets around in my hospital bag. 'We'll change his nappy when he's finished his feed. Did you do the first one?'

I try to think, but much of the evening is already like a half-forgotten dream. 'I think Roz must have.'

Once Teddy finishes feeding I check my phone, but the battery has died. Matt still doesn't know he's a father. I need to find one of the nurses to ask if I can use their phone and am summoning the energy to haul myself out of the chair when a doctor whisks the cubicle curtains open and strides in. He looks remarkably fresh-faced for the time of night, although I'm so tired I'm having trouble focusing on his features.

'Sophie Saunders?'

'That's me.'

'We've arranged a side room for you and the baby.' He smiles. 'If you'd like to follow me.'

Lou steers the wheelchair towards me, but I shake my head. 'I'm not an invalid. I'll be fine if you can take Teddy.'

I shuffle along the corridor a few steps behind the doctor.

'Sophie!' Lou cries, as I cannon into a wall.

'Stop fussing. I'm fine.'

'You are not bloody fine.'

They are the last words I hear as my legs give way and I crumple to the floor.

———

When I wake I'm lying in the side room, wearing an itchy blue gown with a drip attached to the back of my hand. I pull myself up in a panic, only relaxing when I see Teddy asleep in a cot beside my bed. His arms are stretched above his head and he's wearing one of the yellow sleepsuits I bought in Fenwick all those weeks ago.

'You're awake,' says a familiar voice.

Lou is sitting on a chair beside my bed, her legs tucked underneath her. Her hair is all over the place and there are purple shadows under her eyes. She looks like the dishevelled older sister of the glossy woman in her Facebook profile photo.

'Wow, you look like shit.'

She raises an eyebrow. 'I love you, too.' She stretches her legs and stifles a yawn. 'You don't look too hot yourself.'

I hold up my hand. 'What's with all this?'

'It's fluids to rehydrate you. The doctor said you'd lost so much blood you were lucky you didn't need a transfusion.'

I reach over to the cot and stroke Teddy's hair. It's as fine as cobwebs.

'He's been an angel,' says Lou, smiling. 'He's the original contented little baby. Gina Ford would be proud.'

'Just as well, considering I'm going to be bringing him up on my own.'

'What are you talking about?'

'Matt obviously doesn't want to know. If he did he'd be

here.' I wave my hand around the room, almost dislodging the drip. 'But he's conspicuous by his absence, isn't he?'

I don't expect her to answer, but I don't expect to see the corner of her mouth twitch, either. I narrow my eyes. 'Some sympathy wouldn't go amiss. I've been kidnapped by a mad woman, forced to give birth in a cellar, Matt has dumped me and all you can do is laugh. Some friend you are.'

There's a timid knock at the door. Lou runs her hands through her hair and smoothes her rumpled shirt. 'That'll be my favourite ward assistant with some tea. I'm telling you, he's *hot*.'

'Christ, Lou, do you ever stop?'

She sprints to the door and pulls it open. My heart misses a beat. Standing in the doorway is my husband, a plastic cup in each hand and a worried expression on his face.

'She's awake,' Lou says unnecessarily. She flicks a look over her shoulder at me. 'It's time you two talked properly. I'll be in the poor excuse for a café if you need me.'

I want to beg her to stay. I'm not sure I can deal with the disintegration of my marriage right now. Matt nods and she slips out of the room. I watch out of the corner of my eye as he places the cups on the ring-marked cabinet beside the bed. His fingers are trembling. If Lou looked bad it's nothing compared to Matt. His cheeks have a hollowed-out look as if he's sucking on a slice of lemon and he doesn't have shadows under his eyes, he has bloody great bags. The stubble on his chin is more salt than pepper and his complexion is waxy.

He sits heavily in the chair and his eyes scan the room as if he's looking for an escape route. For a second, his gaze rests on the cot. We need to be civil, I remind myself. For Teddy's sake.

Finally, he turns to me and I hold my breath, waiting for the bomb to drop.

'I'm so sorry, Sophie. You have no idea how sorry I am.'

'It's OK. I saw it coming.'

His eyebrows shoot up. 'You'd already guessed?'

'I'm not stupid,' I say hotly. 'I just wasn't sure who. The delectable Susie from head office or the accommodating Kelly from accounts? Or maybe someone else altogether? Why don't you tell me?'

I smile a smile that doesn't reach my eyes and pluck at the hospital gown with my fingers. Matt is frowning as if he doesn't know what I'm talking about and I have a sudden and very real urge to slap his face.

'Who is it?'

'Who's what?'

'Who are you having an affair with?'

'An *affair*?'

'Oh, be a man and come clean, for pity's sake. You've been acting weirdly for weeks. Not interested in sex. With me at any rate. Ignoring texts and calls when I'm around. I know you didn't go to the Indian Village with Greg and the boys. He told me. And that crash on the M26 you claimed you were stuck in actually happened on the A2. Where were you, Matt? And who were you with?'

'I know how it looks, but you've got it wrong.' He reaches for my hand, but I snatch it away.

'I was looking for someone.'

'Oh yes?' I sneer.

He nods miserably. 'I was looking for Leanne.'

CHAPTER FORTY-EIGHT

NOW

'Leanne?'

'I think you know her as Roz.'

The world tilts on its axis and I draw the thin hospital sheet under my chin. 'Why were you looking for her?' I ask in a small voice.

'I don't know how much she told you down in the cellar, but we have history.'

So, she wasn't lying. I wait for my husband to continue. When he does his voice is heavy. 'We met when I was working at a bank in Portsmouth. I'd just been made assistant manager and she was a mortgage advisor who had transferred from the Southampton branch. She was edgy and cool. Nothing like the girls I usually dated. Perhaps that's what attracted me to her. But it was a destructive relationship. We weren't good for each other.'

'She said you lived together.'

'We did. But not how you think. Not how she wanted, either. I'd bought my first house and the mortgage was crippling. I decided to rent out a room, put an advert on the staff noticeboard and Leanne was the only person to respond. I was her landlord.'

'With added benefits.' My voice is bitter.

Matt hangs his head. 'You make it sound as though I'm some kind of sexual predator. But she did all the running. And she wasn't very good at taking no for an answer.'

'She told me you were going to get married, have kids, the lot.'

'That's not how it was. You have to believe me. She has a warped sense of reality. I never made any promises. She knew I wasn't in the market for a serious relationship. I was twenty-three, for God's sake. All I ever wanted was a bit of fun, no strings attached.'

'Who was Tess?'

Matt buries his face in his hands. 'She was a cashier at the bank,' he mumbles.

'And?'

He looks at me with a haunted expression. 'We fell in love.'

A dart of jealousy pierces my heart even though I know how the story ends. 'And Leanne didn't take it too well?'

'She totally freaked out. She trashed her room and made a spectacle of herself at work. I asked her to move out, and let's just say it didn't go down too well. That's when I first realised her edginess was because she was literally on the edge. She was completely mental.'

I wince at Matt's un-PC choice of words.

'She started following Tess and me outside work. She posted long, rambling love letters through my letterbox and dog shit through Tess's. She tried to turn everyone at work against Tess, claiming she'd been sacked from her last job for sleeping with the boss. She even lodged an official complaint about her with HR. It was a nightmare.'

'Did you report her to the police?'

He nods. 'They told us to keep a diary of all the incidents. They needed us to show it was a pattern of behaviour and not a one off. Did you know that stalking behaviour has been identified in nine out of ten murders?'

The temperature in the room seems to drop a few degrees and I shiver. Matt is staring blankly at the wall behind me.

'So, you kept a diary. What happened then?'

'It was the day before our appointment at the police station. Tess went for a run. I would have gone with her only I was nursing a groin injury from five-a-side and I didn't want to make it worse. She set out on her usual five-mile run. It normally took her about forty-five minutes. When an hour had gone by and she still wasn't back I began to worry. I just had a feeling something was wrong, you know? I jumped in the car and drove her route. At first when I saw the ambulance and police cars I told myself it couldn't be her. But it was. A hit-and-run driver had knocked her over at a crossroads and fled the scene. Tess died in the ambulance on the way to hospital.'

The sound of the door handle makes us both jump and we sit in silence as an orderly bustles in and changes the jug of water on my bedside cabinet.

Once he's left I say, 'You think Roz - Leanne - knocked her over?'

A sob catches in the back of Matt's throat and he nods.

'Did you tell the police?'

'Of course, but there were no witnesses, no CCTV, nothing. They brought Leanne in for questioning, but she denied everything. In case you didn't realise, she's a very good liar.'

'What about her car? It would have been damaged, surely?'

'They checked, but there wasn't a single mark on it. They found a stolen van with a dented bonnet nearby, but there was nothing to link it to Leanne. Without a shred of evidence, there was no case. The crime report was filed.'

He sounds so distraught I can't stop myself reaching over and taking his hand. 'What happened then?'

'Leanne turned up at the funeral, all caring and concerned. I almost punched her lights out. I knew I had to get as far away from her as possible, so I put my house on the market and started looking for jobs. When I was offered one in Chester I grabbed it with both hands. I sold up and moved on.'

'What happened to her?'

'One of the cashiers told me she was admitted to a psychiatric unit after having another meltdown at work. It was a relief. I thought I had finally managed to free myself of her.'

'But she kept finding you.'

'How do you know?'

'She told me. She was quite proud of herself.'

'The first time I moved I left a forwarding address with a couple of mates. I never made that mistake again. With every move I became more careful not to leave any clues behind. I had to be. I deleted all my social media accounts, I always rented. I even changed my name. You should really be Sophie French.' He looks at me warily.

'She told me that, too. Honestly, Matt, why didn't you tell me about her?'

He buries his head in his hands again and when he speaks his voice is muffled by his fingers. 'I don't know. I guess I wanted to pretend it never happened. I hadn't heard from her in over eight years and I thought I was free. What you and I had was so... so perfect, that I didn't want it to be tarnished by that evil bitch. What if she tracked me down and tried to hurt you, too?'

'She did though, didn't she? She tried to steal our baby!' My voice is as squeaky as a dog toy. I take a deep breath and try again. 'You should have warned me about her. It was irresponsible... no, *selfish*, not to.'

'You have no idea how sorry I am.'

He looks so dejected that I feel a twinge of sympathy for him. But only a twinge. 'When did you realise she'd tracked you down again?'

'About eight months ago. It followed the usual pattern. First, I'd get a couple of missed calls from an unknown number, then she'd leave a message asking if I wanted to meet up for a drink as 'friends' to talk about old times. Of course I didn't want to talk about old times,' he explodes. 'It was the worst time of my entire life. The last thing I wanted was to relive it.' He leans back in his seat and addresses the ceiling. 'Then she started calling me at the bank. I was pissed off but not overly worried.'

I raise my eyebrows.

'I knew there was no way she could know I was married. But she turned up at Moira's and charmed her way in, claiming to be a friend of my sister. I don't even have a fucking sister, but Moira wasn't to know. I suppose I should have warned her.'

'And Moira told her about me?'

'They had a very cosy chat, apparently. Moira gave her chapter and verse about how I was married and only lived in Brighton during the week. She told Leanne we lived in Canterbury and that you worked at a community garden. It would have been easy to find you.'

'And so she drops a flyer through our door offering me a discount on a haircut.' I remember finding the sheet on the doormat and thinking it was fate. 'What would she have done if I hadn't booked an appointment?'

'She'd have found another way to inveigle herself into your life. She's like bindweed, insidious and impossible to get rid of.'

Teddy stirs in his cot.

'I wonder what she thought when she realised I was pregnant.' I think back. 'She was always so interested in the baby. But not just that. She seemed to genuinely care.'

Lying in a hospital bed watching my husband literally wringing his hands, his face a mask of self-torment, I wonder how I could have been so naive as to let a complete stranger into my life. Deep down I know why. With Matt away all week I was lonely. Since I lost touch with Lou I've never actively sought the friendship of other women. Too scared I'd get hurt again. I have many acquaintances but no close girlfriends, and I thought that was fine. But when Matt became a part-time husband it wasn't enough. Roz filled the hole he left. How bloody ironic. We had so much in common, only now I know it was all a sham. A friendship built on deceit and duplicity that could have ended catastrophically.

'How could I have been so stupid?'

'If it's any consolation, you're not the only one she deceived,' says Matt, his voice low.

My eyes harden. 'You lied to me, too. How are you any better than her?'

'I did it to protect you!'

'You still lied. How do I know it won't happen again? Even my name is a lie. How do I know I can trust you?'

'I give you my word.'

'You tell me - is that enough?'

He meets my gaze, his eyes unnaturally bright. 'Where does that leave us?'

I turn away. All these lies. I can't deal with them anymore. My future has to be based on the truth or it's not worth living. 'Honestly?' I say. 'I don't know.'

CHAPTER FORTY-NINE

NOW

W e sit in awkward silence until Teddy wakes up as abruptly as he fell asleep and, at the top of his lungs, demands a feed. I start to shuffle out of bed, but am beaten to the cot by Lou, who sweeps into the room, orders me back to bed and scoops Teddy out of his cot and into my arms.

Matt looks away as I feed our baby. I assumed he'd be the original hands-on dad, fumbling with nappies and changing sleepsuits, all fingers and thumbs. But he hasn't had any interaction with Teddy since he's been here. He hardly seems to notice Teddy's even in the room. So much for my fantasies about our happy little family. I run my finger across Teddy's forehead and wonder yet again how it all went wrong.

Lou clucks about like a mother hen, re-arranging the few belongings on my bedside cabinet and straightening the curtains.

'There's a couple outside,' she says. 'Look like coppers to me. They were waiting by the nurses' station. Reckon they're here to see you.'

My spirits lift a little. 'Maybe they've found her.'

Lou pats my shoulder. 'Best not get your hopes up, sweetheart. I'll go and find them, shall I?'

I nod and she slips out of the door.

Matt, having spent the last few minutes brooding, has obviously decided that attack is the best form of defence, because the minute she's gone he jumps to his feet, thrusts his hands in his pockets and stalks over to the window.

'We're not all completely blameless though, are we? I thought we were a team, but you made a unilateral decision to name our son. And, not only was I not consulted, you decided to name him after your first love. How do you think that makes me feel? I'll tell you, shall I? Pretty shit.'

'Who told you about me and Ed?'

'Lou. She assumed I knew, of course, but it turns out you're pretty good at keeping secrets, too.' He spins on his heels to face me and my heart thumps. 'Were you ever going to tell me Ed got you pregnant at seventeen and that the abortion you had was the cause of all our fertility problems?'

I'm silent. What can I say that's going to make this any better?

'You let me think it was all my fault. You even made me have the tests, for Christ's sake. I was sent into a room with a little plastic pot and a couple of dirty mags with other men's sticky fingerprints all over them and told to do the business. I didn't mind. I would have done anything for you.'

My heart constricts. *Would have.*

'You call me a liar, but you're no better yourself. You know what they say about glass houses and stones, Sophie.'

I recoil at the naked hostility in his voice. 'I'm -' I falter. The fact is I don't know what I am. Because he's right, isn't he? I kept secrets, too. Big, ugly secrets with lasting consequences. He's entitled to be angry. 'I'm -'

I don't have a chance to finish because Lou bursts in, followed closely by DC Sam Bennett and her musclebound sidekick PC Dillon Grant. They're both in civvies today, but there's no mistaking they're police. It's something about the world-weary, seen-it-all slant of their shoulders.

I can tell by Lou's face that they don't bear good news, but I ask anyway, despising the pitiful tinge of hope in my voice. 'Have you found her?'

DC Bennett shakes her head. 'Not yet.'

'She seems to have vanished into thin air,' PC Grant says.

His colleague shoots him a contemptuous look and perches on the chair Matt has vacated. 'It seems Ms Beaumont has a number of aliases. She also has previous for stalking and harassment. You're not the only people she's become obsessed by, if that's any consolation.'

'Not really,' says Matt.

'We think she probably stole a car, fitted it with false plates and parked it up nearby so she could escape with the baby.'

'She could be halfway to Scotland by now,' adds PC Dillon.

DC Bennett rolls her eyes. 'We're applying for a search warrant to search her flat, so that might throw up some leads, and we're looking at reports of stolen vehicles over the last few days, but the fact is she could have stolen a car weeks ago. She put a lot of thought into this.'

'You seem to be taking it very seriously,' says Lou. 'Is that because you think she's a danger to Sophie, Matt and the baby?'

I watch the detective closely. She pauses and glances at me, as if she's weighing up whether I can take the truth.

'In light of what happened we're treating both the arson at Angela Platt's home and the incident last night as attempted murder. I've also been talking to Hampshire Police about the Tess Andrews case. By luck I managed to track down the DC who filed a report for the coroner and he was only too happy to reminisce. He said he'd always had a niggling feeling something wasn't right, but he was over-ruled by his DI at the time, so it never went any further. I wouldn't be surprised if they didn't re-open the investigation in the light of Roz Beaumont's confession to Sophie.'

'She didn't actually *confess*,' I say.

'But murdering a love rival fits her modus operandi, doesn't it?' Lou says.

Matt is silent through this exchange. He's standing at the window, his arms wrapped around his body. He looks... desolate. There's no other word for it. As though his world has come crashing down around him. I realise with sudden clarity just how much he must have loved Tess. I always thought I was the love of his life, but everything is recalibrating before my eyes. All the things I thought I knew, the things I took for granted, are shifting and reforming into a reality that bears no resemblance to the one I've been living for the last decade. I'm reminded of the kaleidoscope my parents bought me for my seventh birthday. A nondescript, grey telescope-like affair, it used light and mirrors to create complicated, ever-changing patterns. Scenes changing with the flick of a wrist.

My life, my predictable, comfortable, taken-for-granted life, was an illusion. Not light and mirrors like my much-loved kaleidoscope, but smoke and mirrors. I correct myself. Not even an illusion. A *delusion*. Our life together was built on foundations so shaky they crumbled at the first sign of trouble. Because it's clear Matt doesn't love me the way he loved Tess. He was in love with her when we met. Still is, I think, watching the wretched slump of his shoulders. I was his rebound relationship, the one everyone warns you is doomed to fail. I will him to return my gaze, to reassure me with those brilliant blue eyes that I'm wrong, that although he loved Tess, his heart belongs to me now. But he refuses to meet my eye. A single tear splashes onto Teddy's downy head. I wipe it away with my thumb before anyone notices.

I become aware that Lou and the two police officers are watching me. 'Sorry,' I murmur. 'I was miles away.'

DC Bennett hands me a piece of paper on which a jumble of numbers and letters are written in smudged ink. 'I was saying, we have to get back to the nick now, but you need to contact us the minute Roz gets in touch, OK? Phone 999 and give that reference number.'

She must notice the alarm on my face because she adds, '*If* she gets in touch. She probably won't. She has too much to lose. But if she does...'

'I'll phone you,' I say quietly.

'Good.' Her voice softens. 'And enjoy the little one. I know your life will soon seem like an endless round of nappies and feeds and sleepless nights, but in the blink of an eye he'll be setting off to uni and the house will feel very empty without him, take it from me.'

Matt follows the two officers out of the room and I stare at the crime reference number till it blurs with tears. I stifle a sob.

Lou is beside me in an instant. 'Soph, what's the matter?'

'Matt doesn't love me anymore.'

'He told you that, did he?'

'He didn't have to. He hates me.'

'I'm sure he doesn't.'

'I never told him about the abortion.'

Lou sits down heavily on the bed, causing Teddy to give a little whimper. 'Shit. I assumed he knew.' She frowns. 'But he didn't say it was news to him.'

'He was obviously bottling it up. It all came out while you were gone. He's pissed off I named Teddy without consulting him, even more so because I've named him after Ed, but he's absolutely furious I made him go through infertility tests even though I should have realised I was the one with the problem.'

'I'm sure he'll come around in time.'

I focus on the sweep of Teddy's long lashes, trying to swallow the lump that seems to be a permanent fixture at the back of my throat. 'I'm not sure he will.'

I had no choice but to flee. I crawled up the cellar steps, stole through the garden and melted into the night.

The car was where I left it, halfway along an overgrown farm track south of the city. I took a risk, leaving the keys in the ignition, but I'm glad I did. The car started first time, the sound of the throaty diesel engine a salve to my battered psyche.

I felt disorientated, bewildered. Numb. I had planned for every eventuality. At least I thought I had.

I hadn't bargained on Lou coming to the rescue, risking her own life to save Sophie's.

I hadn't planned for the power of friendship.

After all the hours spent plotting, the research, the

spreadsheet, the preparations, what a schoolgirl error to make.

As I turned right and headed towards the A2 and London I heard the faint wail of sirens. I slammed my foot on the accelerator and sped towards the slip-road.

I'd been close, so close, to picking up the second syringe and injecting my own veins with oblivion.

What stopped me? Fear of the unknown? Sheer bloody-mindedness? The knowledge that this didn't have to be the end - that I could still claim my future one day?

I still don't know.

All I do know is this. Lou would have killed me.

Sophie showed me mercy. She spared my life.

Maybe I'll find it in myself to show her mercy, too. Maybe I'll leave her to enjoy her perfect little life with her perfect husband and her perfect baby.

But taking what's rightfully mine has been my raison d'être, my motivation, for so long.

Without it I have nothing.

Maybe I won't.

CHAPTER FIFTY

SIX MONTHS LATER

I pull into the lane that leads to the church and park behind a beaten-up Fiesta. In his car seat beside me, Teddy is gnawing on his favourite teething ring, his bib already drenched in dribble.

'All set for your big day, little man?'

His big, blue eyes light up at the sound of my voice and his arms and legs pump the air in excitement. I pull up the handbrake and check my reflection in the rear-view mirror. Despite Lou's liberal application of Touche Éclat the dark shadows under my eyes are clearly visible. Teddy still isn't sleeping through, and no amount of concealer can eradicate six months' worth of broken nights.

'You don't care how haggard I look, do you, Teddy Bear?' I say, pulling a silly face. He rewards me with a gurgle of laughter, easing the butterflies in my stomach. I don't know why I'm so nervous. Stupid really.

I shiver as I let myself out of the warmth of the car. The forecast warned the temperature wouldn't rise above freezing today and my breath clouds in front of me as I make my way to the passenger side and lift Teddy from his car seat.

He grabs a fistful of my hair as we crunch up the gravel path and through the lych gate into the church. The vicar, a round-faced man with a welcoming smile and a faint stammer, is in the porch, sorting through hymn-books and orders of service. I cough politely and he scurries over.

'Sophie! I wasn't expecting you so early. And bonny T-Teddy, looking very smart, I must say.'

'We wanted to make sure we were the first ones here. I think most of the gardeners and all the volunteers are coming.'

'S-splendid!' says the vicar, looking genuinely pleased. Cam sits just within the boundary of his parish and he is one of our longest-standing trustees and a regular face at our fundraising events and open days.

The double doors to the church are closed but the vicar deposits the orders of service onto a shelf and flings them open. 'Everyone's been very b-busy, as you'll see,' he says mysteriously.

I follow him into the church and gasp in delight. The end of every pew has been decorated with posies of pale-almond hellebores, buttercup-yellow wintersweet and sprays of silver-grey eucalyptus. Twists of variegated ivy and winter jasmine trail along the backs of each pew and in pride of place next to the font is a stunning arrangement of rose hips, red and white amaryllis, ferns and magnolia leaves. The whole effect is one of simple rustic beauty and the scent is mind-blowing.

'Who did this?' I ask in amazement.

'It was R-Rosie's idea, but everyone pitched in. She, Mary and Nancy scoured the hedgerows for greenery and

Martin and Geoff were in charge of the ivy and eucalyptus. They spent yesterday afternoon arranging everything.'

'I had no idea.'

'Rosie was adamant it was a surprise.'

I smile. 'It's certainly that.'

Even though I'm still officially on maternity leave I've been spending a couple of mornings a week at Cam. I know they can manage perfectly well without me, but it's hard to stay away and anyway, Teddy loves going. Everyone makes such a fuss of him.

The door creaks on its hinges and I look up to see Lou sweeping down the aisle towards us. She's wearing a shimmery silk dress the colour of champagne, a matching coat fastened with a diamanté clip, vertiginous nude heels and a complicated organza and feather fascinator. It makes the simple, print dress I dug out of the back of my wardrobe look understated to say the least.

'Bloody hell, Lou. You look like the mother of the bride. It's only a christening.'

She tuts good-humouredly. 'The godmother can't let the side down, can she? How is my gorgeous boy?'

Teddy is already holding out his arms to Lou and I hand him over. He adores her. I call her his second mum. And she's been my rock, too, helping me through the difficult first few weeks when I was on my knees with exhaustion, my hormones all over the place and my anxiety levels still through the roof.

I spent what seems like ages in a fugue state and the few memories I do have of those early days are confused and indistinct. Now that's behind us, Lou is still there when I need her, but we do the fun stuff together now, like trips to the swings and the zoo and coffee and cake in our favourite cafés.

'Did you know about this?' I say, waving my hand at the flowers.

'Rosie may have mentioned it a hundred times or so,' she grins, tickling Teddy till his small body is convulsed in giggles. 'But she swore me to secrecy. And anyway, I thought you deserved a nice surprise.'

Lou started volunteering at Cam not long after Teddy was born. She wanted something to take her mind off the booze. She spends half her life in the garden these days. But she always was an all or nothing kinda girl. Angela is also back at work after a few months off with stress. She walks on eggshells around me and is much less snippy with the gardeners than she used to be. Geoff thinks the arson attack had more of an impact on her than she would ever admit. I think she'll probably revert to type eventually, but I'm enjoying the ceasefire while it lasts.

The door swings open again and this time Rosie bursts in, her face beaming. She sees me and runs over. 'Do you like it, Sophie?'

'I *love* it,' I say, hugging her tightly.

She was pragmatic when she found out I'd had a boy and not the girl she'd been hoping for. 'We're not going to be able to call the baby Little Rosie now, are we?' she'd said, peering at his sleeping face. 'That wouldn't do at all.'

'I was thinking I might call him Teddy,' I'd said, metaphorically crossing my fingers.

Her face had split into the biggest grin. 'Like a real-life Teddy Bear!'

'That's right,' I agreed. The nickname has stuck ever since.

Lou hands Teddy back to me and I nuzzle his neck and blow raspberries to make him chortle. The fragrance of the flowers is wonderful but my baby smells totally delicious. I breathe in his scent of warm skin and Johnson's baby shampoo and watch as a stream of familiar faces arrive and take their places in the beautifully-decorated pews. Angela and Geoff. Mary and her WI friend Margaret. The not-so-new volunteers Derek, Mike, Bev and Trev. Even Martin and his mum are here. Martin is still subdued - they've upped his meds since his manic episode - but he smiles and gives me a little wave.

Lou taps her watch and looks at me.

I shrug helplessly. She doesn't need to tell me the service is due to start in a couple of minutes and Matt's still not here. Bored, Teddy wriggles in my arms. I root around in my coat pocket for his teething ring. He grabs it and thrusts it straight into his mouth.

The vicar glides over, his hands clasped in front of him, and gives me an awkward smile.

'Five more minutes?' I plead.

'Of course,' he says. He knows my situation.

I flash him a grateful smile and stare at the church doors, as if Matt will miraculously appear if I will it hard enough. Minutes tick by and I can tell the congregation is getting fidgety by people's forced coughs and shuffling feet.

At ten past two the vicar approaches again and says in a gentle voice, 'I think we'd better get started. I have a funeral at three.'

I nod miserably and turn to face the altar as the organist plays the opening notes of the first hymn, *Lord of all Hopefulness*, and the congregation stands.

Even though they are behind me I recognise so many of their voices. Lou's confident contralto. Geoff's rich baritone. Angela's reedy soprano. Tone deaf Rosie, the loudest of them all. I want to sing but there's a lump the size of a golf ball in the back of my throat. Because I'm suddenly overcome with emotion. They are my friends, my people, and with them in my corner I know I'll never be alone.

We're halfway through the third verse when the church doors open, bringing with them an arctic blast of freezing air. Teddy sees him first, his face breaking into a gummy smile. Relief floods through me and I turn to watch my husband tiptoe up the aisle, nodding and smiling his apologies to our friends as they jokingly mouth 'what time do you call this?' and 'nice of you to show up'.

'Sorry,' he murmurs as he takes his place beside me and holds his hands out for Teddy.

Teddy drops his teething ring in excitement and tilts his little body towards his father. Matt drops a kiss, as light as a feather, on top of his blond curls.

'Did you get it?' I whisper back, as the hymn draws to a close and the vicar ambles over to the lectern.

He nods and I smile with relief. The woman making Teddy's christening cake was in tears when she phoned yesterday to say her lurcher had slunk into the kitchen when her back was turned and gorged himself on it. She'd promised to work through the night to make us another, as long as we didn't mind a sponge instead of the fruit cake she'd originally baked. I'd urged her not to worry, that we'd make do with a plain birthday cake from the supermarket, but Matt had taken her up on her offer. He wanted everything to be perfect for Teddy's big day.

He'd set off for Faversham with oodles of time to spare. And then, typically, a lorry had jack-knifed on the Boughton bypass and he'd phoned me in a panic when the sat nav warned him it would take two hours to get home.

'I'll be there if it kills me,' he'd said, and I'd felt a frisson of fear.

'Don't say that.'

'It's a figure of speech. I'll be there. I promise.'

Looking sidelong at him now, his blue eyes crinkling as he coos at our baby, I know I should never have doubted he'd make it. I should never have doubted him full stop. There was never an affair. He loved Tess, of course he did. Just as I loved Ed. But he loves me, too. For a couple of days after Teddy and I were discharged from hospital we tiptoed around each other, barely talking, guilt and resentment eating us up. Lou was the one who forced us to sort ourselves out, arriving one evening and ordering us to the pub, where we talked till closing time.

I told him about Ed and the abortion. He talked about Tess and what she'd meant to him. It was liberating, knowing all of him. No skeletons in the closet. No more secrets. I suppose it was the same for him, too, as we've never been closer than we have these last few months.

The vicar clears his throat and Matt slips a hand in mine. Happiness fizzes like sherbet through my veins and I steal one last look back at my friends before the service begins. Lou smiles, Rosie waves, Geoff gives me the thumbs up. A movement catches my eye. I swivel on my heels to get a better look. But I'm too late. All I see is a flutter of midnight-blue fabric before the doors clunk shut.

I rack my brains, trying to picture what everyone was wearing as they took their seats. I realise with a mounting sense of panic that I can't remember anyone in midnight-blue. Biting my lip, I wonder whether I should race out of the church and confront our uninvited guest.

What if it's Roz, finally coming to claim her prize? Because the police never found her, despite DC Bennett's best efforts. In the empty hours between midnight and dawn, when sleep often eludes me, I picture her lying in wait, watchful and ready as she plans her next move.

Maybe she's still obsessed by us. Perhaps she's found someone new to fixate on. I desperately hope she's found someone who will love her back, despite her flaws. Because if life had been kind to Roz she could have been a good person, I know she could.

Matt squeezes my hand, bringing me back to reality. Let her go, says a voice in my head.

You can't spend your life looking over your shoulder, not when the people you love most in the world are right by your side.

I cast one final look behind me.

And then I let her go.

THE END

AFTERWORD

I hope you enjoyed *When She Finds You*. It would be great if you could spare a couple of minutes to write a quick review on Amazon. I'd love your feedback!

ACKNOWLEDGMENTS

Writing a book is always a leap of faith and *When She Finds You* was no exception.

I have received much help and encouragement along the way, without which I would never have reached The End.

Firstly, my thanks go to my wonderful, patient and talented editor, Sacha Black. Sacha's insights and suggestions were invaluable and helped make the book the best it can be.

Thank you to Penny, Barbara and Terry for their expert advice on medical and police matters respectively. Any mistakes are my own.

I owe a great debt of gratitude to my early readers for their feedback and support. You know who you are.

Most of all I'd like to thank my long-suffering husband, Adrian, who inspires me to push boundaries every single day.

ABOUT THE AUTHOR

A J McDine lives deep in the Kent countryside with her husband and two teenage sons.

She worked as a journalist and police press officer before becoming a full-time author in 2019.

Endlessly fascinated by people and their fears and foibles, she loves to discover what makes them tick.

She writes dark, domestic thrillers about ordinary people in extraordinary situations.

When she's not writing, playing tennis or attempting to run a 5K, she can usually be found people-watching in her favourite café.

When She Finds You is A J McDine's debut psychological thriller.

BOOK CLUB QUESTIONS

SPOILER ALERT! LOOK AWAY NOW IF YOU HAVEN'T
FINISHED THE BOOK!!

The prologue followed one of the characters on their way to hospital. Was it Sophie going for her abortion, or Roz going for electroconvulsive therapy?

Sophie has major issues with trust, yet at times she is too trusting. Is it possible to be both sceptical about some things and gullible about others?

Do you think Sophie should have told Ed about her pregnancy when she was seventeen? If she had, what different path could her life have taken?

How do Sophie and Lou's characters evolve over the course of the book?

Did your opinions about any of the characters change?

What choices would you have made differently if you were in Sophie's shoes?

Rosie is perhaps the only completely unflawed character in the book. Do you think it's important that all characters have flaws in order to be believable?

Roz believes in nature, not nurture and that our character traits are determined by our genes. What do you think - are we all, as Roz claims, 'pre-wired'?

Sophie showed Roz mercy. Do you think Roz will reciprocate and leave Sophie and Matt to enjoy their happy ever after?

Do you agree that gardening can help with depression because it allows people to be nurturers, gives them a sense of responsibility and helps them be less insular?

COPYRIGHT

Lightning Source UK Ltd.
Milton Keynes UK
UKHW042111230919
350301UK00001B/166/P